M000113922

THE ROAD
TO THE
SALT SEA

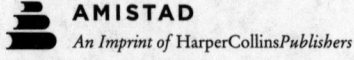

AMISTAD

An Imprint of HarperCollins*Publishers*

THE ROAD
TO THE
SALT SEA

A NOVEL

SAMUEL
KỌ́LÁWỌLÉ

This is a work of fiction. Names, characters, places, and incidents are products of the author's imagination or are used fictitiously and are not to be construed as real. Any resemblance to actual events, locales, organizations, or persons, living or dead, is entirely coincidental.

THE ROAD TO THE SALT SEA. Copyright © 2024 by Samuel Kọ́láwọlé. All rights reserved. Printed in the United States of America. No part of this book may be used or reproduced in any manner whatsoever without written permission except in the case of brief quotations embodied in critical articles and reviews. For information, address HarperCollins Publishers, 195 Broadway, New York, NY 10007.

HarperCollins books may be purchased for educational, business, or sales promotional use. For information, please email the Special Markets Department at SPsales@harpercollins.com.

FIRST EDITION

Designed by Yvonne Chan
Map on page ix © Beehive Mapping
Art on pages iii, 11, 87, 277 © Alicia Tatone

Library of Congress Cataloging-in-Publication Data has been applied for.

ISBN 978-0-06-305085-3

24 25 26 27 28 LBC 5 4 3 2 1

For Jahdiel

no one leaves home unless
home is the mouth of a shark

—Warsan Shire, "Home"

A TRANS-SAHARAN MIGRANT
ROUTE FROM NIGERIA

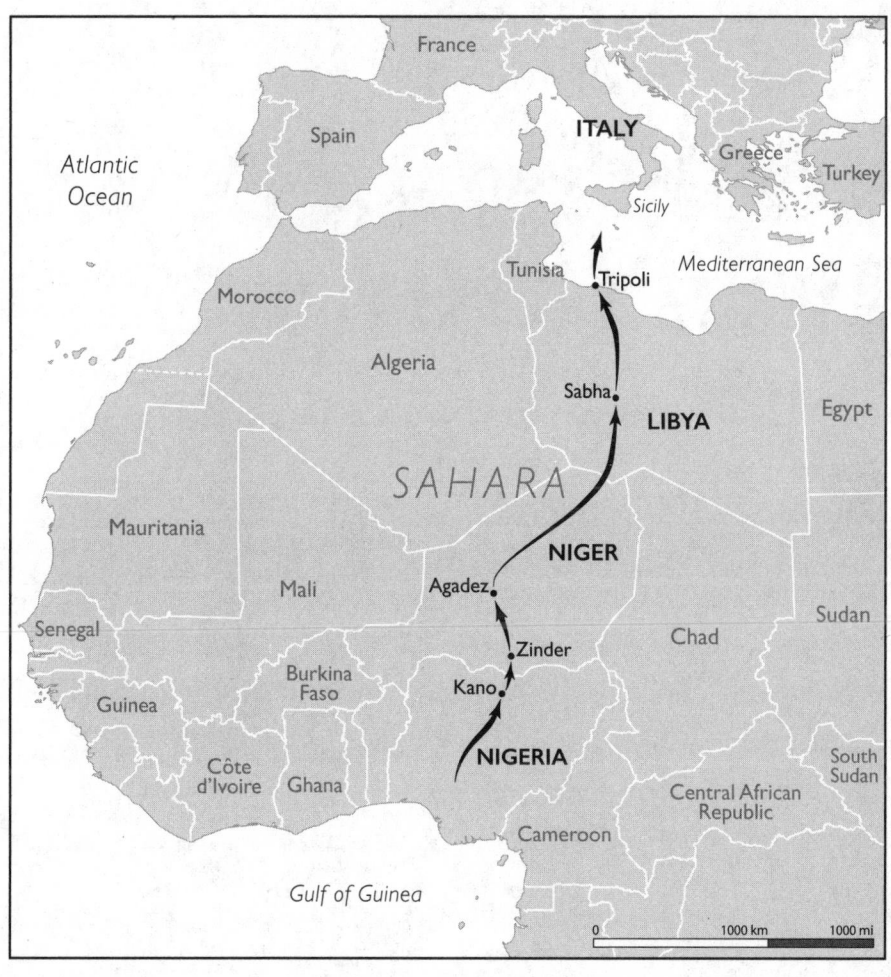

1

After fixing the tire, Able God drove carefully through outlying streets in search of a guesthouse. The darkness did little to ease his anxiety. It would be harder to find him in the dark, when faces were barely noticeable. He turned down a road lined by buildings. He located one tucked within a maze of tenement apartments. The walls were stained brown, there was not a signpost in sight, and a long passageway led to the entrance. It was perfect.

The hotel attendant, a man with bushy eyebrows and a stubbled chin, stood behind the reception desk. There was a telephone on the counter, and a huge black-and-white television hung in a corner, encased in a cobwebbed iron frame.

"You are welcome to Mount Pleasant Guest House. How may I help you?" the fellow asked.

"I wan lodge for room."

"Single or double bed, sir?"

"Just gime sontin!" Able God responded impatiently. He wiped the sweat from his exposed palm on his trousers. The receptionist threw a suspicious look at him. Able God slipped some notes on the counter.

"Once again, you are welcome to Mount Pleasant Guest House," the man said with a smile as he unhooked a key from the rows of keys on the wall. The receptionist led Able God upstairs to a corridor with six facing doors and wiggled the key into one of the door locks, pushing and pulling at the door before it finally creaked open. A rancid smell issued forth. The receptionist handed Able God the key and went back downstairs. In the room, Able God paced manically, shaking his head in panic.

He parted the curtain and gazed outside: nothing but a wall. He went to the bathroom to inspect the gash across his palm. He wet a wad of tissue paper under the faucet and, flinching, wiped the blood off the wound. Back in the room, he sat down on the edge of one of the hard twin beds. A folded, worn-out towel and a chip of soap were arranged at the foot of the bed. The asbestos ceiling was bloated with water and streaked black. The walls were collaged with chipped enamel. The air-conditioning system made a humming sound punctuated by a violent mechanical crunch, like a pepper grinder.

He pulled out his phone and dialed the number Akudo had given him. Five times he called, no response. He called Ben Ten. No answer. A curious thought flashed through his mind. Maybe calling Akudo from an unrecognizable number would work. He scribbled her number with the guesthouse pen on the pad on the bedside table, tore the page from the pad, and rushed downstairs. The receptionist was dozing, his head on the desk.

"Excuse, sir," Able God said.

The receptionist sprang up, wiping a streak of white saliva from the corner of his lips.

"Yes? Can I help you?" He peered at Able God with tired eyes.

"I want to call this number. Can you help me?"

The receptionist shot Able God a look that said, "Boy, you better grease my palms or deal with the police." The man assessed him, his gaze falling on the wound in Able God's hand and the bloodstains on the side of his trousers. At that moment, Able God realized that the receptionist had to be aware that he was in trouble. He had no choice but to pay him some money at this point. Able God dipped his hand into his pocket.

"*Oga*, we no want trouble for this hotel, ooo," the receptionist said, smiling ever so slightly.

"No, my brother, I just wan phone somebody."

The receptionist took a quick glance at the money and bundled it off behind the desk. Able God reached out for the handset and punched the dial. She still did not answer. Shit! He returned the phone to the cradle and went back upstairs.

He thought about calling his parents but immediately shot down the idea. He'd already caused them so much pain and disappointment. They would almost die of shame when they realized their son was running from the law, but that would be better than seeing him presented before the shutter-clicking press and surrounded by armed police officers. He'd be handcuffed together with Akudo, perhaps wearing just his underpants in the police's typical fashion of publicly humiliating suspects before trial. In this fevered imagining, Able God knew they'd allow Akudo to keep her clothes on, but not him. His face would be swollen and bloody after they tried to force a confession out of him. He was all entangled in this. There was no way out.

He ran to the bathroom and retched into the toilet, sweat breaking out on his forehead. He flushed, watching the vomit eddy and swirl around the bowl. He flushed again, watched the water disappear. Still not satisfied, he flushed the toilet again and again. Then he washed his face and looked in the mirror.

He lay on the bed and closed his eyes. No sleep. He felt weak, hollow inside.

A little later the electricity went off. Silence. He squirmed, rolled over. Now he could hear rats scratching in the walls. In the quiet darkness his fear seemed to assume a more fearsome quality, bearing down on him till he gasped for air and drenched himself with his own sweat. He let his mind wander to distract himself from the feeling inside his chest, and his thoughts traveled to his stained work clothes. Time to get rid of them. Guided by the light on his phone, he grabbed his backpack from the bedside table. One by one, he pulled the items of clothing from the plastic bag, spreading them out on the mattress. They represented a past he would be forced to leave behind. That was when he noticed his name badge was missing.

❯ ● ▲ ❯

Earlier that day, Able God had been seated behind the driver, anxious for the vehicle to hit the highway. When it did, to calm himself, he watched trees and buildings rush by. Upbeat Fuji spewed from a broken cassette player in the driver's seat. The Danfo driver kept locking eyes with motorists, grinning as he flew past them. Steering with one hand, he switched cassettes. The broken cassette player expelled a tape, exposing strands of cascading wires, and instantly gobbled a new one. It groaned and spluttered static before coughing out a more upbeat Fuji tune. The driver cut off another vehicle. This time agitated murmurs filled the air. One passenger spoke up, asking if the driver wanted them all to die. Another pleaded with him to take it easy.

Able God was unmoved, or rather, he was too preoccupied with his own anxieties to care. If anything, he wanted to get to his destination as quickly as possible, for with the crisis came a timely solution.

As far as Able God was concerned, there was only one way—they both had to leave. If he escaped without her, then Akudo would take the fall for the crime they had both committed. What would happen to her daughter? If the three of them survived the treacherous journey, they would be on the other side of the sea within days with a new life, and maybe he would be at peace. Maybe he would be able to atone for what he had done.

It was time to pay.

Able God buried his wounded hand deep in a pocket. The other hand, which did not stop trembling, was out. At first, he reckoned it must be because of the shock of seeing so much blood. But several minutes passed, enough time for the initial trauma of the incident to have subsided, enough time that he was able to scrub himself clean and think up a plan with Akudo, enough time for him to flee the crime scene without attention. Fearing someone would notice his trembling, he tucked his hand into his pockets. But that also made him look suspicious, especially when it was time to use his hands for what people used hands for, like paying the Danfo bus fare on his way to the rendezvous spot. The bus conductor, a gaunt-faced man with a receding hairline, gave what Able deemed to be a concerned look when he produced a crinkled note with an unsteady grip, so Able God immediately turned away to avoid conversation.

Able God got off the bus and walked quickly along a bush path near a row of houses close to his neighborhood. Anxiety swelled in his chest, and pain stung his hands. He studied his surroundings, his gaze finally settling on a heap of refuse dumped at the side of the path. Unzipping the corner of his backpack, he smelled stale blood as he peered inside the plastic bag at his stained work clothes. He was preparing to toss the clothing on the pile when he heard footsteps behind him. Seconds later, a passerby asked him politely to step out of the way. Able God stepped out of the way, and the passerby continued his journey.

He decided it was best to incinerate the clothing when he got home. But first, he needed to help Akudo get out of the country.

› ● ▲ ›

A woman he recognized as one of the madams sat frowning on a stool in the doorway of Akudo's room. A group of drunken ladies danced to reggae music pouring from a loudspeaker in front of the other rooms. They smoked and vied with each other to see who could make the most suggestive gyrations with her hips. Awkward and out of step with the beat, the group shrieked with joy and stuck their tongues out whenever the snare drum's rhythm was interrupted by a sharp break or the guitars twanged. Able God greeted the madam and peered into the room, expecting to find Akudo there packing her belongings. The madam spoke before he did. He strained to listen. She said something, but he could not hear over the loud reggae noise from the speakers.

"What?" he said in a loud voice, leaning toward her.

"She has left. She is no longer here," the woman replied.

"Left?" he said, confused.

"Yes, she left. She no longer works here."

"That's not possible," Able God said. "We spoke in the afternoon. That's not possible!"

The sudden fury he felt toward Akudo hardened his tone. There was a tightness in his chest. Her words made him feel nauseated. He drew a sharp breath, then glanced at the plastic bag wrapped around his injured hand. The wound had stopped bleeding, but it still throbbed with pain. The woman sprang up and signaled to the ladies to cut the noise. They obeyed promptly, and silence descended on the place.

"Akudo no longer works here," she said, leaning against the door frame with folded arms. "What is it that you don't understand about what I just said?"

Had Akudo reported him to the police, or had she blamed the death on him? Able God had been careful about removing all signs of his connection to the crime—as careful as his panicked state would allow. Now he wanted to ask the woman if she knew Akudo's whereabouts. He wanted to say finding her was a matter of life and death. He wanted to ask about her daughter. She would do anything for her sweet little daughter.

Able God suspected, however, that nothing good was going to come from his conversation with the madam. Despite attempting to focus his attention on the here and now, he was overwhelmed by a dizzying rush of thoughts about what might happen next. Every moment that passed brought a greater threat to his freedom. Sadly, the window of opportunity might have closed for him after all.

With a hand now trembling violently, he drew the strap of his backpack close to his chest and walked away.

He quickened his steps, then broke into a sprint as he made his way home. A strange fog of fear overwhelmed him, stifling his breath and making his heart ache with unbearable pain, but he kept running. He stopped several minutes later, when he was a little distance from his house. Breathless, his chest heaving, he waited a few seconds, peering suspiciously at his surroundings.

He bounded into the room, where he saw that his door was wide open—or rather, it had been torn off the hinges and was lying on the ground in front of the building. His clothes were strewn across the doorway, the plywood partition torn down. Inside, the table and stools were overturned, and his mattress had been yanked from its frame. Smashed glass bottles and ceramics littered the floor, his transistor radio cannibalized, his curtains ripped apart.

Able God walked in slowly, dazed, then he stepped outside and turned to look at his neighbors, who were sitting in the narrow alley. He scanned their faces for answers, but they turned away, shifted on their low stools, and one after another, went into their rooms.

Inside, Able God paced the house, frustration coiling around his head. Had he had any doubt that the police were aware of his involvement, what he saw erased it. He looked out through the louvered window. He blundered his way manically through the chaos, tossing things aside. He pulled up the mattress, rifled through his clothes, heaped one on the other.

He noticed they had not taken his hidden wrap of marijuana, but his chess pieces were spilled all over the ground. He tried to gather them into a plastic bag, but his whole body trembled now, his eyes smarting with tears. The chess set was not meant to be scattered; the pieces were meant to be neatly arranged. How had the police known where he lived? Maybe Akudo had been arrested, but if so, why was the madam protecting her whereabouts?

For a moment, he thought he heard a rush of footsteps heading toward his room, but it was only in his head. He heaved a sigh of relief and quickly gathered what he could: his chess set, clothes, a toothbrush, a pair of flip-flops. Moving through the city using public transportation would be dangerous, since his bus could easily be stopped at a checkpoint. His search for employment had accustomed him to the landscape of the city. He knew every dirt road, every corner, all the shortcuts. With a car, he could navigate his way through the shacks and the fancy gated housing estates. It would be easy to get to the bus station with a car. He needed a car, but where would he get one? He also needed somewhere safe to stay for the night.

The distant wail of a police siren filled the air. For a few seconds, he paced back and forth, not sure what to do, then a crazy idea struck him. He picked up a kitchen knife and dashed out of his apartment.

Several minutes later, he pointed the knife at a teenager in the dark, demanding the keys to his car while telling himself he was doing what he had to do.

"Don't make me knife you," he whispered. It sounded more like a plea than a threat. He felt like he had lost control of his own body, and for a moment, Able God feared the boy was going to see through his bluster and call his bluff, or perhaps flee with the keys. His hold on the weapon was like that of an addict desperate for a fix. Able God crept closer to the youngster, flailing with the knife as if he were about to strike the boy with the next blow. The young boy instantly turned over the keys. Able God thanked him before realizing he had not meant to.

He drove through dirt streets and bumped down alleyways. Then, at dusk, he heard one of the tires flapping loudly. He checked his rearview mirror, pulled over, and waited a few moments before getting out of the car. A nail had lodged in the tire. Luckily the boy had a tire in his trunk. Able God had to work fast. He pulled out the spare and some tools and unbolted the ruined tire. As he heaved the old wheel off, he kept a vigilant eye on the road. He was almost certain he'd shaken off a police van, although he was not fully certain of anything. Able God could not yet process the fact that when he had started the day, he was a hotel worker struggling to make ends meet, and now he was ending it as a fugitive.

HOTEL ATRIUM

2

Able God jumped off the bus and walked down the palm-lined driveway to the Hotel Atrium. On the ride, he'd done everything he could to avoid creasing his shirt. He had folded a newspaper into a fan to dry his sweat and leaned away from the dirty seats. He had dusted his shoes, adjusted his bow tie, and smoothed his shirt when he arrived—prim and proper. It took him ten minutes to walk through the entrance; two of its gates were reserved for vehicles, but the third was for pedestrians.

"Are you staff?" asked a uniformed guard holding an AK-47. The guard peered out at him through the barred window with the expression of a man who'd just woken up from a nap.

There were three other armed guards in the gatehouse. One sat behind a small desk holding a black ledger. Able God frowned. He always had to deal with this. It was not enough that he had his work clothes on. He had stopped asking himself why he was still unrecognizable after working at the hotel for more than three months. The disrespect didn't always get to him, but that day it did. So, that was the kind of treatment you get with a degree in this country!

"Do you have an ID?" the guard asked when he saw that Able God was not going to respond. Able God balanced his bag on a raised knee and reached into the front pocket for his photo ID. The guard squinted at it.

HOTEL ATRIUM

ABLE GOD ONOBELE

HOSPITALITY EXECUTIVE

"So, because you are staff you cannot speak? Common greeting you cannot greet?" the guard said. There was an awkward silence. Able God clenched his jaw as he tried to push down his rising anger.

"I work here," he said.

"Hey, Mr. Man, I am doing my job here. If you are tired of your own work, you can go back home," the guard said, his voice laced with irritation.

A voice rang out from the gatehouse. "Let him in, Sikiru. You like trouble too much!"

Sikiru hissed and grudgingly opened the gate. Able God nodded in greeting to the man behind the desk, who registered his name in the ledger. The guard gave him the evil eye.

"I want to advise you man-to-man," said the worker behind the desk. "This is not how to behave. You are still very young. Respect is give and take. Don't think because we are security guards you are better than us. We also went to school, even if we didn't go to university—I am an old soldier; you were not born when I fought for this country during the civil war."

The old soldier paused to look at him as though wanting Able God to feel the seriousness of his words before plowing on ahead. He was in his sixties and had a double chin that hung down and quivered as he spoke.

"We work very hard here," he continued. "One day you will need our help, so you should treat us with respect. It's for your own good."

Able God mumbled an apology to the old man while wondering why he was apologizing. The old soldier was right. It would be wiser to avoid conflict with them even if that meant feigning respect. That was what his job meant. He shuffled out of the gatehouse.

Flags of various nations waved along the entrance of the gleaming sixteen-story building. Jets of water shot up from an oval fountain at the entrance, spraying a fine mist over the paved walkway. The fountain's unending cycle of sparkling water never overflowed. Tall bellmen stood on standby as the shiny brass revolving doors twirled. Two men dressed in dark blazers stepped through, attaché cases in hand, then a young couple came after them, all smiles, fingers interlaced. Able God broke into a trot to avoid crossing paths with the guests. Otherwise he would have to follow the twenty-ten rule: acknowledge the guest when at twenty steps away using a nod or eye contact, then at ten steps, initiate eye contact with a toothpaste-commercial smile. It must be brief!

"As staff of this organization, you are not permitted to walk past a guest without presenting them with a slice of our hospitality," insisted Mr. Tanimola Hastrup, a small-framed man, during orientation. "No matter where you are on these premises, when you are ten steps away from a guest, you kowtow, then you put on your hundred-watt smile. You may speak to them softly and say something like, 'Hope you are enjoying your stay at Hotel Atrium. We are glad to have you here.' If for some reason you can't say that, just shut up and put on your hundred-watt smile with a polite bow of the head."

Able God wasn't in the mood to present a hundred-watt toothpaste-commercial smile. He walked around to the rear entrance. He passed the pool with its rows of cabanas and lounge chairs.

He took the granite path around the tennis courts and gardens to the staff quarters, a walled and gated bungalow tucked in the back of the hotel.

He scanned the notice board inside the bungalow to see where he would be working that night. At the Hotel Atrium, *hospitality executive* was a glorified name for a workhorse. It meant working wherever assigned—housekeeping, room service, kitchen stewarding, facility maintenance, front desk check-in, tourist advising, sauna attendant, or waiter at the restaurant or café. But he had taken it all in stride. He had learned from *Think and Grow Rich* by Napoleon Hill that "failure is a trickster with a keen sense of irony and cunning. It takes great delight in tripping one up when success is almost within reach."

That night, he was on room service duty.

Able God was glad the cramped cubicle that doubled as an office and dry-goods space was empty. He sat behind the desk. He dug into his bag, pulling out a dirty vinyl chessboard, a plastic bag filled with chipped chess pieces, and a battered copy of the book *Chess: Improving and Staying Sharp*. His head felt clear again. The mental focus of the game of chess was a rush—the rapid-fire thinking, the problem solving, the strategizing.

As soon as he'd set the board, he tried a few tactics from the book. He touched and then put down pieces, reconsidering his moves. He scratched his head, caressed the pieces before playing, lightly grasping the very top of each piece with his fingers before making a move. He turned the pieces slightly between his fingers and imagined simulating the moves in his phone's DroidFish chess app.

Now thirty-two, Able God had not played competitive chess since qualifying for his polytechnic's team. Back then he'd borrow chess books from the library, memorizing copious notes. He installed chess software on one of the PCs in the computer lab and played till he became one with the software, anticipating its moves and blitzing frequently until all else faded and it was only chess and him. He dreamed of joining the state chess club. He imagined that in a year, if he practiced hard, he could be on his way to the World Chess Olympiad. Maybe chess would be what lifted him out of his wretchedness. Whenever he closed his eyes, he saw himself famous for his opening, just like the grand masters. *Picture the future you want to feature.* He saw himself strangling opponents like Magnus Carlsen, the world's number one, the Mozart of chess. Perhaps aspiring to be like Magnus Carlsen was taking it too far, but he wanted at least to be the best chess player in the country. He had since abandoned that dream for more practical expectations and now played chess to "learn strategies to win in life." That wasn't going too well either.

Someone glanced into the cubicle thirty minutes later. Another worker drifted in soon after, nodded a greeting, and left with some office supplies. More people peered in, asked where he was working the night shift.

"Is that checkers?" one of them asked in a casual voice.

"No, it's chess."

"Chess. I have never heard of that game before. Can you teach me? Is it difficult to learn?"

"No, it's not difficult. Do you want me to teach you something now?"

"Maybe later—my shift is about to begin."

Moments later, Able God opened DroidFish on his phone.

3

efore Akudo, there were other women. The night shift was busy, and orders poured in. Able God was shuffling orders from the kitchen and ferrying food and alcohol on clinking carts. He wheeled his cart through a lobby the size of a basketball court. It had high ceilings with sparkling chandeliers, glass and concrete walls, shiny floors, and planters containing decorative trees. Luxurious sofas upholstered in bright reds and yellows beckoned to guests as smooth music softened the sterile air of the lobby.

He maneuvered his cart past the row of concierges in the booths next to the service elevators before guiding it into the elevator. He rolled it over the rich, soft carpet lining the long, brightly lit hallways. He knocked on doors and floated his well-practiced, hundred-watt toothpaste-commercial smile.

During his first days at the hotel, he had been clumsy and unsure of himself. Sometimes he worried he would run into one of his former lecturers in the lobby or end up cleaning an old classmate's room. The hotel was a haven for strangers in transit, a meeting place for regular visitors and distant travelers alike. What would they think of him when they saw him there? Would they be surprised? Concerned? Would they pity him? Maybe they would just be confused.

The game of chess had taught Able God that a threat was best confronted with a move that strengthened one's position. He wouldn't be trapped into reacting with anger and frustration. His solution to the threat on his livelihood and dignity would be gentle and calculated. Meanwhile, he would do what he needed to get by while figuring out how to get his life back on steady ground.

To ease the drudgery of his work, Able God made it his business to know things. He eavesdropped on fellow workers whispering gossip about guests. Sometimes he joined in the conversation. He knew that some guests padded around in the lobby for no reason at all, sometimes in their pajamas. One guest he'd heard about had woken up in the middle of the night, walked out of his room, descended the guest elevator, and sauntered over to a potted plant to take a piss. The man then closed his fly and went back to his room. No one mentioned it to him the following morning, and he didn't seem to remember.

Able God knew the difficult guests who made impossible requests. He knew that people sold things in the lobby—well-dressed people, people with carry-ons and bright smiles. He knew when the evening guests started trickling in—expatriates with see-through blouses and dyed hair, cutoff shorts, leather leggings, stilettos. A few were dressed in well-tailored skirt suits. Others were marketing executives from banks visiting rich clients. They sat cross-legged in the lobby, fiddling with their cell phones or typing away on their laptops. Some walked up to the counter, then straight upstairs. Others were greeted reverentially by bellmen the moment they showed up at the door.

At midnight, Able God collected the empty trays that had been left out in the hall and walked the floors looking for stray carts to take back to the kitchen, an attempt to unwind before the graveyard shift. His eyes were heavy; he could feel a faint throbbing in the center of his forehead. His muscles ached. Soft instrumental music streamed in from the ceiling-mounted speakers, making him even sleepier.

He needed to stay awake for the early morning calls. He walked back to the storage room next to the kitchen and soon drifted off to sleep in a chair.

If he dreamed, he didn't remember.

A chef woke him at 2:00 a.m. for a room service order. Dr. Ol-amide Badero, a high-profile guest who frequently stayed in one of their best suites, had requested a bottle of champagne. Blinking sleep from his eyes, Able God set the bottle on a silver platter and scattered rose petals over the ice in the bucket. He placed two champagne flutes on the platter, carefully crossing their stems. Linen napkins and two bottles of sparkling water were added to the cart. Everything was just the way Dr. Badero would want it, the chef said. Able God didn't have to wonder why he had requested champagne at that hour. The wealthy guests did whatever they pleased. He had once served a guest who ate pounded yam and egusi soup at midnight. Even though he grumbled under his breath as he went about his witching-hour duties, he had no choice but to comply. Didn't the guests pay all that money to get whatever they wanted, whenever they wanted? Now he rubbed his eyes and let out a big sigh, then gathered himself, and left groggily.

The hotel was mostly quiet, but as he approached the suite, he heard muffled screams. It was not uncommon for sounds to filter into the halls from the rooms. Even though the rooms were supposed to be soundproof, the halls sometimes filled with grunts, squeals, and moans. This noise, however, was different. It was unpleasant and guttural, like the rasping of a dying sheep. When Able God heard it from the staff elevator vestibule, he immediately suspected something was terribly wrong. He abandoned his cart and ran down the hall to locate the source of the noise.

He reached the door with the number 703 engraved on a metal plate. A *DO NOT DISTURB* sign hung on the door handle. He was alarmed to realize it was the same suite that had ordered the champagne. As a rule, he was not allowed to knock when that sign was on a guest's door, so he raced back to his cart and returned to the kitchen. When he told the chef what had happened, a large grin stretched across his face. The chef walked to the telephone to put a call through.

"Good morning, Dr. Badero. My name is Mr. Earnest from the kitchen. . . . Oh, yes? . . . We have your order ready, sir. . . . We are sorry, sir. A server came by but couldn't knock because of the DO NOT DISTURB sign. . . . Yes, sir. . . . He will be right there. We are here to serve you, sir."

He hung up. "You can go up now," he told Able God.

Able God wanted to ask the chef about Dr. Badero—who he was, why he was there—but he changed his mind. Surely he would have another chance to ask. He wheeled the cart upstairs.

▸ ● ▲ ▸

Dr. Badero opened the door. There was not a shred of clothing on him. He was a tall Kanuri man with a big, strong frame and a remarkably handsome face. Able God couldn't quite place his age, but he must have been at least fifty. Even though he did not have large muscles, his figure revealed that he was formerly athletic; he had the kind of body that emphasized the torso and seemed to shrink the waist. His hair was still abundant but irregularly streaked with gray. He glistened with sweat from head to toe.

"Room service, sir," Able God sputtered as he lowered his eyes to the level of the doctor's chest. Able God couldn't look him in the eye, but he wouldn't look away.

"Bring it in and put it down on the table," Dr. Badero said. He vanished into the bathroom, leaving the door ajar. The sound of water from the tap filled the room. Able God wheeled the cart in and closed the door.

A light-skinned woman was hunched up in the corner of the bed, sheet drawn to her chin. Her bare shoulders, emblazoned with what appeared to be a tattoo, suggested that she was naked or at least in her underwear. She stared sideways and rocked gently back and forth. The corners of her lips were bloodied, and a long welt ran across her shoulder. She glanced up at Able God. As their eyes met, she quickly pulled the sheet over her shoulders and then resumed her gentle rocking. His mind scrolled through many questions. From what he could see, there was no latex bodysuit, no manacles or whips. This was something else—something reprehensible had just happened.

Suspicion. Outrage. Moreover, confusion. What was he witnessing? He knew he was not allowed to say anything, no matter how terrible. His job was to serve the guests, nothing more.

"Would you like me to open the wine for you, sir?" Able God asked, raising his voice. There was no answer. The water was still running.

Able God stood with his hands behind his back, surveying the cart. It was all he could do to keep his eyes away from the woman on the bed. His palms sweaty, he recalled what Mr. Hastrup had said about how to treat guests, anticipate their needs, and exceed their expectations. Anything to assuage the oddities of a situation.

"I also brought some bottles of San Pellegrino in case you run out of the ones in your bar."

Again, no answer. Able God looked over at the woman. Her eyes were still unfocused, and she was rocking back and forth. Now that he could see her more clearly, she had a feather tattoo that began on her shoulder. A few seconds went by, then the water stopped running.

"You may leave!" the voice boomed from the bathroom.

"Yes, sir! Please don't hesitate to call us if you need anything else, sir!"

"I said leave!"

"Yes, sir! Enjoy the rest of your morning, sir, and madam!" He prepared to exit with arms stiff. But before doing so, he gave the woman one last look. This time, she did not look away but met his gaze. Her wounded lips trembled. In her eyes was an old fear, and for a moment, Able God thought he'd seen a cry for help on her face, as though her eyes were saying that she did not want to be there and she was not safe. Able God heard Dr. Badero open the bathroom door and scrambled out of the room.

He did not look back. Although he wanted to speak to the chef about what he had seen, he decided against it. The strange sense that something terribly wrong was happening lingered in Able God's mind.

By the time he returned to the kitchen, tiredness overwhelmed him. His mental transmission stalled. He couldn't think straight, but the sadness within him did not recede. He sat in a chair, trying to keep from dozing off. It didn't work. The first light of dawn peeked over the horizon. Awakened by staff arriving for their Sunday morning shifts, he yawned, wiped a rope of drool from the desk, and gathered his things. It was an unusually hot morning. The road was almost abandoned, but he was lucky enough to find a bus to take him home.

> ● ▲ ›

Able God walked past the slaughterhouse, braving the stench of animal offal, stale blood, and decayed viscera. Smoke billowed from burning cow patties. The sound of meat cleavers competed with the haggling of butchers and early morning buyers. He steered through a narrow path of wooden shops that turned into the maze of shacks.

The shacks, numbering over fifty and arranged in blocks, were constructed with corrugated iron roofs that crackled in the sun's heat. Tucked between a labyrinthine food market not far from the slaughterhouse and an abandoned rail line, some of the blocks were used as brothels. The place swarmed with area boys, butchers, beggars, salesmen, haulage truck drivers from the north, streetside casino owners, and pool aficionados. It was the cheapest accommodation available, and he was hoping to save up enough money to get a decent apartment next month.

That morning, like most mornings, the neighborhood was quiet and damp. A drunkard staggered up from the muddy ground and trudged home, the booze worn off. An early morning customer pounded on one of the doors in the brothel section. The pounding swiftly became violent. He seemed drunk and was threatening to break down the door. Able God quickened his pace. Even though the fellow's knocks faded as he walked along, Able God knew it was only a matter of time before more rancor broke out in the neighborhood. People would quarrel about who got to use the communal bathroom first. Sex workers, disgruntled from the previous night's work, would fling sharp words at each other. A neighbor would be caught mid-fornication by his spouse. Objects would fly, wounds would be inflicted, and curses would flow freely. Here conflicts were like a stubborn rash: they never dissipated.

Able God passed the house owned by Old Major, the eccentric octogenarian who was said to have fought in the Burma jungles during World War II and who claimed to have survived thanks to divine intervention.

He passed some old women sitting on low stools in their doorways, their laundry out to dry. One was tossing scraps of food to her mongrel dog. Another was waving a raffia fan vigorously to blow air under her blouse. They were the unofficial neighborhood watch who made it their business to know about things that were not their business. Able God greeted them, but they nodded back at him like he was a stranger. He had never been close to his neighbors. He found the very idea exhausting. They weren't fond of him either.

"He acts like a visitor here. He thinks he is better than all of us because he is educated. What has your education gotten you?" one of the old women once remarked after Able God declined to attend the monthly tenants' association meeting for the umpteenth time.

Able God didn't see the point of an association whose main job was levying taxes on its members in order to benefit the brothels. When the brothels were still fledgling establishments, they had suffered a great deal from police raids until Sir K., a self-appointed fixer, began greasing the palms of the police officers. Sir K. levied all the members of the tenants' association in exchange for "security." The cash was shared among the district's three police stations.

And attending the association's meetings or fraternizing with neighbors would have meant accepting that he was part of the community, or so Able God thought. He did not feel that he belonged there.

His room was so small it only had enough space for a creaky six-spring bed with a gnawed-up bedstead and a wooden partition to separate the toilet from the living space. The bathroom was only big enough to contain the toilet.

How could he forget the day he came home from the polytechnic for his allowance, and his mother said, "I can't continue to carry the weight of this family. It's too much for me." The veins on her neck were as taut as ropes.

That day he hadn't come home to the beautiful house where he was raised. Instead, it was the grimy one-room apartment his family rented after his father lost everything. It was just like the room he lived in now. The rusted hinges of the door screeched at the slightest breeze. The smell of rum, cigarettes, and dust filled the room, along with the stench of kerosene from the stove in the corner where his mother did her cooking. Huge cobwebs hung low from the ceiling, and the room was overcrowded with the few possessions they'd been able to salvage from the old house, mainly for sentimental value, like the stacks of old *Daily Voice* papers. At night, rodents and insects scurried across the floor.

"The state government has not paid us any salary for three months now. How do they expect us to survive? We borrow to eat in this house," his mother said.

"Don't worry, Mummy. I am doing business. Don't worry about me. I will take care of myself," he said. It was an attempt at pacification. She swallowed the wail bubbling up to her lips. He held her.

His father was out on the veranda playing checkers with the crumbling tenement building's other gray-haired tenants. He would sit out there all day and come back in drunk on Ògógóró. He'd scream at Able God's mother, flinging words like *nincompoop* at her and complaining about the government before sinking into a blissful slumber on the only bed in the house. Able God's mother would lie down nearby on the floor mat.

Able God went back to school the following morning. His business was no longer what it used to be, and the money he now made was barely enough to pay one semester of government-subsidized tuition, but if he saved every penny, he'd manage. He did not know what to do for food or accommodations.

Able God started crashing at his friends' places. When he realized he was too much of a burden, he moved on to acquaintances, people from school or the chess club. He targeted the soft ones—gullible teenagers who couldn't say no to a request, born-again Christians seeking new converts, campus pastors hoping to touch humanity with the radiance of God's love. They allowed him two or three days at a time—one even put up with him for a week.

He ate whatever he was given. People were generally willing to share no more than a meal or two, so like a street dog he never ate in the same place more than twice. Soon, the entire hostel became wise to his tricks, and doors were shut against him. He attended every Christian student get-together on campus, where he knew the food would be abundant and given freely without judgment.

Able God's personal effects were crammed under the bed. Clothes draped the walls. A black tie dangled from a six-inch nail. It was the tie he had planned to wear for the job interviews that never materialized: Schlumberger, Total, Mobil, Shell. Then it became the tie he had planned for second-tier interviews, a hope that had also been in vain. Then it was the tie he wore on his sunny afternoon treks to random offices to drop off copies of his resume. It was the same tie he had worn the day he sat down with Mr. Hastrup. That day Mr.

Hastrup had told him he would hire him as hospitality executive, a position he knew had been created to make workers do more for less money.

"We have a special hotel policy of employing hospitality executives to supplement our workforce," Mr. Hastrup said. "You see, working as a hospitality exec is like being an athlete taking part in a decathlon. Only the gifted ones make the cut, my friend."

Able God hadn't been sure how to feel about that, whether to be sorry for himself or to feel good about having found work. Desperate, he accepted the offer.

There was no electricity in Able God's shack, and the room was dark except for a shaft of morning light filtering through the raised blinds. Able God flung his bag in the corner and flopped on the bed. He still felt drowsy, and a small headache was brewing behind his forehead. Above him, the rusted aluminum roof was riddled with holes. During the last rainy season, he'd moved his bed into the corner of the room and collected the water leaking through the roof in buckets.

Able God wanted to sleep without the taint of thoughts in his head. His phone buzzed and glowed brightly. It was his mother. He hesitated before answering, his face hardening into a frown.

"Hello, Mummy."

"How are you, my son? How is work?"

"I am fine. Work is good."

"Good, very good. We are praying for you, my son."

"Thank you, Mummy."

"We have also been expecting your money."

He breathed a sigh. "I will send it to you when they pay my salary at the end of the month."

There was a moment of silence. Able God was tempted to pretend he couldn't hear her and hang up quickly. She spoke before he could make up his mind to do it.

"A mighty prophet of God told us at a church vigil yesterday that you will be very great, rich, and prosperous. He said there are spiritual enemies, and you need to come for cleansing and fortification. It has to be very soon. You need to come home, so find a free weekend and travel down or take time from work if you have to."

"Mummy . . . I don't have a free weekend."

"You must be content with cleaning up after people?"

"Mummy!"

"Able God! Can't you see that the spirits that are against you are so strong that they are trying to keep you away from your place of deliverance?" his mother said. "Do you want to serve others for the rest of your life? Is that what you want to do? I will not allow you to ruin your life! I will not allow that as long as I have breath in my nostrils! You must live up to your name and allow God to intervene in your life."

As old as he was, her words still pierced him. He sat up in bed, as if to thrust away the frustration weighing heavily on his neck and crushing him.

"Your brother told us yesterday that he is coming home in a month. He told us he has a girl he wants to marry. He is your younger brother, and he is already ready to settle down. He has the means to do whatever he wants, and you are three years older than him. Your father and I would have died in wretchedness if all we did was wait for you. Thank God we have Calistus. When will you start doing something for your parents? When will you start taking care of us the way we took care of you? When will we enjoy the fruits of our labor?"

Able God did not know what to say. His eyes smarted with tears.

"Able God? Are you not the one I am talking to? Able God?"

He hung up, his hands trembling. Beams of light streamed into the room as the sun rose, illuminating the dust floating in the air. He buried his face in his hands, the mild thumping in his head now a full-blown headache, then he sank back down onto the mattress and tried to force himself to fall asleep.

4

At Maracanã the shrill whistle pierced the air, and one of the players kicked the ball out of bounds. The boys crouched on the ground or planted their hands on their waists, their dripping chests heaving hard and fast. They snorted, hacked up phlegm. In little clusters, they crossed the street to the communal water tap. Able God, wearing a holey undershirt and rolled-up jeans, flopped to the ground and pulled off his battered tennis shoes. He rested for a moment, tied the laces together and slung the shoes over his shoulder.

The five-a-side players had named the field after the famous football stadium in Rio de Janeiro. Maracanã, where they marked the goalposts with sticks. Maracanã, which was owned by the man who also owned the fenced mansion across the street where they fetched water.

The weekend five-a-side games at Maracanã were mainly for fun—simply a group of football lovers gathering to kill time while they battled for a ceremonial "World Cup." It didn't go beyond competition and fun. Even the most skillful among them dared not dream of more than winning a match on that dusty patch of ground. Not because they could not dream but because there were thousands of boys aspiring to be professional football players in Europe, thousands with magical skills, thousands trying to be like Lionel Messi or Cristiano Ronaldo. For Able God, communing in the field meant he could avoid dealing with his neighbors before his evening shift at the hotel.

Maracanã was once covered with elephant grass, but the Saturday morning games had pushed the green off to the edges of the field, leaving behind a vast expanse of dust on the empty lot.

Able God raced across the street but did not immediately join the straggling line of thirsty players in front of the communal water tap. Instead, he went to the mound of gravel beside the fence, keeping his distance. That's where he usually left his knapsack in the care of a young boy. He set his tennis shoes next to his knapsack and gave the boy a nod that said, "Job well done."

That didn't seem to be enough. The boy gazed earnestly at him like a hungry mongrel expecting something, his shaved head white with dandruff. That was when Able God remembered he still had a leftover croissant he'd taken from the hotel. He handed it to the boy, who chewed noisily as the flakes rained over his body.

Able God joined the water line just as Morufu was hobbling away from the tap. He parted his lips in a smile, musing on how much Morufu had improved as a football player. When Able God first started playing at Maracanã, he hadn't known how to tackle Morufu. Morufu, whose right leg was shorter than his left, played with no less gusto than his teammates. He limped quickly down the dusty pitch, gritting his teeth from what Able God imagined must have been pain shooting through his bad leg. He used either leg to kick the ball up in the air, depending on where the ball was—his bad leg was, as could be expected, less effective, and he often ended up kicking the ball out of play. His foot control was awful, and Able God often found it painful to watch him, even though, deep down, he admired his type of resilience.

When it was Able God's turn at the tap, he removed his vest and let the water stream over his hair, face, and chest. The tap had plenty of water pressure, but the flow wasn't steady. He cupped his hands under the water to wash his face, then scooped handfuls for his dusty arms and legs. He quenched his parched throat and scrubbed his sweaty, mossy armpits. His manager at the hotel, Mr. Tanimola Hastrup, didn't take the issue of personal grooming lightly, especially on Saturdays. He often made unscheduled physical inspections of his workers.

Mr. Hastrup would address the workers while gesticulating wildly with his hands. "You are not only an employee of this organization, but you are also part of our brand. Our policy is to be always prim and proper. We are a world-class hotel organization," Mr. Hastrup would say. "The people who built this hotel and invested millions of dollars in it did it for only one reason—to make money! And you know what? They are paying us to help them make money. So, how do we do that? Very simple. We do that by making our guests feel good, so they come back. In India, they say guests are gods, so we treat them as close to gods as possible."

Beside the fence, Able God dried himself with a washcloth and sprayed on deodorant while the boy watched. He combed his hair meticulously and put on a neatly pressed white shirt that he'd kept folded in his bag. He produced a pair of black trousers and shoes. Within a few minutes, he was dressed for work, white shirt and bow tie.

"Do I look sharp?" he asked the boy, who gave him a shy nod before dashing off.

By then, most of the players had left. His bag slung over his shoulder, he strolled toward the bus stop.

A Danfo lumbered toward the bus stop, its conductor hanging from the door and screaming his head off. The Danfo would not stop for more than a few seconds. Able God walked briskly, then broke into a run.

> ● ▲ >

At Maracanã the following Sunday, Able God infuriated his teammates. He flubbed his passes. When his teammates passed the ball to him, he kicked it out of play. Able God was taken out before the end of the second half, but it was too late for his team anyway. He sat on a mound of gravel, throat parched, face caked with dirt and dust. He watched his team struggle to equalize in the final minutes of the game. Afterward, they walked to the communal water tap, their opponents gloating. He saw the pained looks on his teammates' faces. Ghaddafi, who was on his team, glanced angrily at him, spitting three times on the ground. Able God knew they took the game of football more seriously than he did, so he felt even worse for letting them down. Morufu, who was on the winning team, was untying the laces of his dusty canvas shoes when he announced his plans to go to Europe.

"I am planning to travel abroad to play for the trials at the Barcelona football club. I have what it takes to make the first team! I will play with the great Messi."

The field went wild with laughter. The winners burst out laughing. Even the losers loosened up and joined in the fun. In the end, Able God could not help himself and burst out laughing. He reckoned the win had gone to Morufu's head, and he was glad that the attention had shifted away from him. The waves of laughter faded away.

"How do you want to travel to Europe? Who will give you a Schengen visa?" asked a fellow who called himself Maradona, a scornful look in his eyes.

"You can't wake up in the morning, grab your bag, and limp your way to Europe. I hope you know that," Ghaddafi said, stifling a chuckle.

A pained expression came over Morufu's sweaty face before he feigned a smile. He opted for silence. He stuffed his dusty tennis shoes into his worn-out knapsack.

"Let the old man dream. We are all allowed to dream," Able God said. He felt a bit bad for being complicit in shaming Morufu. He occasionally imagined himself as a grand master at chess with a prosperous career. At other times, he fantasized that he controlled numerous industries throughout Nigeria as a business magnate. He wouldn't, however, be foolish enough to talk about them aloud. They were only phantoms. "You are right, Able God. You don't need to pay money to dream. I once dreamed that I was President Obama!" Ghaddafi said, panting with laughter.

Able God did not laugh with them this time. Morufu got to his feet, his bag slung over his shoulder. He hobbled across the street to the communal water tap. When Morufu was done drinking, he headed off to sit in front of his sister's provisions store.

Since there would be no night shift that day, he had no choice but to go home. He waited ten minutes for the bus. At first, it chugged along steadily, but it eventually got stuck in traffic at a fork in the road. Able God sucked his teeth. Beads of sweat trickled from his armpits and soaked his shirt. He detached his gaze from a smudge on the window and let it rove down the busy street, where he saw a black Mercedes-Benz with tinted windows. He imagined that when he grew wealthy enough to buy a vehicle, he would resist the urge to have his car tinted. Yes, there was a special satisfaction in seeing someone who couldn't see you, and the tinted glass protects the owner from being a subject of jealousy by concealing that person's identity. That, however, was not what he desired. Shouldn't everyone be able to witness his good fortune just as they had seen his misery? That was his dream.

After a few moments passed and the traffic cleared, the bus lurching onward, air blowing in. Able God pulled out his phone to play some chess.

At home, his phone buzzed three times. He fished it out of his pocket to switch it off but paused when he saw his brother's number.

"How bodi?"

"Bodi dey for cloth. Did Mummy tell you I am coming home?"

"So what? I should throw a party because you are coming to Nigeria?" The words escaped before Able God could do anything about it. Laughter boomed at the other end.

"Anyway, I will drive down to pick you up so you won't have to take public transport. That way we can travel home together."

Able God sighed. "Okay, okay. Just tell Mummy that you made plans with me."

"Good. It will also be good to know where you live."

"No! No! I will be at work, and I won't have time to go home, so I will tell you where to meet."

He knew Calistus well; if he brought him there, his brother would trash his flat, ask why he lived in a dumpster, and then send him money later to rent a better place, adding insult to injury.

"Okay, text me the meeting place."

He hung up. Able God took a deep breath as he felt something throbbing in the middle of his forehead, radiating outward.

5

A week later, at Maracanã, Able God sat down on a mound of gravel left behind by the builders after they'd completed the mansion. He contemplated his life, feeling vanquished.

"Aláyé!" Morufu called out as he emerged from his sister's provisions store and loped toward him. Morufu flashed a rotten smile, which for some reason made Able God grin.

"Thank you for defending me the other day," Morufu said.

"We were wrong. We should have known when to stop joking. We should not have made fun of you that way."

"It's okay."

Morufu sat on the gravel with him, and together they gazed blankly in the direction of the fenced mansion.

"Have you ever seen the owner of that big house?" Morufu asked him.

"No. Have you?"

"Yes. People call him Londoner. He lived in London for many years before coming back home."

"He is a been-to." Able God was all too familiar with the term: a been-to was someone who had been overseas and was now living large back home. His brother would never move back home for anything—Able God was sure of that. A been-to's novelty would eventually wear off, like a golden item that ages and loses its luster. Calistus cherished the idea of occasionally coming home. He cherished the pomp and circumstance, the buildup.

"Yes."

"He adds *fucking* to everything he says, just like the Americans do," Morufu added.

Able God flashed a glance at him, smiling. They sat in silence for a while. Morufu took two cigarettes from his pocket and gave one to Able God.

"Whenever I feel the burden of the world on my head, I smoke Igbo with some boys at the end of town," Morufu said. "I feel better when I do that. It's hard to be a man in this world."

Able God appreciated that Morufu did not ask him what was troubling him but instead offered some sort of solution. Although Able God had never been much of a smoker, he almost wanted to ask him where the place was. Anything to shake his pain and sadness. What did he have to lose?

"It's hard to be a man in this world," Able God repeated as he thought about his own condition.

"Do you want to smoke with me?" Morufu asked.

"Yes."

"It is a long walk from here."

"I don't care."

"Okay. I will go tell my sister, then we can go," said Morufu, as he sprang off the gravel mound. He hobbled toward his sister's provisions store. Able God's thoughts drifted to Calistus's impending visit, but he shook it off and stood up. He strolled up to Morufu.

▶ ● ▲ ▶

The two trudged along the garbage-strewn bush path to the wall of an abandoned building, a brick-and-mortar structure blackened by many fires. The ground was gray with ash. Men both young and old sat on the ground, sheets of newspaper spread out under their splayed legs. Some of them looked so dirty it seemed the sweat and grime streaking their bodies had permanently stained their clothing.

Morufu introduced Able God to them, but they were too focused on what they were doing to respond. They hunched over their work like alchemists concocting a groundbreaking potion.

They were crushing things up on sheets of newspaper, using smooth rocks or the bottoms of empty wine bottles. Some of the things Able God recognized—a mosquito coil, dry cakes of cow dung, matchsticks, camphor, and Indian hemp—but others he did not. Some of the boys were crushing mounds of white tablets. Others were emptying bottles of cough syrup into big Ragolis water bottles. To wet their whistles as they worked, one boy circulated a plastic bowl of monkey tail, a drink made of local gin steeped with marijuana leaves. Each man took a gulp before passing it to the next. As they swallowed, their faces twisted and they shuddered, closing their eyes—eyes that were scarlet and watery when they opened them again.

When Morufu offered to take Able God somewhere to smoke, he had not pictured this kind of setting. He had assumed they'd go smoke a joint on some corner or in an empty classroom. Now he felt like turning back. He was not the kind of person who'd hang around a place like that. There was no way he would put those substances into his body.

The boys moved to the next phase of their alchemy. They mixed cocktails of crushed tramadol tablets, codeine cough syrup, and Coca-Cola in water bottles. Three of them gathered the crushed ingredients and rolled up fat joints. The joints gave off a sickly smell, like burning refuse. Able God covered his nose in disgust.

"I have to get ready for work very soon," Able God lied to Morufu, who was chatting with a boy leaning against the fence. The boy wore a filthy singlet and had red, sunken eyes. His body was as slim as the trunk of a sapling.

"What?" Morufu asked.

"I have to go. I have work."

Morufu protested. "No, man! Drink and smoke, then you can go. Abi, you got no liver?" Then raising his voice for everyone to hear, he continued, "This friend of mine wants to leave because he wants to go to work."

Morufu broke into a laugh. Some of the boys laughed with him. The one wearing the filthy singlet passed Able God a joint.

"It won't smell so bad when the drug starts working magic in your body."

Able God steeled himself and brought the joint to his mouth. He exhaled quickly, trying to push his contrary thoughts away. His eyes began to burn. He squeezed them shut and quickly took several drags to get past the horrible tang of the smoke and feel the effects of the drug. Suddenly, he felt a tremendous, incomprehensible warmth rising in his body.

Some of the boys had started squeezing out tubes of glue into an empty plastic bag and were huffing the fumes. Those who smoked did so with their faces turned toward the hot, sunny sky, swatting flies away with their free hands until impish smiles came to their lips and a twinkle to their eyes. One whistled a tune through the gap in his discolored, brownish teeth. Another sniffed the air around him like a dog. They were all suffused with an almost mystical joy. The air was thick with it. They set up dice and card games, placing their bets. The takes were mostly rubber bands because they did not have any money.

They drank from the Ragolis bottles as they smoked. When someone passed a bottle to Able God, he allowed the contents to rush past his lips. The viscous fluid coursed down his throat, some dribbling onto his chin, his sharp-pointed Adam's apple bobbing up and down.

They started chatting. Their voices came loud and slow. Soon, Able God felt laughter rising within him. He laughed, and the sound of his voice returned to him like an echo. He took another swig from the Ragolis bottle. Music rose in his head—a song, a rhythm. As he danced, his gaze fell on Morufu, who was also dancing, tapping his fingers above his head. His movements were jerky as he waltzed slowly through time. Able God held his gaze a little longer. He felt no fear, only stillness and wonder.

Time passed. A group of the boys slumped back against the grimy wall, taking long pauses between talking. Some of them dozed off with their backs to the wall. The man with the filthy singlet curled up close to the wall, muttering to himself. As Able God looked on, an idea filtered through his muddled thoughts.

6

He saw Dr. Badero again two weeks later, after he left room service for his housekeeping duties. It was lunchtime, and Able God had been pacing the hotel, trying to clear his head. He snuck a cold bottle of soda from the hotel restaurant, then skulked around the lobby awhile, gazing out through the silvered glass wall before taking the service elevator to the seventh floor. Whenever he let the memory of his mother's phone call catch up with him, a cloud of despondency descended over him, fogging his brain. He made up reasons why he didn't have to care about what his mother said. His frustration frequently morphed into powerlessness and a desperate desire to find an escape, any escape.

He found Dr. Badero outside on a lounge chair by the pool, luxuriating in a swimsuit, his hairy chest exposed and his rounded stomach glistening in the sun. He had covered his face with a baseball hat. A woman was sitting under an umbrella beside him, sipping a piña colada garnished with a cocktail umbrella. She wore cat-eye sunglasses and a bikini, her dark-skinned body trim and toned. Able God was sure she wasn't the woman he'd seen in room 703, even though he'd only glimpsed her face. The woman by the pool looked calm and happy.

Able God found a seat under the sunshade that offered a prime vantage point. He wanted to be able to get a good look at her without being seen. The woman set her glass on a stool, removed her sunglasses, and undid her bun, running her fingers through her extensions. It was definitely not the guest from 703. She got up and walked over to the pool, her shapely ass jiggling. Water washed down her round, dark face and long eyebrows.

The sight of her body sent a particular sensation unraveling through him. He had never gazed so surreptitiously and so greedily at something forbidden before, and he became embarrassed when he felt an erection pressing against his trousers. She sat on the concrete pool edge and dipped her legs into the shallow end, then watched as a bunch of teenagers laughed loudly and splashed around in the chlorinated water. Able God tried to picture this new woman and Dr. Badero sleeping together and was repulsed by the idea. More so, they couldn't possibly have anything in common. He imagined her as a working-class woman struggling to support her family, while Badero most likely prospered from inherited or stolen wealth. There must be something real beneath that materialistic veneer. He wondered if she also loved chess or enjoyed watching street football. Did she enjoy drinking in roadside bars?

In a way, Able God felt wronged. He had known men like Dr. Badero all his life, men who dominated women—and who hurt them. Men who thought sexual conquest was a God-given right, men who made people like Able God feel ashamed of their bodies and women ashamed of theirs. His looks were not Able God's strong suit; he was a heavyset man of medium height with a big, flat nose framed by a fuzzy moustache. He was not one of those guys women flirt with. He had made a decision to become rich during his time at university, as this was the only way he thought he would attract any attention.

Dr. Badero sat up and looked around. When their eyes met, Able God turned away, pretending to be busy with his nails. The doctor raised a finger to call him over. Able God sprang to his feet and dashed over, his heart beating fast.

"How may I serve you, sir?" He floated his pleasant smile toward the doctor.

"I need a bottle of champagne, a cold one."

"Yes, sir. I will inform a waiter to attend to it right away."

"You have served me before, have you not?" he asked, giving Able God a once-over.

"Yes, sir, during my room service shift. I have been employed here for some months now."

"What is your name?" Dr. Badero asked, peering at his badge.

"Able God, sir!" he said with all the confidence he could muster. He had his toothpaste-commercial smile on, hands clasped behind his back.

The lady decided to jump into the pool, and there was a loud splash.

"Able God! That's a very religious name."

"Thank you, sir," he said, although he did not know what Dr. Badero meant by that. He swallowed his breath.

"You can go, Able God," Dr. Badero said with a knowing smile. Able God walked away. Once out of sight, he heaved a sigh of relief.

A little later, back on housekeeping duty, he imagined the lady heaving herself out of the chlorinated water and going for her towel, her hair wet, her skin slick as a seal. He imagined her toweling her hair elegantly and sipping what was left of her piña colada, then shaking her head briskly, her dark waves flying about. He had the sense that he had seen her somewhere before, although he could not put his finger on when. Able God dwelled on sensual images of the lady for a while, but when a colleague asked why he was smiling, he snapped out of his reverie and rolled his trolley into another room.

> ● ▲ >

On his way home that day Able God had both women on his mind. He imagined the two women did not know each other, but they both served at the pleasure of this rich fellow. What if they did know each other? What if it didn't matter? With a lot of money, you could do anything in this world, even terrible things. He could not get his mind off the look in the first woman's eyes. The more he thought about the women, the more he resented Dr. Badero, which made him feel sad about his life. Agreed, Badero was educated, but education was hardly enough these days. A lot of these big men had blundered their way to riches and success by political connections or embezzlement. For a long time, Able God convinced himself that his job was good for him, that serving wealthy people would bring him close to riches, and he would eventually attract it into his wretched life. "You cannot attract what you despise," he once heard a motivational speaker say, although he sometimes failed to adhere to that principle. He hoped that one day something life-changing would happen to him, like meeting someone at the hotel who would help him land a profitable job or winning a chess competition that would catapult him into fame. Hope is a curious emotion, and whenever he couldn't handle it, he sought pleasure.

Able God fished a cigarette from his pocket, lit it, and began to smoke as he approached the maze of shacks. It was dusk, and the women were out as usual. Some of them were in front of their doors, all geared up and talcum-faced. Some stayed out in the open, in varying stages of undress. They flung furtive glances and hissed like serpents to catch the attention of wandering men. They whispered

words like, "Fine, bobo. Come now make we fuck!" Or "Come inside. I go do you well!" Two hundred naira for transient sex, called
"short time," attracted a flock of men.

Able God was not high today, so his plan was to just pass by.
However, he changed his mind and decided to go in clear-headed.
Able God went up to one of them, a woman of small stature with a
beautiful face, who smiled and guided him through the dark passage
to her room. He knew what to do. He produced money from his
pocket and smoked the rest of his cigarette, squinting in the dim,
red-filtered light of the room as she examined the note. Her nails
were painted but chipped. The rooms had no electricity, so they
were illuminated by candles or battery-powered lamps with weak,
multicolored lights. The ladies would work in total darkness if they
had their way, but they needed illumination, however faint, to check
the authenticity of the customer's cash. They needed to stretch
the notes out, check for disfigurements, and look through the bills
for the transparent emblem before getting out of their leggings or
shorts. Able God could recognize some of them, even knew a few by
name—sweet-sounding false names like Endurance, Precious, Phi-
lomena. The woman, who seemed to be satisfied with her examina-
tion, kissed the money, flourished it, and stuck it under her bra. She
wiggled out of her shorts.

When they had finished, she put her shorts back on and opened
the window to expel the scent of semen and cigarette smoke trapped
in the small room. His dark skin shimmering with perspiration, Able
God fixed his eyes on her, trying to think, but his mind was fuzzy.
She went to the door and creaked it open. He knew it was time to go.
He stood up and left without saying a word.

Able God sauntered into the noisy, cold night. Down the corridor,
he spotted a group of women. They were better dressed, and their

makeup looked expensive. They were smoking and fiddling with their mobile phones as they stood in front of their brightly lit rooms. They paid no attention to Able God, giving him the sense that he was not the sort of client they served. They were different from the desperate ones who had catcalled. When one woman looked up and they briefly locked gazes, his heart skipped a beat. He thought he knew her, but then changed his mind and continued on.

He continued walking till he came to a fence where he joined three other customers who were relieving their bladders while chatting animatedly. He opened his fly and, with eyes closed, let out a pleasurable groan. That was when it came to him: what he had been trying to remember suddenly struck him. He had seen her before; she was one of the women with Dr. Badero. It all made sense. The sex workers typically stayed on the premises, but some ventured out. Home visits were for the chosen few, deemed beautiful and exquisite enough by their madams to serve high-class clients. Whenever the ladies went out, they made more money, which in turn made their madams and Sir K. happy, so no one complained. He knew there was something when he laid eyes on her, but what if he was mistaken? He laughed as he zipped up his fly. How was Dr. Badero any different from him or the men peeing beside him? How? Noticing the men staring at him, he shrugged and made his way home.

7

Able God struggled through the next three days of housekeeping that week. Sir K. pestered him over unpaid community dues. Calistus's arrival was quickly nearing, and every work shift felt more difficult. He emptied trash cans, cleaned windows and toilets, wiped counters, and folded linens. He cleaned the rooms inhabited by guests. He worked full floors from start to finish. He felt unclean and useless, the weight of his insecurities crushing him. His trips to Maracanã and the abandoned building helped ease his apprehension. The drugs put his mind at ease, releasing pockets of tension. The faint regret he had felt about going to such a dodgy place had vanished, and a certain longing took its place. Nothing felt as bad after he'd gotten syrup-high on the sweet, sweet strawberry taste of codeine or inhaled the nasty-tasting smoke into his lungs. The wall gave him solace, injected calm into his body. The drugs made him a little sluggish at work, but the high was blissful enough that he stopped caring about his troubles. But the intoxication didn't last all week. As the days wore on, the fear and uncertainty inevitably returned.

He didn't see Dr. Badero or the woman. He checked the guest list and found out that her name was Akudo Okoh. She had provided no residential address, and the only contact on file was Dr. Badero's.

This was not uncommon, since she was Dr. Badero's guest, but it confirmed his suspicion that she didn't want people to discover her connection with the brothel. He reckoned Dr. Badero would not care where she lived, and Akudo would not want him to know, but he almost admired her double life. After work on the third day, he went to look for her to be doubly sure. What if she recognized him? What if he didn't find her? He could ask around, but then he would have to use her real name, which would make people suspicious. Only the police or a family member would know real names in the brothel.

By the end of the week, Able God finally summoned the courage to try to look for her. He went to the corridor where he had seen the well-lit rooms. He combed every corner and corridor of the brothel that evening, hoping to run into her. He searched the faces of women with see-through tights that revealed a lacy thong, shirts open to reveal naked breasts.

He would approach a closed door, his ears pricking at the slightest noise. Walking through the dark corridor, he slowed down as though treading on a road riddled with landmines. He would rap gently on a door, wiping his sweaty palms on his trousers, his eyes darting back and forth. For a moment, he would hope someone would answer, and the face he would see would be hers. Most times, no one answered, and some even sent curses flying out of the little room mid-coitus.

▸ ● ▲ ▸

Four days later, when Able God saw her again, he was behind the long mahogany reception desk wearing a blue company blazer emblazoned with the hotel logo. She walked in through the revolving doors with Dr. Badero. His bodyguard followed closely behind—he stayed in the lobby during the day and booked a single room whenever his boss spent the night.

As soon as Dr. Badero and the woman entered, everyone's eyes turned to them. People stared only for a few seconds, no longer, as though that was all the time required to get over their surprise.

The doctor, who wore a starched white *babariga* and shiny shoes, did not bother to go to reception. He went straight to the elevator with the woman, one hand on the nook of her hip. Akudo had an impatient look in her eyes. Her Brazilian extensions were piled into a bun high on her head. She wore a tight-fitting blouse, a leather miniskirt, and silver bangles that played on her wrist with each brisk movement. A slim crucifix jiggled between her breasts. The bodyguard looked like a bouncer, with muscular arms and a tight T-shirt that exposed his veined biceps.

The bellhop followed behind with their luggage and, judging from the pile of suitcases on the cart, it seemed they would be staying for a while.

Able God and the other front desk agents nodded a greeting at the doctor as he passed. Dr. Badero, in turn, smiled and waved. The woman did not look at Able God or his colleagues. He watched her from the corner of his eye until they disappeared into one of the guest elevators. His colleagues had started talking about the doctor, so he pretended he wasn't listening as he browsed through the desktop computer's files. He checked Dr. Badero's file and saw that the room had been booked for two weeks. Able God had three more days on front desk duty.

Two hours later, the couple came back out. Dr. Badero walked ahead of her, and she followed slowly, walking sideways like a crab. Her steps were out of rhythm. Dr. Badero quickly exited the building with the bodyguard, but it took her a while to get to the revolving door. She wore a turtleneck and dark glasses. Able God was close enough to see the bruise on the side of her face.

He wanted to ask her, "Are you fine, madam? May I help you?"

She broke into a trot as if she could read his mind. She did not stop. The revolving door spun, and she was gone. Troubling thoughts rose from the depths of his mind. But when a guest walked up to the desk, Able God tucked his worries back into a corner and floated one of his hundred-watt toothpaste-commercial smiles at the man. As soon as the guest was checked in, everything came flooding back: the fear and the sense of foreboding.

He must find a way to talk to her without drawing attention, but he didn't see any way to manage it. She would have to be alone in the suite, and he would have to be stationed on room service or house-keeping.

> • ▲ >

The next day, Akudo sashayed across the lobby to the front desk but did not come to his station. Instead, she walked to the receptionist beside him, a new hire named Tinuke Ishola according to the name tag on her uniform. Able God had met her for the first time just a few hours before, and he was a little puzzled as to why a new staffer had been assigned to the front desk of all places. But the more he questioned the decisions made at the hotel, the more confused he became.

"Welcome to Hotel Atrium, your home of delights. How may we serve you?" Tinuke asked, displaying her professional smile.

"I lost my key card. May I have another one?" the lady asked. Her voice was soft and soothing.

"Of course. We are here to cater to your needs. Would you please give me your room number?"

"Seven-oh-three."

"Thank you, madam. Seven . . . oh . . . three," Tinuke repeated, clicking away on the keyboard.

Seeing Akudo in profile, Able God caught a glimpse of the thick fringe of eyelashes lining her lower lids. The skin of her face was smooth and lightly powdered. Her scent was lovely; Able God could smell her from where he stood.

"I am sorry, madam, but—"

"I am Dr. Badero's guest," the lady interjected, as though she were angry at the impatience in her own voice. "He is not coming here tonight. He will be back tomorrow."

She glanced over her shoulder, tapping the edge of the counter with her long, red nails. For a moment, Tinuke seemed confused. She peered closely at the computer, clicked the mouse once, then twice. She looked up with her official smile back in place.

"Yes, madam, because this room is booked in Dr. Badero's name, and our hotel policy requires that we—"

"I was on duty when they both checked in," Able God quickly interjected. He spoke to Tinuke softly. "Dr. Badero is one of our VIP guests, and she is with him."

Tinuke, in turn, shot a quick glance at Able God from the corner of her eye. A slight frown clouded her smile. When the frown vanished, her smile was a shade less than before—a sixty-watt smile.

"We apologize for the mix-up, madam. We will get you a replacement key right away," Able God said, turning to the guest. Akudo smiled at him, which made his heart flutter a bit. Tinuke swiped a key card through the machine, which made a soft clicking sound, and handed it to her. Akudo snapped it up, glared at it for a second, thanked Tinuke, and left.

When there were no guests at the counter, Tinuke spoke up. Able

God had gone back to his chair and was going through the guest database for Dr. Badero's record. He looked over at the other receptionists, then bit his lower lip slightly.

"Mr. Able God, I'd appreciate it if what just happened doesn't repeat itself. I am capable of doing my job," Tinuke said without taking her eyes off the computer screen.

"Sister, no vex. I was just trying to help."

"I am not your sister. My name is Miss Ishola."

He couldn't come up with an answer to that, and he did not feel he needed to apologize again. As far as he was concerned, she should be thanking him. Had he not stepped in, she would have been on her way up to Mr. Hastrup's third-floor office by then.

Two guests approached the desk, so Able God went back to work. He was glad he'd at least been able to say something to Akudo, even if it was neither what he wanted to say nor the place to say it. She seemed to him like a woman with a good head on her shoulders.

After the guests had been checked in, his gaze fell on a woman walking into the lobby, jauntily swinging her bag. She sat down on one of the lobby seats and crossed her legs. Able God suddenly felt ill at ease, and the blood pounded in his brain. He could have sworn he knew her from university. Hadn't they taken a few courses together in their early years? He was not sure which department she'd belonged to. He thought she was called Nosa, but he couldn't remember her last name.

Able God peered uneasily at her. His head worked out an escape route, but first he had to verify it was her. He would be sure if only she turned her face in his direction, but then again, he didn't want her to see him. His tongue would struggle to find words if she saw him.

When she turned toward him, he realized it wasn't her. It wasn't her. Thank God, it wasn't her.

He turned his thoughts back to Akudo. Now that she was alone, it was time to act. He hesitated for a moment under a cloud of uncertainty. What if he was all wrong and just paranoid? Was this matter worth risking his livelihood? Maybe pursuing this was his way of distracting himself from the low point he had reached in his life. Maybe deep down inside he was angry at Dr. Badero, the moneyed man who changed women the way some people change clothes and disposed of them as he pleased. How had he acquired his wealth? He was sure he'd built his wealth on the blood, sweat, and toil of the powerless.

He tempered his doubts by asking himself if he could backpedal if things went wrong. He figured he could.

8

The following day, around 5 p.m., Able God was slightly drunk and shuffling around Old Major's house like a sleepwalker. He had absentmindedly left his apartment. Someone had told him he had no shoes on, but he had walked the dusty streets sandwiched between wooden stalls, still without purpose. Pedestrians glared at him, but he smiled. He passed a cinema with oxidized posters all over its walls, situated within an assemblage of shacks with labyrinths of underwear and clothes left to dry on washing lines. He strode through the abattoir close to the brothel, which buzzed with loud music, dancing, and drinking, and reeked of antiseptic and cheap sandalwood perfume.

He spotted her, then slowed his stride to a halt to be sure. He felt a pulsing in his veins. It was her, but not in the same glitzy, dressed-up way as when she was with Dr. Badero. She was still without a doubt the most attractive, though. A bit of clarity descended on him, and he quickly made his way back home. Able God blundered through the chaos in his room, searching for his cleanest shirt. After putting on his tennis shoes, he combed his hair and applied talcum powder to brighten his countenance. He finished up his looks by putting on a pair of dark sunglasses. He took his wallet and left.

Able God caught himself walking hurriedly but slowed down. He definitely didn't want to miss her, but he also didn't want to go to her sweating and stinking. A series of questions he had asked himself before unfolded in his mind. If she would recognize him and what that would mean, if his escapade would jeopardize his job. But none of the doubts in his mind made him reconsider his actions.

He moved past several sweet voices beckoning him to their rooms. He did not want any of them, didn't even look at them. Akudo was not around. He walked around and found her at a little yellow-colored kiosk next to an outdoor bar. Lice-infested street boys played football with a bamboo-stick goalpost on the other side of the unpaved street. One was the referee, with a plastic whistle in his hand.

The kiosk bore the inscription *Golden Chance Lotto*. Golden Chance Lotto was a local casino that used several little, yellow-colored kiosks as playing terminals. Able God had never been to this terminal before, despite knowing it was there. He thought he remembered seeing a girl there working as an agent, although he was not totally sure. The girl now rested her back on the front of the kiosk while Akudo leaned forward through the window combing the girl's hair and tying it in a knot. She ran the comb through the girl's hair in long runs. She smiled, appearing at ease. Able God shuffled over to the outdoor bar and took a seat. He was content to watch them, or perhaps he was just feeling sentimental because he was tipsy. Every now and then, a customer approached to place a bet, and they would stop to attend to them before continuing.

Able God became aware of their striking resemblance. Could this be her child? If that were the case, why didn't she protect her child from her way of life? Perhaps that was her intention—to keep her close enough to keep an eye on her, Able God thought.

When they had finished, Akudo brought out a loaf of bread and shared it with the girl. They talked while eating, and later Akudo stepped outside and sat on the concrete ledge in front of the kiosk, watching the street boys play. A skinny mongrel approached her, his tail wagging. She tossed some bread to the dog.

One of the boys broke free from the last line of defense, charged toward the goalie, and took a shot. The ball sailed over the goalpost and flew across the unpaved street before descending a few meters away from her feet. The ball came to a halt as gasps of terror swept through the football field. Some of the boys froze, while others turned away. Maybe they thought she would seize the ball. She walked to the ball, picked it up, and threw it back to them without saying anything.

There was a burst of applause and shrieks of excitement. Akudo laughed. Able God caught himself smiling.

These children lacked guardians and lived in poverty, but they also had freedom. When he was younger, his father forbade him from playing football with the neighbors and instead made him sit at home and complete his homework. His father had told him that he needed to invest in his future. Able God's love of the game was not just for the sake of the community. It was more than just a way for him to unwind after a long week at work; it was also a sign that he was no longer subject to his father's demands.

As dusk fell, more people flocked to the outdoor bar, and a server came over to ask Able God if he wanted anything. Able God suddenly realized he was occupying a seat that should have been reserved for a paying customer. He'd have to get a beer or something.

"Bottle of stout," he said to the server and turned his gaze toward the players kicking the ball around.

Moments later, one of the players, a boy with a dirty vest full of holes, charged the goalie with the ball, but a defender intercepted him, delivering a sliding tackle. The referee's whistle went off. The impact of the collision tossed Filthy Vest into the air, and he crashed on the ground. A cloud of dust whirled up, the whistle shrieking again. The striker clutched his leg, his face distorted with pain. The referee, who seemed jolted by the viciousness of the tackle, blew the whistle again and again. The other players came running, and soon they all crowded around him. Several moments later, Filthy Vest still didn't get up. One of the boys began to cry, his hands thrown back under his head. Another boy revealed a hand stained with blood. That was when Able God stood up and walked over. Akudo got there before him. The kiosk girl followed.

"Make way, make way," she barked, and they made a path for her.

She squatted down and peered at the boy writhing on the dusty ground, the gash on his left leg pouring blood.

"Go back to the shop, Uju. I will handle this," she said to the kiosk girl.

"You, you, and you, pick him up and follow me," she instructed, indicating three boys. They scrambled into action. Akudo led them across the unpaved road to her ledge as the child in the vest screamed in anguish.

"Put him down here," she said, bolting away. Able God, now hunched over the boy, noticed that she was dashing toward her room.

She came back with a bottle of iodine and a cotton ball. Suddenly, a flash of remembrance spread across her face, and she dashed to the room again. She returned with a bucket of water, a bandage, and a teaspoon, which she wedged between the boy's teeth.

"Hold him still!" she said to Able God, briefly glancing his way before turning to the wound. He held the poor boy's legs as muffled screams filled the air, telling the terrified boys to give them some room. He could hear her agitated breath. He could feel the heat of her body and smell her perfume, but everything was different here. Here, she was different. Here, she was free. Akudo shot Able God another look, and he saw a flash of recognition on her face, but only for a few seconds. She seemed to retract it as soon as she realized what she had done. She turned her gaze to the boy in the vest. She patted the boy on the head and said, "You'll be fine, boy. You'll be all right." Able God would see this encounter as a sign that there might be more to come.

9

"hear you are gossiping about me in this compound. I am here to let you know that you do not try that with me," a fellow sex worker said to Akudo. Able God stood at a distance to observe her. He had been watching her for days now. After work, when he suspected she would be there, he'd find a shady spot nearby and keep an eye on her. He would occasionally stroll around while chain-smoking; other times, he would visit nearby areas and ask people about her. He asked in ways that made him appear suspicious. He imagined ways to approach her and have a private conversation, but he later realized that he wouldn't be able to say anything meaningful.

The sex worker wore a pair of leggings, and wisps of unruly hair escaped from her roughly tied scarf. Akudo eyed her slowly and said nothing. She was seated on a stool in front of her room.

"I have been watching you! You think you are better than anybody else doing this job," she added, inching closer, stabbing the air with her fingers. Akudo sprang up and took a step back, her eyes flashing a caution sign, as if to advise her to back off. When the other woman appeared unwilling to budge, Akudo cast a glance around as if to see if those around her would approve of her possible course of action.

No one was near, at least at first. Her daughter had to be at the kiosk. Able God had discovered that the kiosk girl was her daughter, and she assisted her in running a lotto business near the brothel. Akudo had still not mentioned recognizing him from the hotel, and Able God had stopped worrying about it. He understood her motivation in some ways. Perhaps to protect her daughter, she had to keep her two lives separate. She had her own method of safeguarding her daughter.

"Do you think you're better than us because you stay in fancy hotels and sleep with rich men?" she asked, striking a chord. Akudo gave her a push that sent her sprawling on her buttocks, stirring up a plume of red dust. She picked herself up, and Akudo parried a slap hurtling toward her face. Akudo unleashed a series of slaps and swipes at her as the sex worker reeled back, shrieking. A crowd began to gather. Able God sensed an opportunity to get closer without being noticed.

The woman dove at her legs, and Akudo wasn't fast enough to elude the blow. She glided through the air before crashing to the ground, slamming her back against the floor. Akudo summoned enough strength to kick the woman off and jump up. She darted to a nearby rubbish dump and began a frantic search for a weapon; she returned with a gnarled stick. The woman stepped back, cursing and spitting, while two women tried to restrain Akudo.

Everything happened so quickly. Able God had witnessed a few brawls at the brothel, but he never anticipated Akudo getting involved in one. At this brothel, Akudo seemed to be an entirely different person, and this realization complicated his feelings toward her. She was an enigma. Able God went home excited, realizing how much he enjoyed the fight. He was pleased that Akudo had the upper hand. His mood soured, however, as the phone rang. It was his mother.

> ● ▲ ›

Able God gazed into the cloud of dust stirred up by the players dashing about. Sometimes when the whistle pierced the air, the players would stop in their tracks, and the dust would settle. But it was never long before the referee blew the whistle again, signaling resumption of their hectic play amid the haze of sand. The tang of their sweat filled his nose.

He was not in the mood to play football that day, but he needed to clear his mind and reflect on the phone conversation with his mother the day before, so he settled for sitting on the edge of the field.

Morufu kicked the ball toward the opponent's goalpost, falling over in the process. The defenders ran after the ball in their dusty, sweat-soaked T-shirts, their tennis shoes yawning with holes. One of them chest-trapped the ball, then passed it to a teammate, who crossed to Ghaddafi. Ghaddafi bounded down the left flank and fired a shot. The ball soared in a perfect arc, eluding the goalie and landing in the makeshift brick-and-bamboo goal. A burst of jubilation followed. The game was not over yet.

Able God's phone buzzed, and he dug into his pocket for it. It was his mother. He stared at the phone for a few seconds, then tucked it back into his pocket, heaving a sigh. His gaze slid across the field to the abandoned mansion, the communal tap, the mound of gravel, and beyond that, the row of shops down the street. He spotted the boy with dandruff running up and down the road, guiding a bicycle tire with a stick. Able God smiled, stood up, and walked around to the other side of the field.

"Young man, let me play with your tire for a while," Able God said. The boy paused, the tire coming to a standstill.

"No! I am driving to London to see the queen!" the boy said, glaring at him from the corner of his eye.

Able God chuckled. "Your little vehicle cannot take you to London!"

"Yes, it can!" he shouted, moving the tire onward, then up over the gravel mound. The boy lost control, and the tire clattered down the slope. Refusing to be deterred, the boy picked up the tire and steered it carefully back up the mound. When he finally made it to the top, he shouted, "See, I am now in London!"

Able God gave him a tight-lipped smile.

After the final whistle, Morufu beckoned, and they made their way to the abandoned building. Then Morufu left the wall for a few hours. Able God did not mind him leaving. He'd grown accustomed to smoking and drinking without him. Not that he considered himself friends with the other boys, but he was no longer an outsider. He felt comfortable chitchatting with them about nonsense, but he would not go farther than that. Whenever they asked him about his job or where he lived, he withdrew from the conversation.

Morufu came back two hours later with a tall fellow. His head was a mass of bushy hair and whiskers from which two eyes peered out. He wore an oversize, snuff-colored jacket. Morufu was carrying a big leather briefcase covered with faded stickers. They bore slogans like "NO BLOOD" and "GOD'S KINGDOM ON EARTH."

Able God recognized the stickers. They belonged to the Jehovah's Witnesses, a religious group that had made persistent visits to his home when he was a child. They came with their glossy pamphlets, briefcases, and the message of living in God's kingdom on earth. Able God cast a questioning gaze at Morufu, who set the dusty briefcase beside his friend and hobbled forward to speak.

"We have someone here with some very good news. It is a once-in-a-lifetime opportunity."

For a moment Able God was confused. He was sure the visitor hadn't come to smoke and suspected he was some kind of preacher. But the last time he checked, Morufu was Muslim, not a Jehovah's Witness. Able God took a drag on his joint.

At first, the boys did not pay them any attention, but the fellow cleared his throat to speak in Yoruba, and one by one, they turned to listen to him.

"My name is Ben Ten, and I am here to share with you a once-in-a-lifetime opportunity. I am the CEO of Boys International Airport, a travel agency with a proven record of making dreams come true and taking people to the Promised Land."

More than what he was saying, his name drew Able God's attention. Ben Ten the cartoon character? In the cartoon, Ben discovered a strange watch-like alien device that attached itself to his wrist, enabling him to transform into a variety of aliens, each with unique characteristics. Able God wondered if the boys knew this. He wondered if this was all a joke. Ben Ten picked up his briefcase. Morufu rushed to help hold it but was waved off. He found a half-broken brick by the wall and set the briefcase on it.

"I organize travel for clients to Europe, America, Germany, China, you name it."

"Really?" Able God said in a cynical voice, swigging from his bottle. Ben Ten shot a cautionary glance at him, then plowed ahead.

"Although we help our clients travel anywhere overseas, we are offering a direct service to Europe at this time. You do not need a visa to travel with us. We will go by road, and it is far."

"*Alhamdulillah!*" Morufu exclaimed. Ben Ten's words had put a happy glimmer in Morufu's eyes. He lifted his face and cupped his hands up to the sky. The rest of the group didn't seem convinced. Able God thought it was a joke. The news was filled with sad stories of people traveling to Europe by road. Ben Ten was probably just another con man. Able God was waiting for him to talk about the money it would take to make the journey. That would be a deal breaker even for Morufu, who had brought him.

Ben Ten whipped a wrinkled, grease-stained map out of his briefcase and unfolded it on the ash-covered ground.

"This is how the journey will go. From here, we move to Kano and then Zinder in the Niger Republic, then we will proceed to the desert town of Agadez and then up to Sabha before we land in Tripoli, the Libyan capital. From Tripoli, we will take a speedboat across the sea to Europe. Very simple," he said, tapping his fingers on the map.

A few of them moved closer and peered straight down; some craned their necks from where they stood. Ben Ten took some photographs out of his briefcase and passed them around. Pictures of tall buildings with flickering lights, arched bridges, narrow cobblestone streets, and train stations with high ceilings. "Photographs from Europe," he called them. There was no excitement, only curiosity. The photographs looked old and smelled of camphor.

Able God stood up with a grin, wondering what tricks were left in Ben Ten's briefcase. He wondered when the man would get to the point, the point being how much the journey cost.

Ben Ten got out some sheets of paper he called contracts. He read the contract out loud. He said the contract stated they would remit to the last dollar the money committed to the trip. It was in dollars. Thousands of dollars. The contract would give them a minimum of three years to work to pay off their debts when they reached Europe.

"You will not pay anything at the beginning of the trip. You will also work along the way in Sabha and Tripoli. You'll do whatever it takes to earn money: manual labor for building projects, dishwashing at cafeterias, bartending at local hotels," said Ben Ten.

"So, we don't need any money to go on this trip, right?" Morufu clarified.

"That's right." Ben Ten's voice was laced with confidence. "You will work for the money later. We have been doing this for years at Boys International Airport. You can ask around. One hundred percent guaranteed to get to Europe. And not only do we service Nigerians, but people come from all over West and Central Africa to join our trips."

At this point, the boys' interest was piqued. They all huddled around Ben Ten. Only Able God did not move closer—if anything, he was even more amused. He was impressed by how detailed and strategic Ben Ten was for being a crook. He took another drag from the joint, downed the rest of his codeine cocktail, and tossed the bottle aside. His mind went to the boy with the bicycle tire from earlier that day. From a very young age, the idea that life was better anywhere beyond the shores of the country was instilled into every mind. Able God had also been indoctrinated, but he always believed he could make it in Nigeria if he worked hard enough.

For Calistus, it was a different story, but even then, he had traveled to South Africa by plane. Able God would admit his life was far from where it should be, but nothing would drive him to such a level of desperation. He would rather steal than allow himself to be smuggled across the Sahara like an illicit good. There was Chinedu, his former schoolmate whose uncle made it to Europe and ended up working in Finland. Chinedu enjoyed his uncle's largess and received money from him often. That was one success story out of many disastrous ones.

Ben Ten kept speaking, his voice stretching like a broken cassette until it faded away.

Able God stared at him for a few moments, not knowing what to make of his thoughts, before shifting his eyes away. He took another drag and leaned back against the blackened fence. A few moments passed, and Ben Ten got out a notebook for the interested candidates to record their names.

"For this trip, I am taking only two busloads of passengers, so spaces for Nigerian delegates are limited," Ben Ten announced. "Passengers from other countries will join us en route."

The boys clawed at each other's throats, trying to add their names to the list. Dust rose from the ground. Able God smiled as he watched them struggle. Ben Ten ordered them to get in line, the now-crumpled notebook raised above his head. Able God couldn't deny that Ben Ten was a good snake-oil salesman. First he had convinced them of their need for his fake goods, then he had created a sense of scarcity.

Only Morufu did not join in the fray, which did not surprise Able God. He was the middleman; his slot on the bus must have been guaranteed beforehand. Morufu approached him, concern written all over his face.

"Won't you register?" Morufu asked.

Able God was going to tell him he was being duped. He was going to tell him his dream of going to Europe was just a mirage, that Ben Ten was preying on his desperation. But he had not seen Morufu so happy since he'd met him.

"If you have money in Nigeria, you don't need to leave Nigeria. I will be one of those who will make it in this country," Able God said. Morufu burst out laughing. Able God laughed, too. Laughing was a salve.

Later that day, Able God decided to go back to his old shack, although he didn't think it would still be unoccupied. He took the overgrown bush path right after the spare-parts market as a way of avoiding the old women or anyone else who might recognize him. He did not want anyone tipping off Sir K. He looked to the right and to the left as he trudged through tall weeds, braving the stench of shit.

It was dark all around him, and all was quiet but for the distant sound of music drifting out of the brothels.

He sat and clasped his hands in prayer. He hadn't prayed to God since the day he'd taken his last final exam back at university. This was another time of need.

10

"What is Ghaddafi doing here?" Able God asked Morufu, who appeared perplexed by the question. Able God asked again, taking a drag from his joint. Here was Ghaddafi, smoking and playing cards by the wall, days after the game.

"He is joining us for the trip," Morufu answered. "Who doesn't want to make it in this life? We are leaving on Monday!"

Able God wanted to press him further but realized it would take another ten minutes to get an answer, so he remained quiet.

Ben Ten showed up moments later in a black Toyota Camry. He made a dramatic entrance, his vehicle screeching to a halt in front of the abandoned building, the boys shouting and hailing him. He got out of the driver's seat with his briefcase, and someone—a ludicrous caricature of something—shuffled out of the passenger's seat. The stout fellow wore a heavily embroidered white kaftan. Tied across his waist over a pair of brocaded trousers was a red skirt embellished with a beaded eye motif. He looked like a witch doctor, but there was nothing authentic about him, at least not as far as Able God was concerned. He looked more like one of those witch doctors from a low-budget Nollywood movie.

Able God guessed that the presence of the Nollywood witch

doctor meant there would be some kind of ritual. He figured it would be best to enjoy the spectacle quietly and try to forget about his problems, his hopelessness. Part of the distraction was the reminder that no matter how bad things were, they weren't as bad as what he was witnessing.

So, his mouth set in a rictus, Able God watched the Nollywood witch doctor proceed with his performance without any sort of introduction. He shook a small gourd vigorously while incantations burst from his lips. Soon, he was prancing around, chanting and shaking the gourd as though dispelling evil spirits from the area. Able God couldn't control his laughter when he saw how some of the boys looked on with fear-glazed eyes. Able God saw that even Ghaddafi, who had initially scoffed at the idea of traveling to Europe, was swept off his feet by the elaborate scam. Two of the boys burst into laughter, which made Able God a little glad that he wasn't the only one who'd seen through this charade.

Able God began to laugh, causing the believers to look at him. Ben Ten tried to shut him up, but Able God only laughed louder until he was doubled over in a violent coughing fit. Ben Ten charged at him angrily.

"Do you think we are joking here?" Ben Ten demanded, pushing him a couple of times.

"Yes, I think you are joking. The joke is on those who believe in this fraud," Able God said in a voice dripping with ridicule, his fists balled up and ready to strike should Ben Ten push him again. Morufu sprang in between them to calm things down. Able God looked around and saw faces flaring with anger and contempt. Those sitting had gotten to their feet. The witch doctor kept on chanting as though impervious to what was going on around him.

"Abegi, no put san san for our gari! If you are not interested in what we are doing here, don't hinder others," Morufu said in a low tone, his jaw clenched with suppressed anger. He shoved Able God away from the irate group.

"Do you want Ben Ten to change his mind and take his business elsewhere?" Morufu asked. "They will all blame me if things go wrong because I brought you here. Behave yourself or I will remove the teeth in your mouth with my fist."

Able God wiped the smug look off his face. For a moment, he thought about walking away, but he changed his mind almost immediately. He would stay merely out of curiosity. The abandoned building was no one's personal property.

Morufu went over to Ben Ten to apologize. Then Morufu suddenly started laughing. The laugh came as a surprise and helped dispel the tension. It infected Ben Ten, then rippled through the group. Able God wasn't amused this time around.

At the tail end of the laughter, the Nollywood witch doctor finished his incantations and sat on the bare ground. Ben Ten called for everyone's attention, his briefcase beside him.

"Traveling to Europe is very easy, although there are certain risks. Everything in life is a risk. Even common eating is a risk. You can take in food through your mouth and have it end up in your windpipe," he began. "There can be no success without risking something. The road to Italy may be filled with dangers, but we trust in God. We will get to our destinations by the grace of God."

The boys called out a chorus of amens. Able God almost chuckled at the irony of their amens, but then the witch doctor sat down right in front of them.

"On this trip, it is important that you keep your money very well. Remember to change your money into dollars. Don't bring naira on this trip. It will be useless to you. If the police see that you have money, they will trouble you, so you must be smart. Generally, you must be vigilant. Your fellow travelers can steal from you. Yes, it can happen," Ben Ten said, then produced an empty toothpaste tube from his briefcase. He showed them how to cut the tube open halfway, roll up a wad of notes and stuff them inside.

He took a piece of muslin from his briefcase and showed them how to wrap it around their heads to protect themselves from the infernal dust of the Sahara. He explained how to kill fleas and mosquitoes, to wear layers of clothing for the cold nights, to avoid rousing snakes or scorpions or beetles. He advised them to bring dates and mint tea. He advised them never to trust their eyes in the Sahara, because the landscape never stopped changing. He advised them to piss into plastic bottles because they might have to drink it eventually. His eyes, set deep in their sockets, darted to and fro as he spoke and gestured.

Then the ritual began. The witch doctor recited incantations and shook his gourd for a while before asking those traveling on the journey to step forward. His words came out hoarse and raspy, just like the Nollywood witch doctors. Able God couldn't understand why the other boys were falling for it.

The witch doctor paced around, then began circling the would-be travelers. He asked them to repeat phrases after him. He gave them his gourd, which they hit against their foreheads and chests three times each. They repeated the phrases again. The witch doctor goaded them into a kind of frenzy. The phrases were long, and they were shouting, so Able God did not catch everything he said, but he understood what the witch doctor was trying to do.

They proclaimed that they were beneficiaries of Ben Ten's kindness. They invited the gods to visit them with sickness, misfortune, and death should they under any circumstances snitch on Ben Ten to the police or immigration. They invited the gods to visit them with wrath should they fail to remit to the last dollar the amount specified in the contract.

The strange kind of respect Able God had felt for Ben Ten was immediately renewed. Out of nowhere, this odd, unkempt individual had managed to convince a group of boys and grown men to do something utterly stupid, if not actually life-threatening.

Able God found himself floored by the force of his own awareness. He reminded himself how much had changed for him in a short period of time. By the following week, more than half of the boys at the fence would be gone. He would no longer be welcome there after what he'd done to the witch doctor. His friend Morufu would also be gone. The boys at Maracanā would have no one to taunt.

Ben Ten's words echoed in his head: "Everything in life is a risk. Even common eating is a risk. There can be no success without risking something."

11

erhaps after all, some risks were worthwhile. Able God had first believed that Akudo was out of his league and that he would need to be well-to-do for her to even notice him, but the past few weeks had proved him wrong. Years of reading self-help books had taught him to see difficulties as an opportunity rather than an impediment. Perhaps their common desire to break out of life's rut would bring them together in some manner. Maybe she had been shunned just like he had and needed to prove her family wrong. Many individuals might disagree with the methods she had used to advance in life, but he didn't care. Besides, he wasn't in her shoes and didn't know her story. But he wanted to know it. He knew he wanted to be a part of whatever circumstances she was in. Maybe then he wouldn't feel so alone in his struggles.

That morning, Able God stood behind the front desk with his well-ironed uniform, name tag, and fabricated smile. He awoke early that morning, overcome by a strong sense of unease after another night of drinking and spying. He realized he had been so blinded by his fixation on Akudo and her daughter that he hadn't seriously weighed the risks. Maybe he had. He could not tell what he was doing these days. He would lose his job—all Akudo needed to do was tell Dr. Badero about him. What if they had him arrested for harassment?

By afternoon he was overcome with fatigue, and when she walked in with Dr. Badero, Able God's self-consciousness had almost vanished. Akudo gave him one awkward glance. Her gaze had something sleepy about it. She did not address him. They left in seconds to go upstairs. When the front desk phone rang for the umpteenth time later that afternoon, he rolled his eyes.

"Hotel Atrium front desk. How may I help you?"

A female voice was sobbing at the other end of the line.

"Hello? Is everything all right?"

"Am I speaking to Able God?"

"Yes."

"I killed him!"

"May I know who is speaking, please?"

"It's me, Akudo, for Christ's sake! I killed him! He is dead!"

For a moment, Able God cupped his hand around the receiver.

"I hit him on the head. I thought I was going to die. . . ." Her voice choked, and she burst into tears. Able God looked around, listening to her weep in cowed silence, until she hung up. For a moment, he was frozen in place. He tried to make sense of what he'd just heard. Then he slowly set down the receiver, grabbed the master key card, and slipped from behind the desk without telling his colleagues he was leaving. He walked to the elevators. He would use the guest elevator this time. One pinged at just the right moment, its doors parting to reveal two men in suits. He tacked on a smile and greeted the men. Despite the flurry of activity in his brain, he was surprised that the rest of him remained calm. Maybe it was the shock or maybe it was that he didn't really believe her and just wanted to be sure. It was quiet in the guest elevator except for the classical music piped in from the ceiling. Fearing that the anxiety boiling inside him would froth over into a full-scale panic, he walked briskly down the long hallway, not so quickly as to attract attention nor too slowly—something between speed and caution. He slid the card into the key slot and cracked the door open to sneak a glimpse into the room, then quickly entered to find her sitting naked on the floor beside Dr. Badero's supine, naked body. She was rocking slightly back and forth.

Able God slammed the door shut behind him and stared down at Akudo. She was still clutching the phone receiver, which was stained with blood. Blood smeared her face and her breasts. The sheets on the bed behind them were soaked with blood. Her mouth had assumed a miserable arc, there was foam at the corners of her lips, and her tear-stricken face twisted in distress. Broken glass littered the floor. Had she snatched the tumbler from the bedside table and used it to strike Dr. Badero's head?

Dr. Badero's eyes were closed. A fine ribbon of bright red blood trickled down onto the plush guest room carpeting, drawing a short line from his head toward Able God's feet. First he dashed to the wardrobe to fetch a blanket to cover her trembling body. He then removed his company blazer, yanked off the bloodied bedsheets, and helped Akudo into the bed. She curled up with her knees to her stomach and pulled the sheets up to her chin.

"I—" she started, tears spilling down her cheeks. "I—"

Able God grabbed her by the shoulders and looked into her eyes.

"Shhh. Everything will be okay, all right? Let me check him. He might still be alive; we might still be able to save him."

Akudo turned her head sideways and sobbed. He took a deep breath, tried to focus. He recalled his training.

The first priority is to ascertain the guest has expired with no hope of resuscitation. If revival is a possibility, contact the front desk and have them call the emergency number or contact the police or emergency response authorities immediately.

Engage in CPR or other appropriate first aid measures until the emergency services arrive. If it appears that the guest has been expired for a considerable time and you are certain that revival is impossible, do not remain in the guest room or area. After notifying the front desk, exit and lock down the guest room or secure the general area. Await the arrival of hotel management and the police.

Calling an ambulance or the police was out of the question, but Able God could find out if resuscitation might be possible. Crouching on the floor over the doctor, he reached out a hand and placed his index finger on the chubby wrist. He felt nothing—or rather, he was not sure what he felt because his fingers were trembling. Able God wiped his sleeve across the sweat stinging his eyes, then tried to check Dr. Badero's pulse at his neck. That was when Badero's face twitched. He turned his bloodied head slowly, groaning in pain. Akudo bolted to a seated position. Able God looked around, wondering what to do next, maybe something for his wounded head. Maybe he should call the front desk after all.

Dr. Badero's eyes snapped open, and within seconds, his face transformed into something twisted and animated. He reared up with a kind of strangled scream, a sound that could have been rage or maybe anguish.

He hurled Able God to the floor. A sharp pain shot through the back of Able God's head, and his eyes went dizzy. The doctor's naked body was now pinning him down. Badero wrapped his hands around Able God's neck, angry veins pulsing on his forehead. Able God tried to push him away, but the weight was suffocating him. He sucked in air through his mouth as he felt the grip on his neck tighten. He kicked desperately, arms flailing as he tried to free himself from the hands clenched around his throat. He heard Akudo screaming and crying. He became light-headed, and his vision clouded. Akudo's cries became less audible, like some distant sound. He soon realized that he could no longer move his legs. *He felt like he was dying.*

His right hand groped around on the carpet, and he felt a thick shard of glass. He summoned his strength and drove the broken glass into Badero's neck. Able God struck twice.

A terrible scream erupted from Badero's throat, and blood spurted forth like a faulty fountain. He rolled away from Able God and slid to the floor, clutching his neck, cursing and screaming in pain. Able God gasped for air and coughed, then rose to his feet, teetering a moment.

"Oh, my God! Jesus! Jesus! Oh, Jesus! Blood of Jesus!" he heard Akudo screaming in horror.

He then looked at the doctor, drawing in a terrified breath. Dr. Badero tried to stop the bleeding, but blood spurted out between his fingers, and he began to choke. His screams trailed off, and within seconds the only sound in the room was the flapping of his mouth and the gurgling of blood in his throat. He went still, his eyes wide open.

Able God slowly opened his trembling hand, allowing the shard of glass to fall from his grip. He gazed at the deep cut etched across his palm by the glass. He contemplated it for several seconds, his fingers unsteady. Finally, he glanced at Akudo, who had curled up again, her back pressed against the headboard. She was sobbing. He tried to think. The fearful thudding of his heart seemed to echo in his ears. He gasped for air as though he had been underwater and was now struggling to the surface for oxygen.

He dashed to the door, leaving a trail of blood behind him. He was not sure if he had locked it. He had. He then hung up the DO NOT DISTURB sign with his good hand before rushing to the bathroom.

In the bathroom, as he tried to calm himself down, he glanced in the mirror. He could not stand to look at himself. He was the murderer now, not her. The burden, the darkness was now his to bear, and the whole affair seemed like a waking nightmare.

He turned his attention to his palm, running cold water over the gash and wincing as pain seared through him. The sharp burning in his hand persisted even as he grabbed a hand towel to wrap around his bleeding palm. He dashed back to the bedroom. Dropping to his knees beside Akudo, he shook her by her shoulders.

"We have to do something! We have to do something fast!"

Akudo stopped sobbing and shot him a crazed look, snot dripping slowly from her nose. She didn't look away.

"We need to deal with the body and leave this hotel! We cannot call the police; we cannot tell anyone about what happened. Do you understand?"

She said nothing. She just stared.

"If we let anyone know, we are going to jail, and we will not stay there for long," Able God said, panic rising in his voice. With that, Akudo's face twisted in anguish, and she broke down in tears. Her breath was short and ragged, her body heaving with grief.

They both knew what would happen to them if they got caught. The prisons were crowded, so extrajudicial executions were used to decongest the cells. Even armed robbers were shot and their bodies thrown into the bush. Akudo was not likely to be exonerated given that she had tried to kill a rich man, and there would be no escaping death for Able God, the man who had finished him off.

An idea struck him, and he took her by the shoulders and gave her a shake. He turned her body to face him.

"You need to stop crying. First, we need to clean this place up. I will go and get the things we need. Stay in the room and lock the door. Do not open the door for anyone. I will knock three times so you will know it's me. Is that okay?"

She nodded and choked back tears.

"Your shirt is stained with blood," she said.

Able God took one look at his sullied shirt and quickly tucked it in. He pulled his company blazer on over his shirt, covering the stain. Then he made for the door, Akudo tailing him. He stepped into the carpeted corridor, shut the door behind him, and hurried to the broom closet. That was when he remembered that he needed a key card. Able God was going almost mad with fear, a cacophony of thoughts ringing out in his head as he walked toward the elevator. But he needed to maintain composure at all costs. The door could open any time, and there could be a guest or supervisor in the elevator. He took time to breathe deeply, looking left and right. Seconds later, the doors opened.

Thankfully, it was empty.

He stepped in, holding his body stiffly, and the door closed. When he reached out to press the button for the first floor, he felt a sharp pain and peered down into the palm of his wounded hand. Blood was oozing from the gash on his palm. He could not wipe off the blood, nor could he allow anyone to see his hand. He shoved it into his pocket, gritting his teeth. He tapped his feet, his eyes glued on the digital display screen showing the floor numbers above.

7 . . . 6 . . . 5 . . . 4 . . . 3 . . . 2 . . . 1 . . .

The elevator came to a halt, the doors opened, and he was back in the lobby. Nothing had changed; soft music filled the air as shoes

clacked along the marbled floors. Black suitcases rolled on wheels.
Courteous greetings in low tones floated back and forth. The smell
in the air was the same—pleasant, perfumed with many fragrances.
The world moved on, or rather it kept on moving. Dr. Badero, on the
other hand, remained irrevocably dead.

"Where did you go? Why did you leave your duty post?" his supervisor asked him sternly. The supervisor had quietly cornered him
in the tiny office behind the front desk. Able God's mind went blank
from trying to concentrate so intensely.

"Are you not the one I am talking to?" she snapped at him.

"S-sorry, *oga*! I was in the toilet," he spluttered. His wound blazed.

"You were in the toilet for over thirty minutes? And you didn't tell
anyone before you left?" she asked, giving him the evil eye.

"Yes, *oga*."

"People have been concerned about your behavior in this organization. You do whatever you like. You disobey orders. You are even
putting your hand in your pocket while I am talking to you."

"Sorry, *oga*!" Able God said as he quickly slipped his bleeding
hand out of his pocket and put it behind him. Had she seen it?

"You will need to report to Mr. Hastrup's office. He wants to see
you!" she said and left the room. Able God could hear her giving the
other front desk staff instructions. He grabbed a tissue from the shelf
and hastily wiped his bloody hand, which throbbed with a scalding,
persistent pain.

Once the supervisor was gone, he slipped behind a computer and
furiously typed the broom closet's access number into the key cod-
ing machine. He swiped a new card through and was done and gone
before anyone could question him. He knew it would not be long
before security started looking for him. Able God hurried back upstairs, then suddenly remembered he hadn't needed the key card to

begin with; he had the master key. He swore at himself as he opened the broom closet.

He grabbed rolls of toilet paper, cleaning rags, and a mop and bucket. He found a gallon of bleach, some disposable latex gloves, plastic garbage bags, scouring pads and sponges. There was a large laundry cart in the closet, which he thought could be used to dispose of the body. He removed what was in it and loaded it with his cleaning materials.

Able God pushed the cart quickly along the hallway but stiffened and slowed down when a staff member emerged at the end of the hall. Sweat beaded on his forehead. He smiled and nodded at her as she passed, waited for her to disappear, then hastened to room 703.

He knocked three times and waited for twenty seconds, ears straining. Nothing. His heart raced, sweat dripping from his temples. He knocked again and finally heard footsteps. The door opened.

In the room, Able God suddenly became aware of the metallic odor of blood in the air and the stench of shit rising from Badero's body. Able God wrinkled his nose and got to work.

His first task was to clean the blood from the gaping wounds on Badero's head and neck to avoid creating more of a mess. After soaking his sponge in a bucket full of warm water, Able God began to wipe the blood from the doctor's body. He was not sure he knew what he was doing. Waves of pain rippled through the gash in his palm.

"I need some help here, for Christ's sake!"

"No! No! I don't want to touch him!" she shouted, her voice breaking.

He went on, averting his face and gagging a couple of times. When he had finished cleaning up the scene, he rushed to the toilet to vomit.

Next, he laid out a clean sheet on the carpet and rolled Badero's enormous body onto it. He groaned and wiped sweat from his brow. He heaved and pushed and rolled, more sweat pouring down his face. He flipped Badero onto his stomach and carefully rolled up his limp body in the sheets, wrapping him up like an Egyptian mummy. In the end, Able God collapsed on the floor in exhaustion.

The hardest part would be scrubbing all trace of blood from the hotel suite. After mopping and scrubbing for several minutes, he decided it was a futile effort. He glanced at the laundry cart, then at Badero's shrouded body. Once again, he had made the wrong calculations. There was no way his body was going to fit into the cart. Even if it did, where would they dump the body without being caught? There were guards and cameras everywhere and they had no way of getting through the emergency exit. He discounted the idea. In the end, Able God realized they had no choice but to abandon the corpse and try to leave the hotel without arousing suspicion. But then another idea struck him, one that had been hovering at the back of his mind. Ben Ten was his escape.

"I have a new plan," he said to Akudo. "What if you dress up in your best outfit, put on makeup, and go down to the lobby to ask the concierge for a taxi to take you back to school. If they ask for the bill, tell them to add it to Dr. Badero's account. We will meet at the brothel."

"What if they track me down?" Akudo asked.

"If we leave this body here, they will track you down anyway, but I know someone who can get you and your daughter out of the country."

"How? How are we going to get a visa?" she asked, her eyes widening with hope but still teary.

"You don't need a visa. It is by road. No time to explain. We must go now!"

Akudo squeezed her eyes shut in resignation and heaved a long sigh.

"Give me ten minutes to leave the hotel, then you can leave," he said. Moments later he stepped out of the room. He kept going, not looking up or quickening his pace until he reached the lift. It was when he got to the elevator that he noticed his hands were shaking uncontrollably.

He made his way quickly to the staff quarters to grab his bag and hurried toward the gate, his injured hand shoved in his pocket. Outside, the air was hot. He had to get out of the hotel without the guards suspecting anything. When he approached the gatehouse, he noticed there were three guards on duty. He prayed Sikiru was not among them.

It was, in fact, Sikiru who stepped out of the gatehouse to inspect a line of incoming vehicles just as Able God was about to step in. His heart raced as he stood at the registration table to sign out.

Inside, an old soldier sat behind the small desk with the ledger. "Day or night shift?" asked the old soldier. He opened the ledger, his double chin jiggling.

"Day shift," Able God said, watching Sikiru from the corner of his eye, his heart thumping.

The old soldier looked up at him. "Are you done with your shift already?"

"No, sir."

"So why are you leaving?"

He knew what to say. "I am not feeling too well."

The old solider snapped his ledger shut and examined Able God closely as if trying to diagnose his ailment by looking at him.

"What are the symptoms?"

"What?"

"Headache? Aches? Chills?"

"Yes, sir."

"You need herbs. I will give you a list of ingredients to get and how to prepare it. It works like magic. That's the secret of my good health."

"I will be okay, sir. I'll go to the chemist as soon as I get home," he said, dizzy with anxiety. Sikiru was inspecting one last vehicle.

"Nonsense! You won't have to go to the chemist or a clinic if you do what I ask you to do."

"Thank you for your concern, sir. I need to go now, or I will miss the bus!"

"Well, I have tried to help you. You young people nowadays—you don't listen to advice," he said in resignation as he opened the ledger.

The old soldier scanned the first page, arching one eyebrow. He then flipped through three pages in an excruciatingly slow manner, at least in Able God's estimation. The old soldier peered at each sheet, running his eyes from top to bottom and scratching his jowls intermittently. Able God's blood boiled, and for a moment he considered leaving without signing out. What was the worst that could happen if he did that?

"You sign right here, beside your name," the old soldier finally said, jabbing his finger at a page. Sikiru was waving in the vehicle he had just inspected. Able God grabbed the pen with one hand and signed.

"See how your hand is shaking? This must be malaria! How did you allow yourself to get this sick?"

Without answering, Able God turned to leave. Sikiru walked in frowning, his eyes filled with scorn.

"Why is he leaving so early?" Sikiru asked.

"It's none of your business. You are not my boss." Able God talked tough as he left, hoping Sikiru would not stop him or press further. He heard the old soldier telling him about malaria and herbs and the stubbornness of young people. Able God slouched until he was out of sight, then held himself erect and walked rapidly.

THE TRAVELERS

12

Able God called Morufu before driving the stolen vehicle away from Mount Pleasant Guest House, taking shortcuts and backroads to avoid the police. He abandoned it where he was sure it would not be traced to the guesthouse. Since they might be waiting for him at the bus station, he decided to continue his journey on foot, avoiding the main road, and when he reached the lot, he hid behind an empty kiosk across the street while he surveyed his surroundings. He waited till the sun rose, drops of sweat trickling down the edge of his cheek and hesitating at the end of his chin before plunging down to vanish in the sweltering dust. Pain shot through his left shoulder, so he switched his backpack to the other arm. A dull pain stung from the gash on his hand. Despite his sleepiness, he needed to stay alert.

He saw Ben Ten move out of one of the lot's tarpaulin sheds to bark orders at the travelers and go back in. He sent a text to Morufu and took a deep breath. Seconds later, Morufu came out of one of the buses and leaned against an electric pole, his eyes wandering. Their gazes met. He hobbled across the road. Able God nodded in greeting, but Morufu opened his arms for an embrace.

Under the shed, Ben Ten's eyes were fixed on the small black-and-white TV. His pudgy fingers jabbed away at the controller, the screen flashing and the video game bleeping spasmodically. Ben Ten's challenger, a young shirtless boy, sat on a bench beside him tapping furiously at his controller. A car battery powered the TV. It was propped on a stool and connected to the TV by a tangle of multicolored wires and a pair of rusty clips. This game center was not much more than a rectangular structure made from pieces of tarpaulin nailed across a rotten wooden frame. Able God kept his wounded hand buried deep in a pocket.

"We are no longer accepting customers. Only those who filled out the forms and swore the oath will travel! All our seats have been taken," Ben Ten said without looking up at Morufu.

His hands still clasped behind his back, Able God lowered his eyes and held still as if he could make himself present in the room only by not moving. But he could not concentrate. Outside the game center, vehicles revved their engines and honked their horns as they prepared to begin the long journey north. Hawkers haggled with bus passengers under a darkening sky. Voices crackled out of megaphones, calling out routes. Able God struggled against the growing sense of unease gnawing at him. As far as he could see, his fate was in Ben Ten's hands. He was a dog under the table waiting for crumbs.

"My friend here was joking the other time. He was high, so he didn't know what he was doing. When he got back to his senses, he realized his mistake. That's why he is here," Morufu said, sidling up to Ben Ten, his hands clasped behind his back, his body listing toward his shorter leg.

"I see," said Ben Ten with a smug, self-satisfied expression. Suddenly, "YOU WIN" blared from the TV. The shirtless boy shrieked joyfully, and Ben Ten flung the controller to the ground in frustration. He whirled around, craning his neck, the bench creaking.

"You see, I have lost the first round to this small boy because of you fools!"

"We are sorry, Mr. Ben Ten. Make una consider his case. He is your brother. Please help him," pleaded Morufu, who clasped his hands in front of him. Able God smiled tightly as pressure mounted in his chest.

"Why are you speaking for him, Morufu? Can't he speak for himself?" Ben Ten asked, casting a disdainful look toward Able God.

"Please help me, sir," Able God quickly jumped in. He had been careful not to speak because he suspected his words would make an already indignant atmosphere boil over. Whatever was left of his ego had been crushed after he left the hotel. If there was any chance at all that he could start over, it was now or never. It no longer mattered to him if the journey was successful as long as it put distance between him and his past. He did not have the luxury of options.

"Please help me, sir, in the name of the God you serve!" Able God implored, trying to appeal to Ben Ten's religious faith. His calm demeanor gave way to a look of desperation, which somehow managed to wrest a smile from Ben Ten. Able God wasn't sure if that was a good sign or not. Seconds stretched out.

"I will forgive you because Jehovah forgives and forgets. You should thank your lucky stars that we have one space left in the Nigerian group. Take your belongings to the bus and wait there like the others. Add your name to the manifest. And remember, I will be watching you. If you provoke me, I will abandon you in the Sahara. Now, will you let me play my game in peace?" Ben Ten waved them off.

Able God felt a rush of relief.

"Yes, sir! Thank you, Mr. Ben Ten! Thank you," Morufu said.

Ben Ten went back to his game with its spasmodic, explosive sounds, and Able God and Morufu left the center.

Cross-country buses filled the station and lined the side streets leading to the gate: eighteen-seaters, luxury buses, Siennas. Hawkers, pedestrians, and conductors milled about with candies, biscuits, hard-boiled eggs, and whatnot. Candles flickered in the stalls. The smell of piss and diesel filled the air. The ground was greasy and riddled with gaping potholes. One end of the lot was bordered by a low concrete wall, along which a gutter gurgled with iridescent waste and green water. The electric poles appeared stunted, the cables hanging dangerously low, nearly grazing the luxury buses. As the two made their way through the crowd to the two eighteen-seater buses waiting for them, Able God surreptitiously scoured the surroundings like an animal aware that predators lurked nearby. He was careful not to look anyone in the face, and it wasn't until he had reached the bus unrecognized that it occurred to him that he had not thanked his friend.

"Don't thank me. Don't thank me at all," Morufu said, cutting off Able God and patting him on the shoulder. "We are brothers, and that's what brothers are for."

Able God nodded slowly, eyes shining with genuine gratitude.

"Where is your jacket?" Morufu asked.

"J—?"

"You need to buy a coat. It will be cold in Europe. Even in the desert at night."

"Okay."

"And you need some iodine for your hand before you get an infection. There's a chemist here," Morufu added after getting a look at his hand. Morufu did not ask how he'd gotten wounded. Maybe Morufu had noticed how tense his friend was. But Able God was still glad his friend knew when not to meddle in his private affairs. With Morufu he felt no judgment. He needed no explanation.

The minibuses' back and side doors were wide open. Although the spaces in the back, in between the seats, under the seats, and on the roof of the bus were crammed with the travelers' belongings, there were still some empty seats. Heavy winter coats, sweaters, and scarves hung everywhere in the bus—another sign that Able God was ill prepared. He had only his knapsack, which he shoved into the back of the bus. He'd hastily packed some clothes, his chess set, some food and drugs, a set of plastic cutlery, and a pack of cigarettes. He felt weak, hollow inside. His body ached terribly.

Morufu's legs were weary, so he hobbled over to an abandoned sofa, its upholstery cracked with age and black with mold. Three other passengers were already sprawled across the disemboweled sofa's exposed springs. Able God left to search for some first aid for his wound. He hated the smell of iodine, so he'd try to find a bottle of mentholated spirits somewhere. His anxiety had not abated, but it had been tempered by hope. He was still on high alert. They could come for him. They could be anywhere.

He found a pharmacy tucked between an empty stall and a gutter full of green water. The wooden house had been painted with what appeared to be a miserly amount of white emulsion paint. Bottles, small boxes, sachets, and packets crowded roughly made shelves. The attendant, a woman in her sixties, didn't seem like she wanted to be there. It took a while for Able God's request for a bottle of men-tholated spirits and a pack of cotton balls to register and even longer for her to hand over the items. All the while, Able God was looking around, fidgeting, and tapping his feet, his mind tangling with ur-gency. He stared at the gutter as he waited. Its green water seemed to gleam as if coated with oil.

As his eyes skimmed over the lot, a man leaning against a bus caught his eye. The man's face was grooved with wrinkles, and a cigarette smoldered in his hands. The fellow took a drag from his cigarette, the light end brightening, and blew the smoke slowly out, never taking his eyes off Able God. Then a smile swept across his lips, as if he were in on some secret. At least, that's what Able God thought. His heart fluttered. No, it wasn't a flutter—it was more like a thump. Adrenaline pumped through his veins.

"Madam, you are wasting my time!" he shouted at the poor old attendant.

Back at the bus, he inhaled, shut his eyes, and dabbed at his wound with a spirit-soaked cotton ball. First, his hand felt cold, then a terrible sting jolted through his body. He gritted his teeth.

The evening was gathering darker and deeper, which gave Able God a sense of relief. The darkness was a good cover, but he'd still have to be careful. He climbed on the bus and took a seat by the door. That way he could maintain his surveillance and make a quick break in case they came for him. He would sleep once the bus was on the move, but true rest would never come if the memory of his mistakes remained. He was ready to live with that, or so he thought. Able God reminded himself of Chinedu's uncle, who made it to Europe. "Be calm and do whatever they ask, and everything will be fine," Chinedu's uncle had said when Able God asked him how he survived the journey. He didn't think much of it then, but now it made so much sense.

Beckoning to a hawker, he bought two sachets of water, ripped one open with his teeth, and drained it in a couple of gulps. He paused before finishing the second one. Able God had barely been able to eat anything since the incident, but he took care to drink water.

A bell rang once, then twice, and a robed and barefoot evangelist shuffled toward the bus. His robe was surprisingly clean, and he wore a sash of blue cloth across his chest. Pacing back and forth while speaking about hell and damnation and salvation, he rang his bell, but no one seemed to pay him any attention. People simply went about their business. It was as if he wasn't there at all. But Able God could not take his eyes off him—not because people like him were uncommon in parks and marketplaces but because the man reminded Able God of the barefoot prophet.

13

ble God's father had been enjoying plates of pounded yam, egusi soup with croaker fish, and bottles of stout in the company of three of his friends, making wisecracks and laughing as men often did when they gathered to drink. Their father preferred to have his friends over for drinks, something only well-off men did. Even the fact that they were laughing with bits of spicy food filling their mouths wasn't at all surprising—men in beer parlors had done that for ages without anything going wrong. Only this time, something did go wrong.

Able God and his family lived in a government-reserved area, a gated community with tall electric poles and tangles of black cables running alongside the electric wires in front of the houses. The thick cables meant the homeowners had telephone service. Almost everyone who could afford a landline also had a satellite dish. Theirs was a wide, orange-colored dish that sat on the rooftop deck of their house.

From a fifty-inch color TV in the living room, the boys enjoyed channels such as E! TV, Spice Network, TLC, and MTV Base. In the evenings, when their father returned home from work, he'd turn to the news channels, mainly BBC, CNN, or Sky News. Sometimes their father called the office while he watched a news program, tak-ing copious notes. Usually, it was some scoop for the foreign news section of the *Daily Voice* newspaper.

"There is news breaking in Copenhagen now! Let's see if we can run it tomorrow morning!" he would shout into the receiver, his eyes shining with excitement, mustache twitching. The journalists at the *Daily Voice* referred to him as Mr. Onobele. Mr. Theophilus Onobele, the editor-in-chief and a portly, dark man. Mr. Onobele, who went about with a sternness that easily morphed into verbal reprimands. Mr. Onobele, who was prone to perform random acts of kindness at home and in the office. Mr. Onobele never missed a Sunday evening get-together with his friends.

After collapsing in a heap of laughter, Mr. Onobele started cough-ing. Able God's mother hurried out of the kitchen with a glass of water, and he grabbed it, spilling almost half on the floor. He drank the water, then tried to speak. This forced a horrible sound from his body. His efforts to wash down the fishbone with more water failed. He even tried swallowing a wad of pounded yam to push down the vicious bone. Within minutes, everyone had crowded into the living room. Mrs. Onobele was in full panic mode, and one of Mr. Onobele's friends was slapping his back. Able God and his brother looked on helplessly. Mr. Onobele barked out another cough, expel-ling a clump of bloodstained sputum, and their mother broke down crying.

In the hospital, the doctor performed an endoscopy and re-moved the fishbone with forceps. Mr. Onobele was discharged that day and sent on his way with a mess of antibiotics. Able God hoped they'd eventually look back on the incident as their family joke. He was wrong.

For weeks, Able God watched their mother blame herself for

what happened. She hadn't brought the water quickly enough or she'd added too much pepper to the soup. Then she started blaming others. She blamed Able God and his brother for not coming out of their rooms quickly enough when they heard their father coughing. She blamed their father's friends for visiting. That's the one she got stuck on. Perhaps his friends were convenient targets, but her dislike of them persisted.

She became increasingly unfriendly when they showed up. She greeted them with derision, her lips somewhere between a smile and a frown, like someone trying to be courteous even as something boiled up inside and threatened to froth over.

"What business do his friends have here except to spend our money and eat our food?" she muttered one day when their father was not around. The question was addressed to no one in particular, but Able God knew it was meant for him and his brother. He also knew it was not about food or money but a call for solidarity, a cryptic warning to stay away from their father's friends. It was not long before those men took the hint and stopped coming over.

Once the men had been dealt with, their mother acquired a new set of enemies. They were largely imagined obstacles to their father's advancement—his colleagues at the office, his distant cousins from the village, an assortment of witches and wizards, or a stranger she'd bumped elbows with at the market. Then she began fearing her husband's enemies would come after her children.

"When Satan wants a man, he goes after his family," she said. A previously nominal churchgoer of the Anglican Church, she made Sunday attendance mandatory in the house. Special prayer meetings were added to the mandatory Sunday services. She even joined a women's prayer group called Women Winning with Warfare Prayers. Then there were the visits to every crusade or revival held in the city.

It was not long before she sought further spiritual reinforcement from barefoot prophets.

> ● ▲ ‣

"There can never be too many prayers, my sons. Do you want the witches and wizards from your father's village to have power over us?" she would tell them whenever one of them asked why they had to go to another place to be prayed for. Being Yoruba herself, she was also quick to point out that the witches on their father's side of the family were particularly cruel, owing to their Ibo ethnicity. The boys would manage a nod and seal their lips, making no objection. Not that they had any choice. Able God was ten years old when his mother took him and his brother to the prayer mountain to see a prophet who, according to his mother, knew the future like the back of his hand.

The church was a wooden structure built among boulders on a hill. How could Able God forget how difficult it was to walk up the bush path to the top of the hill, his mother huffing and puffing, his brother stopping every now and then to swat away bugs or complain about an itch. Able God was ready to faint with exhaustion, but he was also furious because their mother made them do this. Once his foot caught on something and tipped him forward. He landed on the ground, bruising his knees.

"We are almost there. Ten more minutes," his mother said, gasping for breath. Able God dusted the sand from his knees, looking up at his mother with tears in his eyes. He felt a kind of gentle disdain for his mother, but he picked himself up and trudged on.

When they finally reached the top of the hill, Able God could barely move his legs. His knees stung and his waist ached from hiking. His brother, Calistus, broke down weeping, and their mother had to carry him the rest of the way on her shoulders. They paused for several minutes to collect themselves.

There was a sign driven into the ground that had the Yoruba words ORI OKE MORITEMISE, AKA MOUNTAIN OF ACHIEVEMENT. Gray rocks of various sizes and shapes massed everywhere, and a few clusters of trees provided shade for the pilgrims who'd come to pray on mats or between the rocky crevices. Songs and prayers and chants floated in the air.

As they walked toward the church, a huge man emerged from the doors. His face was lined with deep creases, and his eyes were red and piercing. His Adam's apple protruded from his thin neck. He wore a dirty white sutana tied at the waist with a blue rope. He was barefoot.

Able God's annoyance transformed into fascination the moment he laid eyes on the gigantic prophet. What struck Able God most were his ponderous feet. He'd never seen feet so large. He wondered if there was a shoe size big enough for the prophet.

His mother kneeled to greet the prophet, and the boys prostrated themselves before him.

"The Lord bless you, my sister," he replied with a toothy smile, his raspy voice as enormous as his body.

He led them into the church, a bare building with a dozen benches and a simple altar. The altar was a three-legged stool that had been propped against the wall. A cross and a bell had been placed on top of it. A portrait of the sacred heart of Jesus hung above the cross. The air smelled of *turari*.

As soon as they sat down, the prophet rang the bell twice to begin the prayer session. The idea was for the session to lead to revelations about the visitors even before they could wedge in their request.

"Holy Michael!" he said loudly.

"Mimo!" Able God's mother responded, dropping to her knees. She glared at the boys, who took the cue and kneeled.

"Holy Gabriel!"

"Mimo!"

"Your children have come before you. Show them the way!"

"Amen," they all chorused.

"What is hidden belongs to you, oh Lord, but you reveal it to your holy prophets. Open my eyes that I may see."

"Amen."

The prophet suddenly began praying in strange tongues. His eyeballs slid down, showing the white of his eyes. His lips and nose quivered. He showered the air with spittle. Just as it seemed as though his prayers were coming to an end, he began to shake as though tortured by something he did not want to escape his body.

Able God cast a glance at the prophet from under his half-shut eyelids, a method he had devised to peep at girls in Sunday school during prayers. That way, he could still see while his eyes seemed reverentially shut. Able God peered at the prophet's tortured face as he prayed. He glanced down at his dusty, ponderous feet. The prophet's face relaxed, and his lips moved to speak, his eyes still closed.

"You are here because of your sons?"

"Yes, Baba!" his mother responded, her voice thick with desperation.

"Hmmmm . . . Which one of your boys is Calistus? I hear a voice from heaven for Calistus!" He shook vigorously.

Their mother pushed Calistus forward by the head. His round innocent face shone with sweat, wetness sliding down his neck and grubby collar. He shuffled to the prophet on his knees. Calistus wrung his hands, grinning, his left eyelid slightly open. The prophet looked down at Calistus, then shut his eyes. He rang the bell, and another trembling fit gripped him.

"Thus saith the Lord, you will bring glory to this household, and your name shall be great."

"Amen!" they chorused. Again, Able God's mother's voice was the loudest. Able God's was only tepid. It seemed odd to him that the prophet called his brother first given that Able God was the firstborn—so how could Calistus be the one to bring glory to their household? He recalled the story of Jacob and Esau from Sunday school and how Esau had snatched his brother's birthright.

"Is this the younger brother of Calistus?" the prophet asked his mother.

"No, Baba! This is Able God. He is my firstborn!" she said awkwardly.

"Ha ha! Let me pray for you, my son!" he said after emerging from his trance.

The prophet prayed half-heartedly for Able God. When he had finished, he turned to their mother to warn her about her husband's relatives.

"Whenever they send you any gift from your husband's village, read Psalm 91 over a bowl of water and sprinkle it on the gifts to drive the evil spirits on the gifts away. Then give the gifts to the poor."

Able God's mother nodded vigorously. "Yes, Baba! Thank you, Baba!"

"Whenever they want to visit your house, do the same thing. Read Psalm 91 over a bowl of water and sanctify all the rooms. Do it the night before they arrive," the prophet said.

Before they left, Able God's mother dug into her purse and got out some money for the prophet with the ponderous feet. She thanked him, and they left. The journey back to the main road was easy because it was all downhill, but Able God couldn't stop thinking about what had happened.

His mind went to Bible stories about brothers from his Sunday school classes. There was the story of Cain and Abel and how Cain had killed his brother out of jealousy. There was the one about how Esau had sold out his brother for a plate of porridge. Had Esau thought his brother had cheated him and their mother was complicit? Hadn't Esau tried to kill Jacob?

Time passed, and eventually the trip to the prayer mountain no longer bothered him. Soon, the grimness he had attached to the event simply tapered off. Able God thought the moment would come when he'd be able to look back at that day with amusement and laugh about the big-footed prophet and his wrinkled face. But in the years that followed, he would experience many things that would disturb him and make him relive that fateful day.

14

By the time the evangelist shuffled away, Able God was overwhelmed with sadness. Shaking it off, he glanced at an imaginary watch on his wrist. His eyes followed Morufu, who had joined Ghaddafi, then turned to some of the boys and a group of rowdy bystanders who'd gathered in front of a newspaper stand illuminated by a fluorescent lamp. Pedestrians drifted by, squinted down at the evening paper, hissed, and left. Some hung around and shook their heads sadly while they read the headlines. The newspaperman, a toothpick sticking out of the corner of his mouth and a paper rolled up under his armpit, was leading the discussion. They were engaged in rigorous debate, shouting and spitting.

Able God almost wanted to walk over to them, ask them if they remembered the now-defunct newspaper called the *Daily Voice*, and tell them who his father was. Would they believe him if he told them his father had once run the *Daily Voice*? Even Morufu knew nothing about that part of his past. Frankly, Morufu knew almost nothing about him, yet he had helped him. Fate had rewarded him with the kindness of a *stranger* to make up for his misfortune.

A uniformed traffic officer showed up at the newspaper stand. He clutched a baton, and a white turtleneck peeked through the open buttons of his worn uniform. His trousers were loose around the waist and gathered into folds by his tattered belt. Traffic officers were usually harmless. There had even been cases of them getting beaten up by irate motorists, but that didn't stop Able God from imagining a series of worst-case scenarios.

Reflexively, he slunk into his seat, where he'd be protected from view. He could feel his heart pounding in his chest cavity. For a moment, all eyes were on the police officer, and the newspaper stand was quiet. From the quiet, a murmur slowly rose again, and the shouting and spitting resumed. The officer joined in the debate, shouting and waving his baton. His English trailed off into Hausa. It didn't take long for Able God to realize the officer had had too much to drink and was in no condition to scour for lawbreakers, but he was afraid all the same.

He peered out at the officer a couple of times, then decided to leave the bus, slipping out through the back. When he felt he had created sufficient distance from the officer, he filled himself with cheap gin from a plastic bottle at a roadside bar. He lurked behind kiosks and stalls, hoping to move through the world unnoticed. He bought another plastic bottle of gin.

Several times he dug his phone out of his pocket. He even dialed his mother's number once, but he couldn't summon the nerve to speak to her. On the one hand, he didn't want his parents worrying about him, thinking he had vanished. On the other hand, he didn't want his parents to find out about the trouble he was in, even though he figured that would happen eventually. Sooner or later, the police would find out where he lived and who his parents were.

He shook his head and muttered to himself, too consumed by trying to stay vigilant. Panic made him consider abandoning his phone. He kept looking at it like it was some strange object.

The officer was gone when Able God returned, and Morufu was back on the bus. Morufu gave him water for his face and told him to sit down.

"This time next week, we will be in Europe. Can you believe that?" Morufu asked heartily. Able God managed a smile.

The sky was now pitch black, and after a while, the bus station cleared out. Long-haul trucks returned from their trips, the acrid smell of diesel filling the air. They eased into parking spots lined with black patches of oil. Hawkers counted their money, took inventory of the rest of their goods, and ducked behind abandoned vehicles to wash their arms and faces with sachet water. They made their way home one after the other. Conductors and touts went to roadside bars to drink. Traders packed their goods into well-fortified storage rooms and blew out their candles or oil lamps. A loudspeaker at a distant mosque blared a call to prayer.

Night bus drivers, eyes red from sleep, emerged from their hiding places. Some turned toward the fence to piss. Some squatted beside the wall to do ablutions before praying and taking to the road. Others went straight to inspect the engines of their vehicles. Ben Ten came out of the game center, his phone's flashlight illuminated, and announced it was time to go. Two drivers, a young man with a sharp goatee and a shortish, bald man in his fifties wearing a dust-stained djellaba, showed up.

Able God tried to suppress his doubts about the trip. He grappled with a thought that kept sliding away—what was that chess term again? Chess terms or famous moves somehow helped him put things into perspective, like a proverb or the self-help author Napoleon Hill would do.

Within ten minutes, both of Ben Ten's minibuses were filled with passengers. Somehow, he'd managed to squeeze twenty-five into each vehicle. Ben Ten, Morufu, and Ghaddafi were on the first bus. Able God was assigned to the back row on the second. He took a window seat and nodded a greeting to the boy next to him. He didn't recognize the boy from the abandoned building. The boy glanced at him once and looked away, his face strained with worry.

The first bus roared to life and zoomed off. Then the driver of the second, the shortish man, turned to the passengers and called for prayers. He had a thick mustache and eyeglasses that slipped down the ridge of his oily nose. One of the boys led them in a long, rambling prayer until people began to shift in their seats and cough.

"In Jesus's name we have prayed," the driver cut him off to a resounding shout of "amen."

Finally, the engine's gears ground violently, and the bus jerked forward, spitting up clouds of dust and exhaust. The driver picked up a rag to wipe the film of dust from the windshield. His bald head shone with sweat under the park's fluorescent light. The bus drove down the street, around the corner, through the intersection, and onto the highway. Pavement stretched ahead as far as the eye could see. Cool air rushed in.

Minutes into the journey, Able God turned off his phone and leaned back. When he closed his eyes, he saw Dr. Badero's face and the blood on the floor, so he kept them open. The cut on his hand blazed every so often, as if to remind him of what had happened and hold him to account for ruining his own life. A long lasso of guilt encircled his neck. The wound would fester and eventually heal. Time would do its work on his memories, too, but what had happened would always remain.

Zugzwang.

Yes, zugzwang. That was the word. A chess term for the obligation to make a move even when any move would be a bad one. Able God knew he had to be anywhere but there.

He sighed.

He closed his eyes and began counting, hoping the rhythm would carry him off to sleep.

1 ... 2 ... 3 ... 4 ... 5 ... 6 ...

15

Traffic roused Able God. Sounds ebbed and flowed with the morning breeze. He sat up and yawned, the ache in his body worsened from sleeping in an uncomfortable position for so long. He could not believe he'd slept through the bumps on the road, the police and military checkpoints, and even the short rest stops. He reminded himself that there was still reason to be suspicious. What if they weren't really going to Kano? What if they were being kidnapped? What if the police picked him up at a checkpoint ahead?

He looked out the window to see crowds of people, rundown buildings, mosques, auto-rickshaws, motorcycles, bicycles, boys selling sugarcane from wheelbarrows or laden down with bags or wheeling fifty-liter jerricans, street kids with begging bowls.

"Are we in Kano?" he asked the boy next to him.

"We are in Sanbongari Park in Kano," he responded without meeting Able God's eyes. He was staring out the window. Able God reached for his phone. It beeped and vibrated with his parents' panic once it was on.

"ARE YOU AVOIDING US BECAUSE OF MONEY? VERY RUDE AND STUPID OF YOU. CALL ME BACK WHEN YOU GET THIS," his dad had texted.

"WHERE ARE YOU? YOU HAVE NOT BEEN PICKING UP YOUR CALLS. WE ARE WORRIED," his mother wrote.

"CALL US, WE ARE PRAYING FOR YOU," she added.

Able God immediately switched off his phone and returned it to his pocket. The first bus had already pulled over at the park by the time the second one arrived. Passengers got out and gathered around Ben Ten, who told everyone to huddle closer as though preparing to share a secret he didn't want the world to know. Able God did not squeeze his way into the cluster of travelers or stand on his tiptoes or crane his head. But he did try to listen to what Ben Ten was saying as the man took a wad of hundred-naira notes out of his briefcase.

"This is for what you are going to eat this morning," he said, stroking the cash with his fingers like he was about to dole out millions. "We will leave here for Zinder by noon. Make sure you don't leave the park—otherwise we will leave without you."

With that, he began peeling off notes for them. Each boy took his share and walked off to the food canteen or the beer parlor in the park. Waiting to take money from Ben Ten made Able God feel like an *almajiri* boy begging for alms. To think that just a few days ago his life was different seemed unreal to him. Able God immediately sent a barrage of ill wishes to Akudo, wherever she might be. But he knew his bruised ego was the least of his problems now. He told himself he had made the right decision to leave, and he was not going to suffer for another person's crimes. The group shrank until it was Able God's turn. Ben Ten hesitated, sizing him up condescendingly before handing him his cash.

Able God dug his hand into his pocket and looked around for Morufu. When he finally found him, they shared a spliff. Afterward, they went to a *mai shayi* joint to have scrambled eggs, bread, and steaming hot choco. They kept talking about football, politics, and women as they ate. Able God was fine with whatever as long as it occupied his mind and distracted him from his current reality.

But then it was time to leave, and he had to sit alone with his thoughts on the bus. He was in a sea of unfamiliarity. The buses were briefly delayed when the older driver announced that a traveler was joining them. Moments later, a portly woman clambered onto the bus.

"Please dress for me small-small, my dear. I don't want to sit in the middle. God bless you," she asked the boy in the back. Surprisingly, the boy complied, and the woman heaved her body into the window seat. The boy was now sitting right next to Able God. He smelled of charred wood. Although Able God was not surprised to see a woman joining them, he wondered what her story was.

The woman shifted in her seat, wedging herself into the allotted space. Once she got settled in, she removed her slippers and stretched her dusty legs out as far as the cramped bus allowed.

They thought it was finally time to go, but Ben Ten stepped out of the other bus and instructed the driver to check the engine again.

"It's better to be late than sorry," he said with a serious face.

The driver pulled up the cushion of his seat to expose the engine underneath and bent over it, poking around, tightening screws, and tapping at it. He rubbed his eyes in the crook of his arm, then continued his work. His eyes were red and unblinking. Thick, prominent veins stuck out at his temples.

Meanwhile, a flock of hawkers, merchants, and scroungers besieged the bus with their pleas and petty goods, clamoring for the passengers' attention. They offered sweets, packs of cigarettes, sliced bread, wristwatches, and belts with shiny buckles for sale. A beggar squeezed into the swarm and craned her neck through a side window of the minibus. Her bulging eyes were milky-white with blindness. One arthritic hand rattled a dry stick at the passengers while in the other she held a plastic bowl that jingled with coins, the fruits of her begging.

The beggar raised her voice in spurious invocations.

"May you not be annihilated before your time! May the road not yawn open to claim your souls! May you not sow for another man to reap!"

The blessings rolled off her tongue in a singsong moan, her bulbous, glaucoma-eaten eyes staring directly at the woman seated near Able God, who dug frantically into her purse and dropped a folded bill into the beggar woman's bowl. The beggar rolled back her lips, revealing decayed teeth, and thanked her profusely before fumbling her way to the next bus.

No sooner was the beggar gone than a hunchbacked Hausa man took her place at the window. He held a cardboard sign in his hands. A harsh gabble poured from his throat. The sign accomplished the task his larynx strived so hard to do but could not achieve—though it was clear that the mute fellow's miserable attempt to speak was simply a ploy to stir up sympathy. On the piece of cardboard was written a poorly spelled message.

HELP ME. I AM A DEF AND DUMM. I HAVE 2 WIFES AND 13 CHILDRIN.

The woman turned her face away from the window. The Hausa man drifted off but reappeared seconds later beside Able God's seat, searching his face for even the slightest sign of sympathy. Able God grimaced. Soon enough, another person replaced the hunchback. A little later, a froth-mouthed preacher in a worn-out jacket replaced that person. Brandishing a battered New Testament, he stepped onto the bus.

"My brothers and my sisters, I have come with the glorious gospel of our Lord and Savior Jesus Christ of Nazareth. You must have asked yourself this question: If you die today where will you spend eternity? My mummy, my daddy, my brother, and my sister, one day the trumpet shall sound and anyone whose name is not found in the Book of Life will be thrown into the Lake of Fire. My mummy, my daddy, my brother, my sister, give your life to Christ today! Tomorrow may be too late. . . ."

The preacher went on and on about hell and the Lake of Fire. To end his sermon, he launched into a lengthy prayer. When he had finished, he began handing out a stack of soiled pamphlets while saying something about the fortune it had cost to produce them.

"The gospel needs money. No amount is too small or too big. Give toward the success of the gospel of our Lord and Savior Jesus Christ. Give and you will be blessed and shall prosper. Give to support the man of God. Sow into this bus ministry, and your troubles shall disappear."

The woman handed a crinkled note to the evangelist. He thanked her and everyone else on the bus, bowing his head and smiling, still expecting more money. When nothing more was forthcoming, he shuffled away.

"*Oga* driver, are we going to sleep here today?" the woman asked.

Able God was glad she had spoken up. He had been shifting in his seat, sweat pouring down his face.

The driver ignored her, but soon the buses began moving and merged onto the highway. They journeyed past grasslands and villages and hills. After gazing through the window for a long time and trying not to think, Able God got out his phone to play chess but stopped himself when he remembered he needed to save his battery. A feeling of deep sadness overwhelmed him, but the sadness was strangely reassuring. It had become familiar.

All the passengers on the bus were asleep except Able God. The boy beside him had draped his arms across the seat in front. Every twenty minutes or so, the boy would murmur something unintelligible in his sleep, then raise himself up, his eyes darting to and fro as though he had woken up in hell, before sinking back down. Able God was concerned the first time it happened, but he got used to it after a while. The woman slept, resting her back on her seat, her face tilted upward, snoring through half-open lips.

Able God turned his gaze back to the window and watched the changing landscape, a world of beauty and barrenness.

16

They approached the Nigeria-Niger border checkpoint, a place demarcated by green-and-brown striped barrels and an arched concrete gateway with peeling plaster. The gateway bore an inscription.

BONNE ARRIVÉE AVEC ZAIN

BIENVENUE À MARADI

Two Nigerian soldiers with assault rifles slung over their shoulders focused on the buses and waved them to a halt. Able God had been nursing a headache, but when the vehicle pulled over, he felt a wave of fear pass through him. The travelers woke up, yawned, and looked around, ill at ease. One of the soldiers came over to the bus and peered suspiciously through the windows at each of their faces.

"Oya, everybody get down," he barked. For a few moments the travelers looked at each other anxiously. Able God could feel sweat trickle down the back of his shirt. He wiped his sweaty palms on the seat of the bus. The soldier would probably demand their passports, and Able God was almost sure none of them had anything close to that. He didn't have any form of identification himself and doubted the other passengers did either. Passports were for real travelers who flew by plane.

Able God saw that the other bus had already been emptied of its passengers, and Ben Ten was having a few words with the soldier. The woman asked the soldier why they should get down. The soldier replied sternly that it was not a request. They all spilled out of the bus.

"Where are you going? Bring out your passports and let me check them!" the soldier shouted at the first busload of boys. A murmur swept through the crowd. Able God felt a wave of apprehension wash over him. Ben Ten approached the soldier with another guard at his side. "Mr. Sergeant, my name is Ben Ten. I am in charge of this delegation."

"What kind of name is that? Is that the same Ben Ten from cartoon movies? Is that the name on your passport?" he asked, measuring up Ben Ten as an immigration officer might. Ben Ten opened his mouth to say something, but the officer interrupted him.

"Mr. Man, show me your passport or I will shoot you!"

"Rambo," the other soldier interjected, "I have had a man-to-man talk with my friend here. He said we should go and settle this matter inside."

"What kind of man-to-man talk is that?" Rambo asked incredulously. The other soldier leaned forward and whispered something in his ear. He shrugged, then they led Ben Ten into the customs building by the side of the road. Soon, Ben Ten was back aboard the bus, and they were ready to move. The soldiers came out with smiles on their faces and waved the drivers onward. There were more checkpoints after crossing into Niger before they reached Zinder, but they never took long to clear. Ben Ten managed everything. Able God saw Ben Ten's prestige grow with each stop. The passengers became more and more relaxed.

The woman on his bus even said, "I like those who know their job. Ben Ten knows his job."

Able God was not one to be swept off his feet by Ben Ten's antics. In his mind, he had plotted ways of leaving the group in case anything strange happened. Crossing the border hadn't eased his fear of getting caught by the police. He didn't expect Interpol to work well in West Africa, but that didn't make him feel any better. What if he got arrested for something else, and they found out he had committed a crime back home? In that case, they might decide to send him back home to face criminal charges. Would he go back to Nigeria if he thought turning himself in was a better choice?

Zugzwang.

It had been five hours. Zinder was brown with dust. They soon reached a scattering of whitewashed mud-brick houses. Tuareg nomadss herded their cattle and scrawny camels across the fields, niqab-wearing women trekked home with their children, unveiled women with henna-reddened hands and feet hurried past, and farmers returned home after a day's work, carrying their tools. A line of old tractors stood against a wall, and an overstuffed Peugeot station wagon groaned down a dirt road. The people in those parts were mostly light skinned. Able God remembered encountering some of them back home. They came in droves to major cities in Nigeria, mostly to beg for alms. They were known for shuffling after their prospective benefactors and sometimes even clutching onto them with unyielding tenacity, stubborn as leeches.

It was dusk when the buses reached the bus station. Stalled vehicles honked. Pedestrians streamed into the road as soon as a motorist so much as hesitated. Hawkers milled about, hoping to benefit from the jam, dangling their wares in car windows. Exhaust-belching motorcycles tried in vain to weave their way through the confusion. The place smelled of cow dung and dust. The first bus parked close to a mosque, and Able God's bus followed suit.

A money changer was waiting for them as they climbed out of the bus. They lined up to exchange what they had for CFA francs. Then they ate whatever they found for sale in the parking lot: biscuits, bread, soft drinks, and coconut. Able God found a leaking water pipe. He slapped cold water on his face and gargled with it. Meanwhile, Morufu filled a bag with supplies for cocktails and smokes.

"Let us celebrate and be thankful to be done with the second leg of the journey," he said, rolling a joint on a flat stone.

"There is a mosque there," Able God told him.

"The mosque is empty, and we are far away from it. Anyhow, I will soon say my prayers," he said, as if that somehow made up for smoking near a house of worship.

They spread mats on the ground and lay down to smoke. Ghaddafi joined them eventually. They made cocktails. They did not say much. They were too tired for that, and Able God just wanted his headache to go away. He hoped the drugs would give him sweet dreams. Morufu and Ghaddafi soon went to a gutter near the parked buses to do their ablutions, then they prayed to the east.

The sunset stained the landscape a deep bloodred. Darkness unfurled across the horizon. Soon, some of the travelers spread out their mats and pulled out coats and blankets, ready to sleep. Able God inspected the gash across his palm, half crusted over, half bloody. Leaving the wound uncovered and dry would help it heal, not that he had any other option. If it got infected, he would wait it out and hope for the best. Able God turned his gaze to the brightness of the stars in the absence of electric lighting. He tried to relax and rid himself of the feeling of uselessness that crept up on him in moments of calm. A thought struck him. Although he'd tried to picture Italy over and over, his mind's eye could only conjure the shore. He needed to see something. He needed something to hold on to.

"Not too long from now, I will be in Italy," he whispered to himself. He said those words again and again. He said them until the words became soundless on his lips.

17

orufu's idea was one Able God was glad to follow. He would've welcomed any idea that involved taking drugs. Ghaddafi also agreed to tag along, so they devised a simple plan: ask around until they found something. The three wandered away from the bus, walking on dirt roads and passing earthen houses. They ducked behind the market stalls and left the stultifying heat for the shade of acacia trees. All around them, men towed pushcarts loaded high with bundles of sticks or tanks of water. They wove their way through the street market, Able God stopping to buy a handful of chocolates from a hawker. He waved them invitingly at Morufu and Ghaddafi.

"No, thank you, my friend. Too much sugar spoils the teeth," Morufu said as he hobbled along, sweating and panting from the trek.

Ghaddafi took some, and Able God ate one and then shoved the rest into his pocket. Soon, the emerald-green domes of the Grand Mosque of Zinder were in view. They passed house facades made of plaster decorated with colorful geometric motifs of various shapes and sizes, some adorned with stucco. They saw signs they couldn't read because they were in French.

The first person they approached looked as though they'd asked him to carry out a murder.

"No Englis!" he said, shaking his head before hurrying away. Able God was confused—surely, the stranger must not have understood their request to react like that. Able God wondered if Niger practiced sharia law or some strict customary rules, in which case their undertaking would be more precarious. He didn't want any trouble. The second person they asked was an old man with a twisted smile. He looked them up and down slowly.

"Do you want trouble for yourself with police? Drugs bad in Niger Republic," the man said, shaking his head, irritation written across his face. What was with these people and the way they shook their heads, Able God wondered. The sun rose, and Able God could feel his pores crackle with heat. Ghaddafi cornered a third person in a small shop. The man was wearing a full-length gown and skullcap.

"*Comment allez-vous?*" Ghaddafi called out in what was perhaps the only French he knew.

"*Lafiya lo,*" the man responded in Hausa. They shook hands and conversed in Hausa for almost two minutes. Able God hadn't realized Ghaddafi spoke Hausa, but he was glad they'd managed to find some common ground. The fellow was cheerful and friendly. When they finished talking, Ghaddafi told his friends, "He said he will take us where the street boys brew tea in small blue teapots."

The walled compound had no gates, but the entrance was guarded by two boys with ashy limbs and dust-caked clothes. They had shaved heads and scar-speckled bodies, and their faces were scorched by the sun and stained with sweat. Machetes in hand, they approached the trio before they even reached the compound and surveyed them with bloodshot eyes. Able God wiped the sweat from his face, his shirt sticky and smelly. His heart was uneasy, but at the same time, he felt a certain sense of familiarity. Strange how some things never changed.

The benevolent go-between addressed them in Hausa. Ghaddafi spoke a few words, too, then pressed some cash into their hands. They were allowed to pass through the mud-brick compound gate into a courtyard shaded by corrugated iron sheets. Clothes hung from sagging clotheslines, and the smell of detergent lingered in the air. Empty cans of beer and cigarette butts littered the floor. Inside were more filthy boys, covered in burn marks, knife scars lacing across their bodies.

The boys were lighting cylindrical coal burners with shallow bowls and holes in the bottom. Red-hot coals filled the tops of the bowls, which the boys fanned with flag-shaped straw fans. They put long-spouted blue teapots dented with age over the coals. When the water boiled, they added tea leaves. When that was done, they fished out little bags of sugar and an assortment of small, thick-walled glasses and stainless-steel cups from their duffle bags. Able God caught a whiff of fresh mint in the air. It became so strong that he could no longer smell the detergent.

The concoction process was so elaborate that Able God was convinced what he was witnessing was more than just tea being brewed; it was part entertainment, part performance ritual. They filled the glasses and cups with tea from the pot, starting to pour from a low height, then raising the teapot high before bringing it low again as the glass filled. Then they emptied the glass back into the teapot with a flick of the wrist. They repeated the process again and again, pouring, tipping, pouring, tipping. They chattered in Hausa as they made the concoction. Occasionally, they would pause to take a sip from the glass, tasting for sweetness or strength. When they were satisfied, they served the tea in three rounds.

The first cup is as bitter as life, the second is as sweet as love, the third is as soft as death.

Able God drank from the first cup, savoring its minty and sugary taste.

The first cup is as bitter as life....

Able God drank his second glass all at once. Maybe this came before the drugs, he told himself. When would the real thing come? He cast a glance at Morufu, who was busy enjoying his tea unperturbed.

The second is as sweet as love....

Before the final round, the boys opened their knapsacks and poured a granulated substance into the teapots. Able God's curiosity flared up. What was that? It reminded him of the abandoned building. The tipping and pouring took longer this time.

The third is as soft as death.

He felt something radiating from his belly barely a minute after finishing the third cup. The warmth felt like a gift, rising up his forearms and spreading in his chest. His neck grew warm. He felt a warm wind against his face. The tension in his shoulders eased, and a smile crept along his lips. Something about this newfound ease both irritated him and made him feel at home. His fear melted, and his anxiety vanished, leaving space for simple things. Able God wondered why he had not let himself enjoy the simple pleasures of life. He wondered why things had to be so difficult, why he had to fight so hard.

He remembered that he still had some chocolates in his pocket and fumbled for them. Unwrapping one, he sank his teeth in. His teeth broke its chewy surface, his lips parting as the gooey caramel glided into his mouth and down his throat. And while his tongue played with the flavor and saccharine goodness, it found some caramel stuck in the far reaches of his mouth. It quickly went to work prodding and dislodging the rest of the caramel. He threw his head back in delight.

Some of the boys lit cigarettes; others were kicking around beer cans. Morufu touched his own face and laughed out loud. Ghaddafi crawled across the dusty ground and grabbed the legs of one of the boys.

Able God opened his mouth to speak, or maybe to laugh, but his voice stuck in his mouth, as though caught in some tunnel of misconnection. Able God needed a smoke, but he figured he wouldn't get one because he couldn't speak. Nothing came out of his mouth. He stood up and felt suddenly woozy. A crushed beer can flew toward him, making a clattering noise as it landed just a foot away. He lurched backward and kicked the can. It sailed straight into the face of one of the boys. He staggered forward—he must apologize, he did not want any trouble. The guard boys could plant a machete in his head. Still, nothing came out of his mouth. Laughter cracked the silence. The boy he had hurt was laughing. There was a cut on his face, yet he was laughing. Able God thought it was funny, so he laughed, too. Yes, he could laugh. He looked around for the can and kicked it again. He searched around for Morufu, who liked to play football, but somehow, Morufu was not in his peripheral vision. He laughed. He kicked.

18

Thirty minutes into their journey to Agadez, the pilot bus heaved to the right side of the road, a maneuver the passengers in the other bus didn't see as unusual. The two buses had been engaging in some kind of speed chase on the road where the distance between the buses shrank until the one ahead swerved to the side to allow the one behind to speed past. But this time around, the pilot bus clanged and brawled, eating up the road as it groaned along nosily before stopping. Their driver reacted quickly, slamming on the brakes, but it was too sudden. The steering wheel trembled in his hands as the bus lumbered across the road, lurching over sand and stones.

Able God held onto the back of the seat in front, pressing his feet against the floorboards, his face stiff with fright. The woman sitting in his row, whom he now knew to be Patricia, screamed, "Jesus!"

The driver swore and took a few moments to collect himself, then poked his head out the window. "*Kuna lafiya?*" he screamed after honking his horn.

The only response was the intermittent roar of the engine as the bus tried to come back to life, then the thunder of mechanical components as a thick, dark cloud billowed from the driving compartment of the first bus. The smell of gas filled the air. Their driver sprang out of the bus, headlights on. Patricia shouted for him to open the door. Passengers tumbled out into the dying light of the day. The road was empty and almost silent except for a sharp wind. The dunes rippled out all around them.

Able God had a slight headache, but it was probably just the stress of the trip. A sense of dread settled in. Although he wasn't as scared of being followed as he had been back in Nigeria, he didn't feel safe yet. He would never feel safe after what he'd done. He remembered the hand-painted message he'd seen on the rear fender of a trailer near Zinder. He could still see it as clearly as if he were looking at a photograph: NO PEACE FOR THE WICKED. Was he a wicked person?

There were times along the journey when he attempted to make sense of what had happened and give himself reasons to feel sorry for himself. He told himself that when Dr. Badero strangled him, he could have been acting in self-defense intuitively, and that maybe he could have talked him out of it to calm him down. Could he truly, though? Did Badero not aim directly and quickly for his throat? When that argument fell flat, his guilt transformed into justification. He latched on to the notion that he himself had no option but to act in self-defense. He didn't murder him, he wasn't wicked, and what occurred was nothing but a freak accident.

Ben Ten took a few walkabouts around the vehicle to check the tires. The pilot driver lifted the hood and stuck his head down into the bus's engine compartment while the second driver stood by. He shook his head after a while, then the three of them conferred briefly.

Ben Ten gathered the passengers beyond the road's edge. "Sorry for the technical problem," he said. "We will be on our way soon."

"What if robbers attack us?" Patricia spoke out from behind.

"No one can do anything to us here."

"How do you know?"

"Madam—"

"Why didn't you rent good buses with the money you took from us?"

There were a few glares and grumbles. Able God hadn't realized that Ben Ten had taken money from people. Didn't Ben Ten say they would work to pay off their debts? His mistrust of the whole arrangement magnified.

"Did I collect a kobo from you?" Ben Ten responded in wide-eyed anger after a moment of silence.

"You said we will work along the way. Are you not going to make money from our sweat, or are they going to pay you stones?"

By this time, she had pushed her way through the crowd and was closer to Ben Ten, her fists planted on her hips.

"Madam, you will talk to me with respect!"

"Respect? If you had respect for us, would you put us in these wretched vehicles?"

People began to turn toward Patricia, their eyes urging her to keep quiet. She remained incensed, her face stiff with defiance.

"I don't like your attitude," Ben Ten said, backing away.

Morufu hobbled after him and tried to reason with the visibly irate Ben Ten. Whispers broke out in the crowd. Two emotions fed the murmur: fear that Ben Ten might not have been making empty threats, and anger that Patricia might have destroyed their hopes with her tongue. Able God did not know what to feel.

Ben Ten shouted angrily, addressing everyone. "Do you know how expensive it is to plan a trip like this? You ingrates! You should be thanking me for lifting you out of your wretchedness, but instead you dare open your dirty mouths to insult me."

Now it was clear Ben Ten saw Patricia's protest as representative of all their voices. The whispers quickly changed into a buzz as everyone talked at once.

"If you are not satisfied with what I am doing for you, then it's okay. We will go back to Nigeria as soon as the bus is repaired," his voice quaked. A barrage of pleas and disavowals rose up. Ben Ten moved toward the broken-down bus, Morufu sidling over to him.

A boy next to Able God quietly asked, "Is he really going to send us back after all the journey?"

Able God simply shook his head. He was not shocked. He knew Ben Ten was bluffing like back at the abandoned building or at the game center. The tactic was meant to quell any dissenting voices and to make them realize he was fully in charge and could destroy them at any moment or make them beholden to him. That way he would be able to use them as he wanted while constantly feeding his own ego. But what choice did Able God have? Would he rather stay in Nigeria and face the consequences of his actions?

Ben Ten moved angrily away from Morufu, but Morufu pursued him, leaning forward and pleading desperately.

"As soon as the bus is ready, we are going back home, and there is no amount of begging that will make me change my mind," Ben Ten said.

He stamped over to the functioning bus, swung the doors shut, and took the driver's seat. All the while, passengers swarmed after him, pleading in the name of God and more deities than he knew existed. Able God was an unwilling participant, his half-open mouth mumbling words he didn't mean.

It was not long before Ben Ten, still looking incensed, locked the doors and rolled up his window. They lingered for several minutes before the crowd dispersed. Morufu and Ghaddafi sat on the bare ground to share a cigarette. A boy sat beside them, tears on his cheeks.

A group went to confront Patricia, and an altercation broke out. She had been standing alone. While some lobbed insults at her, others urged her to beg Ben Ten for forgiveness. But she did not budge. She tied her wrapper into a knot, ready for a fight. Soon, more passengers sat on the ground, angry and sad. Able God joined Morufu and Ghaddafi and listened to them trash-talk the woman who had crushed their dreams. Able God overheard someone say they should have her killed and leave her corpse by the roadside for what she had done.

Everything was silent except for the rustling of sand, the faraway barking of a dog, and the metallic noises of the drivers working on the faulty bus engine. Going back home was not an option for Able God. But what if he escaped to another part of Nigeria? Not that he hadn't considered that before he decided to flee. A thought pounded in his head, and he slowly walked up to Patricia. She sat on a piece of cloth that she'd spread on the ground.

"Madam?" he said to her quietly. She looked up, flicked her flashlight on, and pointed it directly at his face. Able God blinked. She looked him up and down, then hissed.

"Please, madam, I think he will change his mind if you talk to him," he said.

"Talk to him? He thinks just because he can organize a trip, everyone should bow down to him as if he is a god. Over my dead body!"

"These boys are desperate; they might try to harm you on our way back!"

She sprang to her feet, tightening her wrapper. "Harm me? Let them try it, and they will know I am not ordinary. He is taking you all for a ride and you keep quiet? He is not God! Why is he acting like he is God?"

"I am not here to fight with you, madam. Surely you must have children?" he asked, hoping to appeal to her maternal instinct.

"Why are you asking me if I have children? What is your business with me?"

"If you have children, then you must be making this journey because of them. For the sake of your children, please go and beg for his forgiveness."

She closed her eyes and pointed a finger in the direction of the dunes. "Before I count three and open my eyes, I want you to vamoose!"

Able God walked away. He did not want trouble and was too tired to insist. There was nothing else to do now but hope that Ben Ten would have a change of heart. His thoughts faded away from the present moment, going back to his painful past. If he could turn back the clock, if he could start over, where would he begin? Perhaps the Hotel Atrium. If he hadn't worked there, perhaps he wouldn't be on the run now—or would he have ended up here anyway, stranded in the middle of nowhere? Would fate have found a different way to bring him here?

19

Strains of the dawn call to prayer floated in from the outskirts of Zinder. The sun skimmed over the horizon, rising ever so slowly as if careful to wake up. The night had been warm, and Able God struggled to sleep, but the heat had been the least of his worries. Stones and gravel dug into his back through the flimsy mat, but even that discomfort did not really bother him. He was more worried about the prospect of going home. He could relocate to another state in Nigeria, but the law would easily catch up with him. He considered staying in Zinder, but that was too close to home. His sleep had been tortured, filled with so many thoughts and dreams that he could barely distinguish between the two. Just before dawn, sleep finally settled into his head like a harmattan mist. It was short-lived, though, interrupted by the honking of the buses' horns.

He jerked awake and sprang to his feet. The engines of the buses were running, and Ben Ten was calling the passengers to gather. He then signaled for the vehicles to be turned off. Patricia stood beside him, gazing down with her hands clasped in front of her. She had a patterned silver scarf wrapped around her head and a chewing stick wedged between her lips. Ben Ten hacked up some phlegm before speaking.

"I want to tell you that you have nothing to worry about," he said, and the passengers murmured in relief.

"What happened yesterday was a case of many people suffering for the sins of one person. That one person has seen the error of her ways," he said without turning to Patricia. She unclasped her hands and planted them on her hips.

"So everything will go ahead as planned. Our drivers managed to fix the vehicle, and we will be on our way soon." He made his way to the pilot bus.

The travelers followed him, offering up an outpouring of gratitude. Able God saw Morufu's tired face light up with hope, and Ghaddafi ran excitedly to the side of the bus to gather his sleeping mat and roll it up under his armpit. Able God wondered if he should feel joy or simply try to disappear. He was not in the state of mind to figure out how Ben Ten had settled his score with Patricia either. Moments later, Ghaddafi waved him over.

"We are going to Agadez! May God be with us! May God be with us!" he said with a big smile, squeezed Able God's shoulders, and headed over to the pilot bus. Somehow, Able God's eyes stung with the spray of his words, and when he got to the bus small tears were trickling out. He wiped them off with his sleeves and clambered into the bus.

The buses blasted through a sea of drifting sand for several hours. There were no roads and no clearly defined paths. At one point, the drivers stopped to let some air out of the tires, explaining that it was to get better traction in the dunes. Then they stopped to rest for the day. The night was cold and the wind boisterous. The rustling murmur grew into a crackling roar, hurling an eddy of sticks, stones, and sand up into the air. The passengers fled back to the buses, their prayers loud as the storm raged on. Patricia began singing songs of deliverance in an off-key voice. Suddenly, Able God's bus was lifted and slammed down into the sand with a fierce jolt. Cries erupted.

After an anxious night, they set out in the predawn fog and drove without stopping. As the mist burned off, Able God felt as though the heat of the desert were fanning out to consume them. The buses rode over terrible bumps and fishtailed in the deep sand. He closed his eyes and tried to let his exhausted body rest.

▸ ● ▲ ▸

He was already awake when they finally reached the Agadez bus station. He glanced out of the window, surveying city streets jammed with pedestrians, auto rickshaws, and cars. The station was even more crowded. People arrived by the busload or crammed in the backs of lorries. Droves of men, women, and children milled around. Agadez was the rendezvous point for the most important leg of the journey.

"On Monday, we will make the trip across the desert to Libya," Ben Ten told the group after getting off the bus, looking into faces drawn from the long journey. "It will take us six days to drive across the desert. We will enter the center of the city, eat, and rest. We will spend some days here, okay? Once we get to Libya, Europe is not that far again. All of you will achieve your dreams in Jehovah's great name."

A chorus of amens followed, as the travelers nodded like schoolchildren.

Ben Ten plowed ahead. "This is Agadez, the gateway to the desert. If you have done your research, you will know that they speak French here, so you don't need to talk to anybody. Let me do the talking.

"For the Christians here, this place is also a Muslim land," Ben Ten added after a moment's pause. "This is how Muslims greet each other, in case you don't know: you must place your hand on your chest and say, 'As-salaam aleikum.'"

Brushing away imaginary obstacles, Ben Ten went on, "We will get a room in a place they call the ghetto. Also, no drugs or alcohol in the city. This place is not like Zinder. The police are always patrolling. If they catch you, you will go to prison. There is no *banamish* in this prison, meaning no freedom. Don't cause trouble for the rest of us."

A short, turbaned *coxeur* showed up to lead the way to lodging in one of the city's ghettos. He shook Ben Ten's hand enthusiastically and waved at the passengers.

The passengers left their drugs and liquor in the buses, turning their pockets inside out to make sure they hadn't left anything incriminating in them. Able God grudgingly removed the rolling papers from his bag and waited for Ben Ten's instructions.

Ben Ten took roll call, then herded the group through the dusty mud-brick labyrinth of the city. They moved through a tangle of cattle herds and three-wheelers. They passed through the central market. They walked past shops, offices, and coffee stands. They walked past rickety buses full of people—people who might have been going home.

Able God was surprised that the people of Agadez went about their business and appeared to take little notice of them—not that it bothered him. In fact, knowing there were no eyes on him gave him a sense of ease. He had never been so unsure of his future, never been so afraid. Able God wondered if there was a bright side to his predicament. What if Europe, indeed, had better things in store for him? He had heard that in Europe they played chess in city squares—maybe he would start with that. Maybe someone would recognize his talent and get him into a tournament. Maybe he would be able to get a job, and his certificate would not be totally useless after all. If he returned home wealthy and powerful, he might be absolved of his crime, like the second coming of a disgraced politician.

If time passed, then maybe his sins would be forgotten. Maybe, in the end, he would make it. But first, he would need to survive this journey. Once again the words of Chinedu's uncle rang in his ears. *Be calm and do whatever they ask, and everything will be fine.*

It was a short walk to their lodge, one of many in a group of bungalows in a flyblown yard surrounded by mud-brick walls. There were big blue barrels of water inside the compound, and a dusty white Toyota pickup was parked in the corner. The building only had one window, and the only ventilation came from an electric fan that emitted a bone-crunching noise. The plaster walls were cracked and peeling and covered with graffiti. The travelers removed their shirts and lay flat on their backs, tired and drenched in sweat. Some of them took turns relieving themselves in the adjoining squat toilet. This added the stench of human waste to that of sweat and body odor. Patricia spread her wrapper on the floor and sat down. She fanned herself with one hand and pinned her nose shut with the fingers of her other hand, irritation on her face.

The floor was hard concrete, and the mats covering the tattered mattresses were infested with cockroaches, but it didn't seem to matter to anyone in the room. They seemed happy to have a place to lie down and stretch out. Able God was glad to be out of the bus. The boy beside him had refused to respond to his attempts at conversation, and he had become increasingly irritated with Patricia. Able God was eager to forget his own troubles, so he thought about what might have made the boy join the caravan. When he was that age, he didn't speak much either. He'd been a subdued, insecure child who struggled to understand why his parents preferred his younger brother.

Ben Ten led them all in a prayer of thanksgiving, calling roll before going outside with one of the boys. Shortly after, he came back with rice, beans, and stew. A slender teenager with upright posture, dark skin, and big, bright eyes followed Ben Ten into the room. He wore unmatched shoes and had a slovenly appearance. The teenager stood against the wall with a suitcase between his legs.

Ben Ten introduced him. "This is Pepe. He is from the Democratic Republic of Congo, and he will be joining us on this trip. Thank you very much."

Attention turned to Pepe, but only for a moment. Ben Ten had barely stopped speaking when they tore into their food. Ravenous, they ate with one hand while swatting flies with the other. They huddled around in groups with as many as four people sharing a single plate of food. Able God, who sat with Morufu and Ghaddafi, shoveled handfuls of food into his mouth. He tried to eat as much as he could before the food vanished. When the plate was almost empty, Morufu grabbed it and swept the last grains of rice and beans into his mouth, then licked the bowl clean.

"What will you do when you get to Europe?" Ghaddafi asked Able God as he licked his fingers. At first, Able God wasn't sure what to say because he hadn't been expecting the question.

"I will become a professional chess player," he said after a pause.

"What does that mean?"

"Chess is a game."

"It's a game for very intelligent people, and it's very difficult," Morufu interjected.

"Chess is not difficult. It's easy if you know how to play it," Able God said.

"Teach me how to play it," Ghaddafi said.

Morufu let out a volcanic, barking laugh.

Able God grabbed his bag and got out his chess set. He unfurled the dirty checkered mat and poured the pieces out on the floor.

"The first thing you need to learn is to recognize the pieces and what they do. It's like football, where you have different players doing different things on the field," he said. Ghaddafi nodded attentively.

Able God shifted his gaze to the boy who didn't speak much. The boy had been watching them out of the corner of his eye.

"You can sit with us. You can learn how to play, too," he said, beckoning to the boy. The young lad didn't respond. He looked tired and rundown. Able God shrugged and turned back to the board.

"This is the pawn. Pawns are the foot soldiers. They are the servants. You must learn to use them well," Able God said, picking up a black piece. For the next five minutes, Able God was so occupied with teaching Ghaddafi chess that he did not notice when the boy sat down beside him. He smiled a little when he finally noticed.

Ten minutes later, Able God was distracted by Ben Ten, who'd begun speaking to some of the boys. He was loud and animated as usual, and those in the room had no choice but to listen. Ben Ten told stories of crossing the Sahara, of bandits emerging from behind bushes or inside caves and pouncing on cars. Bandits armed with belts of ammunition, automatic rifles, and even grenades. He spoke of how drivers sometimes missed the trail because of a desert storm or how cars broke down. It was almost impossible to survive once one was stuck in the desert, he told them.

"But we have nothing to worry about," he assured them. "God is on our side. The God that has been on our side since the beginning of the journey will not leave us now. You see, there is another path, unknown to the bandits. It's longer, but it's worth it."

Ben Ten paused for effect, picking at the edge of his nostrils with his fingernails.

"Can someone tell me what is written over there?" Ben Ten asked, pointing to a sentence written on the wall across from him.

L'EUROPE OU RIEN. DIEU EST LÀ! MIEUX VAUT MOURIR EN MER QUE DE MOURIR DEVANT SA MÈRE—SANS RIEN.

No one said anything.

"Pepe! You're from Congo; you speak French. What does it say?" he asked as he directed his gaze at the new boy, who was leaning against the wall.

"Europe or nothing. God is there! Better to die at sea than to die in front of your mother—without anything," Pepe mouthed slowly.

Laughter rose from the room. Able God, however, did not find it amusing.

"That is what I call determination. You see, without determination, you cannot do great things in life. You can ask this anywhere. You must be determined in your heart. This journey is fifty-fifty, so if God says your time on this earth is up, then so be it. If it's not your time to go yet, nothing can stop you. Not even the Sahara can stop you."

His voice was laced with pessimism. Able God wondered why he hadn't mentioned the real dangers of the journey while they were in Nigeria. Able God exchanged quick glances with Morufu and Ghaddafi, then scanned the faces of his fellow travelers. He saw a mix of confusion, blossoming fear, and the specter of hope. He told himself it was too early to give in to despair.

Ben Ten went outside after finishing his speech, and the room fell silent. One boy tried to call home, then another.

Able God got out his phone, too, and turned it on. A text message rolled in, but he didn't have enough reception to make a call. French words appeared in the top corner of his phone. He opened the message, which was from his father.

SOME POLICEMEN CAME TO OUR HOUSE ASKING QUESTIONS. WHAT IS GOING ON? WHAT TROUBLE HAVE YOU GOTTEN

YOURSELF INTO? SOMETIMES I WONDER IF YOU ARE REALLY
MY SON.

He tried to turn off his phone, but his hand had begun to shake
again. "Don't yield to despair," he told himself over and over again.
Ghaddafi wanted to resume the chess lesson. Able God declined. He
lay down on the floor and studied the pattern of the mildew on the
ceiling. But he couldn't sleep, so he sat stiffly upright, staring. After a
while, he glanced over at the quiet boy.

"Why don't you call your family?" he asked, not expecting an answer. He looked away.

"I tell my mama say I get job for wharf, so she no go expect my
call," the boy said, which surprised Able God. He gave the boy a look
that said he understood. Why the boy felt he had to lie to his mother
or avoid getting in touch with her was none of Able God's business.
The important thing was that at least he knew something about the
boy. Able God lay back down. The mildew was now cloaked in darkness. Mosquitoes began to buzz in his ears.

20

The call center was a kiosk made of corrugated aluminum and shelves stacked with phone pouches, counterfeit batteries, chargers of all shapes and colors, earphones, used phones, cannibalized phones, and whatnot. Old, spliced wires were strung along wooden poles in the four corners of the kiosk. There were more wires tangled in a heap, peeling and exposed. A big extension box dangled precariously against the aluminum wall on the left, and numerous phone chargers blinked like disco lights. At this point, the travelers couldn't use their phones because their networks were out of reach, so they'd gone in search of satellite phones that could call anywhere in the world.

Able God, Ghaddafi, and Morufu found the call center after walking about twenty minutes. The vendor, a Tuareg man without a turban, sat in the kiosk. He had a wild beard and piercing red eyes. He reeked of garlic. They exchanged greetings with the vendor. It was clear he spoke little English, so Morufu brought a half-clenched fist to his ear and mouthed "phone call" and "Nigeria."

"Ha!" the vendor exclaimed, flashing his ruined teeth. He reached out to the extension box to unplug a small SAGEM 3020. Before giving Morufu the phone, he punched in some numbers from a scratch card. Morufu dialed with trembling fingers, a frown of concentration on his face. Sweat beaded on the side of his head and around his lips. The phone rang, and he turned on speaker mode.

"Hello?" a female voice boomed from the other side.

"Suliat?" he asked.

"Baba Majid?"

"Yes, it's me!"

She erupted in a high-pitched cry that lasted several moments, then began sobbing. The sobbing didn't stop. There were children screaming and laughing in the background. Morufu's eyes reddened as he fought back tears. Able God looked away, trying not to cry himself. He knew Morufu had a family, or rather he had assumed so. Surely a grown man like him must have one, and he often alluded to being a family man. But Morufu had never really spoken about them to Able God. A tear now rolled down his cheek, and he quickly wiped it away with the crook of his arm.

"Are you well? How is your journey going? Where are you now?" Suliat fired off questions in rapid succession, her voice shaky. Morufu's lips parted in a smile, then he gathered himself and spoke.

"Everything is going smoothly."

"*Alhamdulillah!*"

"We are in Niger Republic."

"Niger?"

"Yes, Niger, a desert country. We have one country remaining, then we will enter Europe."

"It's not too far again!" Suliat said in a voice thick with excitement.

"Yes, it's not too far."

Suliat tried to get a word in but was interrupted by Morufu.

"How is Majid?" he asked.

"He is out playing. Let me go and get him."

There was a sound of steps, then silence, then a scrambling noise.

"Baba! Baba!"

"Majid, my boy!" Morufu cried, his tears mingled with laughter.

"When are you coming home, Baba?" his son asked.

"Very soon, my son."

"What is 'very soon'?"

Morufu broke into laughter.

"'Soon' means it won't be long, Majid. Your father will come, and it won't be long," Suliat explained.

"What do you want me to buy for you when I come back?" Morufu asked his son.

There was a momentary silence.

"I want a toy!"

"Yes, I will buy you a toy. I will send you one!" Morufu said, his eyes radiant.

Majid squealed excitedly, and the thudding footsteps and screams of the other children rang out.

"Majid! Majid! Where are you going? Your daddy is still here! Hello? Hello?" Morufu called out. He was met with silence.

"Hello? I am here, Baba Majid," Suliat said.

Morufu turned off speaker mode and walked off to converse privately with his wife. When he returned, his eyes were red with tears. Morufu handed the phone to Ghaddafi, asking if he needed to call his family, but he shook his head. Morufu turned to Able God.

"I was able to reach them before the network went off," Morufu said with a smile and handed the Tuareg vendor a crinkled note.

◗ ● ▲ ◗

They left the kiosk and made their way through the narrow, dusty streets to the central market. Morufu seemed distracted and was almost hit by a turbaned man driving a motorcycle taxi, but his eyes were filled with joy. Able God had seen him happy a few times before, but this was different. There was something of a fierce quality, a kind of delight mingled with determination.

A withered-looking donkey was tethered to an electric pole on the street that led to the central market. The beast of burden twitched under a swarm of flies, slapping his skinny tail around. There was a large herd of goats in the center of the market, corralled by a low fence made of sticks. There were local merchants selling clothes, sandals, and backpacks. There were piles of fruits, vegetables, and grains. There were little tourist shops with overpriced goods—used household items, Tuareg crafts, swords, leather pouches, handwoven blankets, and jewelry.

"I will come back when I have money again, but I need to see what I am buying with my eyes first!" Morufu said when they reached the bustling market and eased into one of the tourist shops. A light-skinned man in a gray kaftan, his fingers decked with rings, got to his feet and flashed a gold-toothed smile. Morufu gave the shopkeeper a nod and went about examining the goods in the store. He picked up an ivory statuette with impossible limbs, inspected it, and put it back. Able God followed him in, the smell of incense filling his nose. Morufu beckoned to Able God and Ghaddafi after some minutes of walking around the shop.

"My friends, what do you think I should buy for Suliat? I want to send something nice for her. I want to send a good toy to my son, too," he said, excitement in his eyes.

"Jewelry—she will appreciate it!" Ghaddafi piped in.

"I agree," Able God said. He added, "A bead necklace is good, or bangles."

They looked around again and Able God found a dusty old

View-Master lying beside an ancient bedside lamp. When he picked it up, he could not help but smile. His father had bought one of those for him as a Christmas gift when he was young. It came with film reels that plugged into the side of the toy. Each reel contained full-color images of places around the world and happy-looking people, the View-Master offering a new spectacle with each click. He recalled asking his mother why the people inside were so tiny. For some reason, which in retrospect now sounded strange, his mother always responded to his question with a smile and the words "God made them that way."

Able God felt the old familiar anxiety and melancholy.

"God made them that way," Able God muttered to himself. It would be a perfect gift for Majid, he thought. The boy must be filled with mirth and wonder like his father.

"What you want to buy, mister?" the shopkeeper asked Morufu, a frown carved into his face. It occurred to Able God that the shopkeeper had been tiptoeing behind Morufu for some time before finally asking the question. Morufu walked out within seconds. Able God figured he was angry about things other than the shopkeeper's quiet scrutiny. He shuffled along the road a few meters, kicked a plastic bottle violently, then halted.

When they returned to the ghetto, Morufu said, "I spent my last cash to call my family." The fierce excitement was gone.

"There is no food in the house, and my son was sent home for not paying his school fees. If I can get cash, then I can send a Western Union to her. There must be a Western Union center here somewhere."

Able God had no doubt there was a Western Union or some other wire transfer service in Agadez. He just wasn't sure there was a solution to Morufu's money problems.

"Didn't Ben Ten promise to give us jobs along the way to pay for our trip?"

"Ben Ten is a bastard *mehn*!" Ghaddafi said.

"That woman asked the same question, and he did not answer her. I wonder how they settled their matter?" Able God wondered.

"How else would they have settled it? She slept with him, of course!" Ghaddafi said.

"Did you witness it? How do you know that?" Able God asked. Able God couldn't imagine Patricia doing what Ghaddafi said. In fact, he was convinced of the opposite: Ben Ten must have made a deal with her to keep her quiet, not to make a fuss about the jobs he'd promised. A move in the game of chess often revealed something— usually an attack on the opponent. But a crafty player knew how to use his moves to conceal. Ben Ten struck Able God as a crafty player in the game of life. Able God knew he was hiding something but didn't know what or why. All the same, nothing could be worse than what he was running away from—or so he thought.

21

The building's electricity had been cut off, and a dim hurricane lantern sat on the floor of Ben Ten's room, casting shadows across their faces. Most of the boys in the large room were either asleep or scrolling on their phones. Mosquito nets ran from corner to corner. A low murmur came from those still awake, and occasionally a mosquito droned close to Able God's ears. He could make out Morufu's heavy breathing and the strain in his voice as he spoke.

"Are we going to work here in Agadez tomorrow?"

"No, my brother."

"Why not?"

"Because we cross the desert in two days, and one day of work will not make you any money."

"I see."

"Yes. There is work in Libya. We will stay in Sabha for some time, then move to Tripoli, where you will find more work. You see, you are not going to cross the sea just like that. You need money to buy tickets for the boat. You also need money to live on when you get to Europe before you find a job."

There was silence. Able God found what he said sensible. If he didn't know better, he would have been coaxed by those smooth words. There was nothing illogical about Ben Ten's plan.

"My family is hungry back home. I need to send something to them. I don't know what to do," Morufu said, his voice cracking. There was another pause. A sniff, some coughing, then Ben Ten spoke.

"You brought me most of the clients on this trip. I cannot let your family go hungry. Over my dead body!" He lowered his voice. "It cannot happen."

"*Merci beaucoup!*" Morufu said in an energized voice.

"I will give you some money to send to your family. You can pay me back anytime you want."

"*Merci beaucoup! Merci beaucoup!*"

Able God was not sure what surprised him more, Morufu's outburst in French or Ben Ten's offer of help. He did not know what to make of what he'd just heard, but he was glad for his friend. Majid would have his View-Master, and he would see pictures of places beyond the shores of Nigeria. Maybe his father would tell him he now lived in one of those places and that he would soon send for him and his mother. Maybe his son would have something to look forward to, to be proud of. Or maybe things would go terribly wrong, and they would all die. Able God realized it was time for the backup plan that had been floating in the back of his mind to materialize. He needed to prepare for the eventuality that he might have to separate from the group and make the journey on his own. He did not know, however, what that would look like or when the right time would be. He took comfort knowing the option existed even though it would be another zugzwang.

"Let's keep this between me and you—that's the only condition," Ben Ten whispered.

"I swear to God, it won't be a problem."

"I don't want the other passengers to think I am Father Christmas!"

They both broke into laughter. There was a light rasping sound, like something being dragged across the floor. More laughter echoed from the room.

"Sleep very well. You don't need to bother your head," Ben Ten said.

"May God bless you, *merci beaucoup*."

> ● ▲ >

Able God woke up to the clanging of pans as Patricia loomed over bodies sprawled all over the mats.

"Wake up! Wake up! Time for prayers!" she barked, then continued banging on the pans. The travelers grumbled under their breath, and the Muslims among them complained that their sleep was being disturbed before shuffling out of the building. The off-key singing started. Patricia belted out the songs in a terrible falsetto as the others sang along groggily in the background. After the songs came the prayers. This time Patricia asked one of the boys to pray, so he quickly mumbled a few words and said amen. Patricia didn't end the session there but offered her own prayer, which went on for minutes. Apparently the boy's prayers had been insufficient.

Morufu and Ben Ten had left by the time Able God woke up. They had loaded the pickup truck with the big blue plastic barrels of water, which meant they must have gone to fetch water from the mobile tankers waiting on the outskirts of the city. Water was a problem in the arid heat of Agadez. But Able God knew it was just a pretext for money to change hands. He was not even annoyed that Morufu hadn't deigned to tell him, just glad his friend would be able to sort out his family problems. Able God only felt bad that he hadn't been able to convince him to buy the View-Master.

The day wore on, and still they did not return. The heat of the Sahel stung like a whip. With no food, the boys began to grow restless. They gathered in clumps, and their whispers soon became a loud buzzing as they all seemed to talk at once. Able God knew that they would soon turn to him as one of the oldest passengers around, so he came up with an idea. Each traveler would contribute something toward lunch. As easy as it was for them to agree on the communal project, they found it hard to reach a consensus on what to eat.

"Rice! Everybody eats rice!" one boy said.

"Tapioca! I want tapioca," Pepe said.

"What's tapioca?" another boy asked.

"I know what tapioca is, but who eats tapioca for lunch?" commented another.

"This is not a restaurant where you pick a menu! We are in the fucking desert!" said another.

A wave of laughter went through the assembly. Able God figured rice would be the easiest thing to cook, and they all agreed. With Ghaddafi's help they passed around a duffel bag. Most contributed cash, but some dropped in bouillon cubes, bottles of vegetable oil, or sachets of dry pepper. A group went to the market to get rice, while another, Able God's group, walked to the next compound to borrow cooking pots. They made a fire from sticks they'd gathered in the area, and although it took several minutes, lunch was finally ready—a pathetic version of the jollof rice they called "concoction" back in Nigeria.

They had no plates to eat from, so they served the rice on whatever they could find—the pots they used for cooking, pans, flasks, metal trays, and sheets of paper. They ate with their bare hands in groups of six or so. Only Patricia had a plate all to herself.

In the end, all the travelers got enough rice to fill their bellies, making Able God feel good that he had helped. After lunch, Able God sat with Ghaddafi along the fence and smoked. He could no longer keep what he knew to himself.

"Ben Ten decided to assist Morufu," he told him in a whisper.

"With money?" Ghaddafi asked.

"Yes."

"We also need money, s—"

"Ssshhh! Don't let others hear you."

"Why?" Ghaddafi demanded in an angry voice. "Is that why they left us hungry here?"

"Keep your voice down, Ghaddafi!"

He realized he'd made a mistake; he shouldn't have told him.

"They are both in this together, I tell you. How much is Morufu getting for arranging this trip?"

"Morufu is a good man!" Able God snapped at him. There was silence. Then Able God said something he shouldn't have. "If not for Morufu, I'd be either dead or in prison right now!"

Ghaddafi glanced at him sideways. Able God wished he could shovel the words back into his mouth, but what Ghaddafi said next changed the trajectory of the conversation.

"I no fear prison because I was there. I am not afraid of death. We will all die one day. What I fear most in this world is poverty. Poverty is not good," he said, and he took a long drag from his cigarette.

22

Ghaddafi had been locked away for three years for stealing three yams from a merchant. Somehow, his file vanished, or at least that was the official report, so the magistrate court never got to his case. He languished in jail for many months, and later he was transferred to prison, where he spent another year awaiting trial. When he finally got his day in court, he was sentenced to one year's imprisonment.

"Three years? Why?" Able God asked, stunned.

"I did not have a lawyer. I am a nobody; my parents are paupers. There was no help coming from anywhere. I only looked to God," he said to Able God, squinting against the late evening sun. Able God wiped the sweat from his forehead with a finger.

"When I was discharged from prison, I made up my mind to start life again, standing as a man," he continued. "I tried to work at a factory, but they wouldn't give me a job. The manager said it was because I am an ex-convict. Then I tried the transport business, same thing. No one trusted me with their vehicle."

He paused as though searching for an appropriate tone—somber or pained. "When getting a job didn't work, I tried to learn a skill. First, it was as a cobbler. I didn't finish that one because my master accused me of stealing his money. I tried carpentry but the master sacked me when he heard I was ex-convict."

Again, he paused as though to let Able God absorb the details.

"I will continue to face my challenges, and I know one day I will make it."

Ghaddafi's words deflated Able God, and for a moment, guilt and shame overwhelmed him. There he was, standing before a man who had paid too steep a price for a petty crime, his life ruined because he was poor and without connections. As much as Able God would love to find common ground between them to make him feel better, he knew he was nothing like Ghaddafi. Able God wouldn't even be on this journey if he had summoned the courage to face the consequences of his actions. Life had given him everything Ghaddafi could only dream of, and yet they were there together.

The pickup truck lumbered in through the entrance carrying barrels sloshing with water. Ben Ten gathered the travelers and went on about how long it took to load the barrels with water and how they needed to stock up on water for the journey across the Sahara. Morufu looked exhausted but happy, a little smile on the corner of his lips.

Able God felt his muscles tighten in exhaustion. He walked into the building before Ben Ten finished his speech and lay down on the mat. Before he drifted off to sleep, images of the Hotel Atrium passed before his eyes, then he saw the room where it all happened.

He woke up to the sound of shouting and running in the compound. For a few moments, he thought the building had been invaded or, rather, they had come for him. He leaped to his feet and scanned the area for an escape route.

It was only the sound of travelers playing football in the yard.

He dashed to the window to be sure, and there they were, kicking a small leather ball around with a single goalpost demarcated by cans and clouded with dust. Taking a deep breath, he realized his shirt was drenched in a cold sweat. A sudden rush of blood made him dizzy, so he sat down. Why couldn't he remember if he'd had a nightmare? He wasn't sure if thinking the building was being invaded had been a dream or if his mind had panicked as he woke up. The room felt warm.

Again, his mind went back to the Hotel Atrium. He recalled the moment before he got the job, right after the final interview question five months ago. Mr. Hastrup's office had been AC-cold. It had smelled of expensive perfume. There had been a moment of silence, a moment he'd thought would be like other moments. Then he'd heard the scrawling of pen on paper. Mr. Hastrup dropped his pen and interlaced his fingers across his stomach.

"When would you like to start?" he asked.

"What?" Able God replied.

"We want you to be one of our hospitality executives."

"I—I don't know what to say, Mr. Hastrup," he stuttered, doing his best to smile.

"You don't need to say anything. Welcome to Hotel Atrium, and congratulations," he said, stretching his hand out for a handshake.

"Thank you, sir, thank you, sir."

Able God had thought he would be rejected, like all the previous times, which would have been extra devastating because the job was a glorified menial position. Now that he had the job, it didn't make him feel any better. The trip back home was replete with auto-suggestions and chess principles. Before he got home, one of them stuck. *Enjoy the journey on the way to your destination.* The hotel received people from all walks of life. Didn't people say, "You are only four persons away from anything you need"? He told himself that day he would work diligently at the hotel, he would open his eyes for opportunities, and one day, his time would come. He would persevere.

23

Sunday was their last day in Agadez, so Able God decided to venture out of the ghetto. He left the travelers to their lazy card games and headed out alone. He wasn't particularly in the mood to talk to Morufu or Ghaddafi, feeling betrayed that Morufu hadn't trusted him enough to tell him about his arrangement with Ben Ten. But despite his mild anger and lingering mistrust of Ben Ten, he was glad Morufu's family would get what they needed. He wondered what Morufu had gotten for Majid.

Able God walked through dusty side streets, the sun beating down on his face. He walked past a lot where buses and trucks were embarking and disembarking. A swarm of *coxeurs* jostled with hawkers ready to provide services to inexperienced travelers. A man in a dashiki sat cross-legged on a rug in front of his stall. In twenty-four hours, they would set out from that bus station. Someone yelled something at him from the station, or so he thought. He looked over his shoulder, then picked up the pace.

He walked on till the foot traffic thinned and the heat became stifling. He could walk away now and never go back to camp, but Agadez was too close to home. Maybe when they crossed the Sahara, he would have created enough distance between himself and his past.

He passed goat herders and women draped in indigo-blue veils. Stiff-legged, he stopped for a rest. He worried he'd gotten himself lost, but then he noticed he was standing in front of a church, or rather what remained of a chapel—the large windows and doors were gone, the walls charred, and the roof torn apart. The chapel's arches were still intact, but most of the walls had collapsed, and it seemed as though vandals had made off with many of its bricks. Blackened roofing sheets lay mangled on the ground. Burnt beams of wood stuck out through piles of debris.

He tilted his head up to see the pinnacle of the chapel, but the sun blinded him, so he ambled closer. He looked around to be sure no one was looking and peered inside.

A place of worship that was once a source of forgiveness had been reduced to ashes. He had heard of religious riots in northern Nigeria and the Sahel region, so this could be one instance. He wondered if God was still there. Could God still inhabit something so charred and dilapidated? "God does not live in temples made by man," he corrected himself—a lesson from Sunday school—but soon realized he might have been referring to his own redemption, his own resurrection from the ashes.

His instinct had been to go back to religion whenever everything else failed. For him, religion was a familiar friend. He'd picked up the idea of autosuggestions at the polytechnic, but he'd been suckled at the breast of religion. And yet nothing had brought him pain in this world that wasn't connected to religion in one way or another.

Debris crunched under the soles of his shoes as he approached the entrance of the chapel. The smell of old smoke and wet wood filled his nostrils. He slowly put one foot in front of the other, careful not to step on sharp objects. Flies buzzed around.

Inside, most of the pews were splintered, smashed, and

scorched. The floor was strewn with bibles and hymn books, their edges charred. There were torn pages and half-burned bibles. He felt something brush against his leg, and he jumped, looking down to see what it was. A cockroach scurried off into the debris as Able God looked on in disgust.

He walked toward the blackened cross behind the pulpit, cleared the debris around him with his feet, and kneeled down. He clasped his hands in prayer and inhaled sharply.

"Dear Father..." he said, pausing to catch his breath and wipe the tears from his eyes. "Guide me on this perilous journey; protect me from evil."

He heard someone shout words in Arabic, so he wiped away his tears and sprang up to see who had spoken.

A man stood at the entrance of the chapel. He wore a scarf around his neck and a fedora. The man kept on speaking, and although Able God didn't know what he was saying, he knew he was being berated by the man's forceful words. There would be some sort of confrontation if he did not leave. He bowed politely and darted out of the chapel.

He walked hurriedly back to the ghetto, looking over his shoulder the whole time. He arrived drenched in sweat but also feeling strangely unburdened. Morufu was smoking outside with some travelers.

"Where have you been, my friend? I have been worried about you," he said with a serious expression. Able God didn't know what to say, so he mumbled something and tried to smile. Morufu approached him as though to sniff out his mood and find out what he was thinking. He tossed his cigarette butt on the ground.

"You know I am not a busybody," he said, his eyes searching Able God, "but I have been watching you since we started this journey. I

want you to know that you can tell me anything. You don't have to
keep your problems to yourself. You are my brother."

"I'm okay, bro," Able God said.

"You see, in this life, you don't know who can solve your problems
until you speak up," Morufu said, then paused as if trying to decide
whether to speak again or not. He leaned closer.

"I spoke to Ben Ten about my family problems yesterday, and he
loaned me money," he whispered.

"Really?" Able God mouthed, feigning surprise.

"He was nice. He even said I can pay him back when I make
enough money in Libya."

"Good, good!"

"Please don't tell anyone."

"I won't."

"Thank you."

"What did you buy for your son?"

Morufu's face broke out in a smile. "I purchased an old View-
Master from the store we went to that time. But first, I lambasted the
vendor for not treating us well. He understood enough English to
know I was not happy."

Able God laughed heartily. Happiness radiated through him.

> ● ▲ >

They gathered in the compound with their jackets, knapsacks, and
sunglasses. After pouring water from the big blue barrels into smaller
bottles and fifty-liter jerricans, they were ready for the journey—at
least physically. Able God felt ready but was afraid of facing the unknown. He thought about telling Morufu to send a message to his
family in case he didn't make it. But what if Morufu didn't make it?
He could tell Ghaddafi.

At the bus station, the group moved through columns of vehicles parked head to tail with their lights on before coming upon their vehicles.

The bald driver had not returned, nor had the goateed fellow. Instead, Ben Ten introduced them to five new drivers, whose faces they couldn't see because they had *tagelmusts* wrapped around their heads. They wore dusty sandals, grubby trousers, and loose shirts brown with filth.

They emerged from five dirty white Toyota Hilux pickups with darkened windows and ripped-off license plates.

"We are in good hands," Ben Ten said, bubbling with renewed optimism. "These drivers are from the Tebu tribe, and they know the Sahara like their bedrooms. They call them *passeurs*. I can't count the number of people these drivers have taken across the desert. Many of them are in Italy, Germany, and Greece doing well. They are sending money home to their families."

One of the Tebu *passeurs* produced a sack and fished out some cloths for those who didn't have a head covering. Able God took one to use as a blanket instead.

It turned out the drivers could speak neither fluent English nor French, so they communicated through gestures and monosyllabic words. At their direction, the passengers tied small jerricans of water to the edge of the pickup truck so that they dangled outside the truck bed. Fifty-liter jerricans filled with gasoline were stacked in the back of the truck so they'd be able to refuel in the desert.

In no time, they were crammed in the back of the pickups. Some sat on the edge, facing outward, legs dangling, straddling sticks wedged under the lip of the truck bed to keep them from falling off. Others had no choice but to sit on the jerricans. This time, Able God was grouped with Morufu, Ghaddafi, and the boy who didn't say much. Ben Ten was in the front seat with the driver. The caravan of vehicles was ready to go. One roared to life, then the others, and soon they were rumbling back and forth, trying to find their way out. Ben Ten asked the travelers to close their eyes in prayer.

Able God looked around as they skirted sparse border towns and villages surrounded by date palms and clumps of grass. Soon sparse vegetation gave way to sand dunes. His mind went back to where it all started, the abandoned building. He wished he had something to smoke. Not a strong drug like Colorado, which when he first took it, shot so much energy into his heart that he felt like he'd been pierced by hot metal. He'd felt a strange sensation at the back of his head and couldn't breathe. And he saw things even though he couldn't remember what exactly. They told him it was because it was his first time.

The other boys seemed to have their intoxication under control, judging by the way they moved about like zombies and stuck out their blue tongues as if to taste the air. But then there was that one time when things got out of hand, and a boy clutched his chest screaming. He kicked and begged God to stop his pain while they held him down and dowsed his head with water. But he managed to break free and ran off screaming, then plunged into a nearby gutter. Eventually he blacked out and was revived. Although the incident had terrified Able God, he kept showing up. Remembering, Able God's lips parted in a smile, and he closed his eyes as hot air grazed his cheeks.

24

Nothing had prepared Able God for the Sahara, not even Agadez with its dry air and dusty winds. They left Agadez for the ever-lasting sands, blasted past the airstrip, and passed through the only police checkpoint in the area. Able God summoned up childhood memories of the Sahara he had seen on TV. He imagined the silk tents as they drove past tattered earth-colored shelters. He imagined distant oases with sparkling ponds bordered by green palm trees. But the burning sun soon overtook him and evaporated all thought and imagination from his head.

Arid grassland, rocky hills, and plateaus faded into gravel plains and sand dunes. One moment he saw herds of goats prodded on-ward by young boys. The next, it was a sea of emptiness. The tem-perature soared while heat radiated from the ground, licking up the moisture in the air and shimmering on the horizon in a silvery haze. Even the breeze was hot.

Able God felt sweat pouring down his face, blurring his vision. A mighty headache brewed behind his forehead, spreading in both intensity and reach. After a while, the dry air teased the remaining moisture from his body. His skin dried up, as though his pores could no longer produce sweat. He could feel every part of his body itch as his skin crackled in the dry air. Soon the saliva dried up in his mouth, and there was nothing to moisten his tongue or his parched lips. He exhaled hot air, his throat scorching with every breath.

He looked at the sullen, muslin-wrapped faces surrounding him. He rarely exchanged words with the people stuffed in with him in the pickup. Words were expensive. They all battled their own discomfort, trying to conserve their bodily fluids.

His eyes fell on the quiet boy. Under his hoodie was a smudged and frowning face. His eyes looked strangely melancholic, as if he were longing for something unknown. Peeling his gaze away, Able God opened his jerrican and took a miserly sip from it. The water was warm by then, but it sent a refreshing jolt through his body anyway. His body ached for more, but he could not afford to drink more. He put the cap back on. That was when he noticed the quiet boy had been watching him. Able God saw that the boy's jerrican was empty and for a moment felt drawn to share some of his with him but decided against it. He could share later if they made it, but not now. He looked away.

Hot sand beat against their pickup with a sound like heavy rain as they barreled through golden dunes and bumped over barren rock. A time came when they spoke up, grumbled about the chassis becoming too hot to sit on. One person suggested they pad their seats, so they carefully removed a few layers of their cloth head coverings. That created a new problem: their faces were exposed to the desert's unforgiving elements. Dust filled their ears and noses and reddened their eyes, provoking bouts of coughing and shortness of breath.

After nine hours in the heat, Able God's tongue had shriveled in his throat. He wanted to strip bare, but he couldn't. His skin was caked with dust, even where he'd kept himself covered. He could hear expressions of exhaustion rising from the boys next to him, the rasping of their breath, and the sound of their clothes flapping in the wind. Terrible smells wafted from their shriveled lips. Some of those lips moved in prayer until they were too tired to move. Further requests to God were offered in the realm of the mind for those who could still think clearly. The quiet boy was sobbing on the shoulder of another passenger.

There was nothing to hold on to—no hope, no newfangled dreams, no bitterness, no memory of love, nothing but his instinct to survive. Able God was grateful for every breath he drew, every hour that ticked by. His concern was not about the future but surviving the next moment.

He tried to distract himself by gazing at the vast expanse of sand stretching out before him. There was nothing much to see. It was all dry land and rocky mountains with a sprinkling of trees and plants.

Once, they blasted past an upturned vehicle caked in dust. Another time, it was a dead camel fossilized by the fiery heat of the Sahara. Able God was surprised at his lack of reaction upon seeing the camel. He was supposed to be scared—if a camel, known as the ship of the desert, could succumb to the environment, then what would become of them? But Able God was not afraid. To be afraid meant to be worried something terrible would happen, but no peril could be worse than what he was already experiencing.

After eleven hours in the desert, the sun finally went down. Deep shadows climbed up. One after another, the travelers removed their head wraps and covered their noses instead. The temperature dropped as the wind began to gust. Cold air tore through their layers of clothing and chilled their pores.

Tire tracks blew away in the wind, and the vast expanse of sand quickly became disorienting. The drivers didn't seem affected, though. Only a few paths crossed the desert, and one wrong turn would lead to oblivion. Ancient caravans and nomads navigated the trackless terrain of the desert by the wind, moon, sun, and stars, and the Tebu drivers were known to have learned the ways of old.

The first thing of beauty showed up: the night sky sparkled brilliantly. Now Able God could watch the stars. But by this time every muscle in his body ached, and he could not turn his neck without difficulty. He devised a way of looking just above the horizon by raising his head ever so slightly.

His father could identify the constellations just by looking at them. Whenever the electricity went off in their house, which was almost every night, they would sit out in the courtyard and enjoy the evening, looking at the constellations and watching the stars.

His father particularly loved spotting the Big Dipper on the northern horizon.

"See that?" he would say, pointing to the sky. "That's the Big Dipper, one of the brightest constellations!"

His father always had something to say when the moon came out or when the stars seeded themselves in the sky. It was his father who had told him when he was just a boy that some stars were bigger than the earth, bigger even than the sun—that they were not as small as they appeared to his eyes. Able God got confused when his father began telling him about the solar system and the Milky Way. Later, the books in their house and his formal education would teach him how infinitesimal Earth was in the grand scheme of things. His knowledge of the universe made him feel diminished.

He sure didn't need astronomy to feel diminished right now. If he were to die in this desert, no one would find him. The universe did not care if he survived this ordeal or the next one. Surviving was up to him and him alone.

> ● ▲ >

"Use your sticks, don't remove your shoes. Be careful of snakes and scorpions. They are buried deep in the sand," Ben Ten loudly warned the travelers when they stopped beside an arid bush just before sunrise to stretch and relieve themselves after nine hours of driving.

They were surrounded by sand dunes, but they'd stopped by a thicket of twisted dry brambles. There were old shoes and bags scattered everywhere, burned rubbish in little piles, and lumps of ashes.

The passengers wandered off to pee. Some dug holes in the hard soil to shit in while others squatted over sheets of paper or plastic bags. The Tebu *passeurs*, to everyone's surprise, reached under the driver's seat and brought out pistols, which they shoved into the back of their trousers. The *passeurs* seemed unaffected by the journey—the only trace of their long travel was the dust that had settled over their *tagelmusts*. They stood ramrod straight, spat on the ground, and smoked cigarettes after removing their *tagelmusts*. Ben Ten went to gather some dry twigs and started a fire under a copper teakettle.

Morufu hobbled over to Able God, the foot of his bad leg scraping along in the sand. He gave Able God a handful of dried dates. Able God thanked him and checked the sand for scorpions with his stick. They sat down and ate together silently.

Able God was painfully thirsty. He could neither chew nor swallow without considerable pain, so he nibbled at the dates like a mouse. He could still feel sand in the back of his mouth. As he ate, irritation tightened his throat and made him empty his lungs in a rasping cough, date flecks spraying everywhere.

Morufu couldn't even chew. He sucked on his dates, crushing their flesh with his parched lips, sucking the mush. His voice box bobbed, and his throat quivered. Because his breathing had become pained, his mouth made sucking and wheezing sounds. His sleep-deprived eyes were red. A network of long veins ran over the ashy skin of his neck. The hunger, journey, and anxiety had been hard on everyone. But they'd known what it would be like before they started the journey. They had chosen it.

Able God suddenly remembered the boy and felt a stab of guilt. He looked around, but the boy was nowhere to be found.

"Where is that boy?" he asked Morufu.

"He is in the pickup, sleeping," Morufu said.

"I don't think he has eaten anything." Able God rose to his feet.

"Do you want to feed him in his sleep?"

"I will wake him up."

Morufu coughed, beating his chest with his palm as Able God walked away. Able God found the boy curled up in the back of the pickup, snoring heavily, a thumb stuck between his lips. His dusty face was visible through his hoodie. A thin line of drool trailed down from the corner of his mouth to his jaw. For a moment, Able God stood looking at the boy. It dawned on him how young the boy must be—not even on the cusp of puberty, really, in his infantile position with his thumb in his mouth. He tapped the boy, who stirred and farted loudly. Murmuring something undecipherable, the boy yawned and sat up. He blinked, peering around wide-eyed as though he had woken up in hell, then sank back down and was soon snoring. Able God sighed and walked back to the mound of sand.

"That poor boy is too tired to eat," Able God said.

"When hunger beats him, no one will tell him to wake up and eat," Morufu responded, his voice sharp and quick with a tinge of irritation.

Able God gave him a questioning look. "He is a boy. He should not be here. Did Ben Ten make a deal with him, too?"

"He is not the only boy here."

"But he is the youngest!" Able God said. "What could force a boy of his age to make this kind of journey?"

There was a pause. "He will grow up fast. He'll learn how to be a man," Able God said.

"The desert is not a place to become a man. Even animals die here," Morufu said in a strained voice.

Beyond the conversation about the boy, Able God could tell Morufu was frustrated, if not disillusioned. This was not just because he seemed to have no desire to open his mouth except to eat.

"*Inshallah*, God willing, we will make it to Italy," Able God said.

"*Inshallah*," Morufu replied absently.

Able God said no more. He ate the rest of his dates, listening to Morufu wheezing beside him. Ben Ten finished his tea, dusted himself off, and announced that it was time to leave.

"Let's go! Sharp, sharp! No time to waste!" he yelled.

The passengers moved to their respective vehicles. The quiet boy was shaken awake, and they were soon ready to continue the journey.

> ● ▲ >

The following morning, they halted to refuel. Able God helped unload two jerricans from the back of the pickup he was riding in. The containers felt heavier than Able God remembered—he was nearly at the end of his strength. Finally, it took five of them to carry a single container over to the gas tank.

After opening the jerricans, the driver stuck a long rubber hose into one of them to siphon out the gasoline. He sucked on the end of the hose until his mouth filled with fuel, which he spat into the sand. Gasoline fumes rose up into the dry air.

While the trucks were being refueled, some of the passengers

wandered off to piss, while others guzzled water from plastic jerricans covered with sackcloth to help keep the water cool or ate the
provisions in their bags. Dizzy with hunger, Able God sat down on
the coarse sand to eat with Morufu, Ghaddafi, and the quiet boy.
Morufu got out some dates and chewed them quickly like a rabbit.
Ghaddafi hurriedly dug his teeth into an unpeeled orange, sucking
and squeezing out the juice as if his existence depended on it. Able
God poured some *gari* into his cup and added half a day's ration of
water to it, about half a pint. He shoveled the food into his mouth
and then paused to look at the boy, who was scrawling arabesques in
the sand with a piece of stick.

"Take. You need to eat for strength." Able God handed the rest of
the food to the boy.

Then he dug a packet of Rothmans out of his bag, lit up, inhaled, and exhaled. Able God stared blankly into space before
sweeping his gaze from the vast swaths of dry land to the gently
rolling hills cloaked in sparse vegetation. He squinted as the hot
air burned his face. Shoes of various types and sizes were scattered
all over, gray and covered in dirt. Trash-strewn areas and used tires
littered the ground. There were tracks in the sand, tracks made by
cars, animals, and humans. The last driver was refueling, and Ben
Ten was sharing a bottle of gin with the other Tebu *passeur*. Strong
sunlight now broke through the thick gray clouds, and soon Able
God felt the sand beneath him growing hot. The smell of rubber
filled the air.

Able God's gaze fell on a flock of vultures on a small heap of sand
surrounded by dry grass. They were pecking at something. Able God
could not see what it was from where he sat, but he could hear them
clacking and hissing. It was not long before Patricia rose to her feet
and plodded over to the heap. The vultures winged off just before

she got there. Pulling her skirt up and squatting, she began to relieve herself.

Able God turned away, but he snapped his head back when he heard her loud scream. She pressed a hand up against her mouth in shock as she moved away from the mound of sand, choking back tears. One of the boys ran over to see what she'd seen. His face transformed into a mask of terror and shock. Another boy went to look and gasped in shock, moving away in revulsion.

Another boy joined him, then another. Able God sprang to his feet after instructing the quiet boy to stay put. Ghaddafi and Morufu followed him. Able God caught a stench of decay, which worsened as he approached. A corpse was lying in the grass. Only the head and limbs were visible above the coarse sand. A green Nigerian passport was half-buried atop the heap of sand. His eye sockets were hollow, empty, and buzzing with flies. His mouth was wide open, his teeth bared, his tongue protruding from between his lips.

The second corpse was a few meters away. Belted trousers brown with dust sagged around his knees. His boots were torn and riddled with holes. His upper body appeared to have either decomposed or been eaten by animals. The skull was all that was left of his head; his dust-colored rib cage had been almost totally shorn of flesh. The ruin of his flanks had been detached from his protruding hip bone. Able God stood there with his mouth agape, too shocked to move or peel his eyes away. The spell in which the horrific sight held him was loosened by Ghaddafi's exclamation.

"A'udhubillahi mina shaytanirajim!"

Morufu put his hand to his head. A crowd had gathered around them. Ben Ten arrived at the scene, took one sweeping glance at the corpses, and shook his head sadly.

"Nigeria! I am sure the people who organized this man's trip did not hire experienced drivers," Ben Ten said. "For some people money is much more important than human lives. So sad. So terrible. May God rest their souls." He spat. He unearthed the man's passport, dusted off the surface, and flipped it open. The wind blew across the sand, mixing the smell of decay with the odor of old urine. Ben Ten covered his nose with one hand as he peered at the passport.

Able God glanced at Ben Ten. That bastard always had an excuse for everything, but he was too sunk in distress to react to Ben Ten's words.

"I don't think this one died here. Maybe he died in the mountains. Whoever found his dead body put his passport on his grave so someone could identify the body. So sad!" he added to buttress his reasoning, then put the passport back where he'd found it.

"I don't know what happened to this other one," Ben Ten said, heaving another big sigh.

A peculiar kind of tension rattled through Able God's body: tension from the realization of a present and imminent danger, something that was no longer distant. He snatched a breath, then another. Sweat gathered on his forehead, at the tip of his nose, and formed a line over his lips.

In this moment of darkness and fatigue, Able God fell prey to the emotion that had possessed him in the hours following Badero's death. He felt a stab just below his ribcage as his mind rehashed the scenes from the hotel room. The images flitted past quickly and stopped at him descending the elevator, hands trembling, the elevator button dinging and lighting up until the very last ding. *Ding ding ding.*

Ben Ten's voice snapped Able God back from his thoughts. He ordered the group to get back in the trucks. He told them there was nothing more to see. Those who died had not been careful enough, but they would be safe.

As Able God walked back to the pickup, he told himself that Badero's body would not end up like the corpses in the desert. Instead, it would be pumped full of embalming fluids to prevent immediate decay. He would be well presented for his burial. At least his family and loved ones would be there to lay him to rest, but here—if Able God perished here, his corpse would be dishonored and feasted upon by animals. One more reason to stay alive.

25

One sulfurous day blurred into another. Able God felt his veins swell and snake along under his skin, pumping, throbbing, ready to burst. The long hours spent speeding through a cloak of fire and fending off the hot sand nearly drove him mad.

Three days after entering the desert, someone tumbled out of the truck.

They had been sleeping slumped against one another when his body hit the ground with a loud thud. He fumbled for a few seconds before lurching after them, screaming, his head bleeding and his sandals slapping his heels.

Able God saw that it was the quiet boy. Able God screamed, his body suddenly soaked in sweat. Everyone screamed. Morufu banged the roof of the truck and shouted at the driver to stop, but he didn't. Able God screamed till he felt he had lost his voice, his heart thundering in his chest. The more he shouted, the more dust blew in his mouth and nose and eyes. Ben Ten called back loudly that they couldn't stop. He said other things, too, but the Tebu *passeur* didn't stop.

At first, when the lost boy screamed, the echoes in the hollows of the dunes answered him, but eventually, the distance and the engine's revving drowned out his voice.

The poor boy ran after the truck for a while, sobbing and yelling, until he vanished into a cloud of dust. When the dust settled, he was far away, a tiny dot on the horizon. Able God tried to keep his composure, but his body trembled. One of the boys started crying. Another started to pray, and the travelers—including Morufu and Ghaddafi—joined in, opening their palms to pray in Arabic. Able God concluded that if they did not band together, they would lose more passengers. The most vulnerable would be the first destroyed, but everyone would be affected. He tried to steady his breath before speaking.

"Heaven helps those who help themselves," he said, raising his voice above the howling wind and the roaring trucks. He looked around, searching their faces. "We need to work together. That's the only way we can survive."

Able God could hear only little sobs around him. His chest ached with terror. He swallowed to wet his throat. Warm sweat trickled under the collar of his shirt.

"Let those who want to sleep move inside while the rest of us keep watch from the edges. That way, no one else will be caught dozing. Make sure you always hold on to your sticks. Never let go. We'll take turns sleeping so we can protect each other. We will all get to our destination safely in Jesus's name."

They all shouted amen, then started to shuffle around, twisting and turning. Sweat and dirt mingled. Able God took the first watch as the truck sped across the endless sand. He stared off into space as the caravan passed a row of abandoned vehicles left to rust, overturned vehicles, skeletons of dust-streaked vehicles, and charred cars blackened with smoke.

He watched the landscape rush past and thought about the dead corpses. He wondered what could have killed them. Hypothermia at night? Dehydration? An animal attack? After a while, his mind moved to what he had been trying to avoid: the boy they had left behind. The boy who was not dead yet. The boy who, in a few days, would be a corpse, too. His mother, whom he had deceived, would never discover his whereabouts. His corpse would never be identified. He would end up buried without a name or proper grave. Even Able God didn't know his name.

For a few moments, visions of the decomposed bodies alternated with images of the boy trudging through the sand. Able God's head swirled with Morufu's words: *He is a boy. He should not be here. The desert is not a place to become a man. Even animals die here.*

Then sound and color shuddered and bled. His eyelids grew heavy. He shook himself alert and tapped his feet against the edge of the pickup to prevent himself from falling asleep.

Time passed. He had no idea how much, but he knew the journey would be long. They would stop again. Maybe they would see other unspeakable things. Maybe more people would die. Maybe it would be his turn to die next. If he did die, they would bury him in the sand with his limbs sticking out. There would be no passport to place on top of the pile.

> ▸ ● ▲ ▸

"Let us pray that the border patrol will pick him up before the bandits. Who wants to die?" Ben Ten said. The Tebu *passeur* had stopped before linking up with the paved road that led to Sabha. They'd all gotten out of the truck at an abandoned fuel station and gathered around Ben Ten.

"As you saw, stopping in the desert would have been very risky," he said. "I am trying to help everybody here. That's all I am trying to do. You should be grateful for what I have done for all of you."

A rigid frown clamped Ben Ten's desiccated face, his beard brown with dust. They were too morose and dog-tired to respond, so they just stared back at him with blank, sleepy eyes. A sense of profound sadness filled the air. Able God stood close to Morufu. Ghaddafi was out of sight. Able God looked at Ben Ten with unmitigated contempt, his mind clouded from the constant trauma. He was no longer willing to suppress his doubts.

By then, Able God no longer wanted to hear anything Ben Ten had to say. His skin was burning, his head ached, and he swallowed with difficulty. His hands and feet were swollen in his sandals, and the soles of his feet stung. He felt simultaneously foolish and terrified. He felt foolish for his naïveté. How could he have hoped things would bode well for him on this path? What greater peril awaited them? A fly settled on his lips. He waved it away, cursing under his breath. He tried to think. What if he disappeared and found his own way as planned? They were already in Libya, and the Mediterranean Sea couldn't be that far. He could work in the city until he'd made enough money to hire a smuggler who would make the journey less perilous for his travelers. Should he make the plan alone and not include Morufu, who had done so much for him? But then, he wouldn't be here if not for Morufu—but where would he be? Prison. Able God realized that he would feel less conflicted about his decision not to turn himself in back home if he got to Europe. Reaching his destination was a nonnegotiable for him.

Able God glanced at Morufu, noting the puffiness under his eyes, the veneer of fatigue and anguish on his face. Maybe he was in pain because of his leg. His skin was brown with dust. His eyes, which once sparkled with optimism, were now clouded by thirst and hunger. How long before Morufu realized Ben Ten was bad luck?

"Praise the Lord!" Patricia suddenly hollered. One boy offered a hallelujah in response.

Able God remembered that she'd been sitting exhausted on the ground with her mouth in a miserable arc just moments before. She was now on her feet, tightening the scarf on her head.

"Praise de leeving Jesus!" she yelled. A scattered response answered her. She raised her voice in song:

> *Praise da Lord!*
> *O sing o sing o!*
> *Praise da Lord!*
> *Praise His Holy name!*
> *O sing o sing o!*
> *Praise da Lord!*

She clapped as she sang. One after another, the boys joined in, clapping and yelling. Able God did not participate at first but slowly became infected by the animated atmosphere, the rhythmic clapping of hands, the tired faces brightening with hope. Their hoarse voices rose higher and higher, piercing the air and drifting in and out of tune. Able God soon found himself clapping and singing. After a few moments, the woman changed her song from a song of praise to something aspirational. Again, they sang after her, this time their voices loud and forceful.

> *Because He lives*
> *I can face tomorrow*
> *Because He lives*
> *All fear is gone*
> *Because I know He holds my future*
> *My life is worth living just because He lives*

Tears tumbled down Patricia's face, and some of the boys closed their eyes as they sang. Some looked up into the sky as they held hands, eyes glazed with unshed tears. Even Morufu and Ghaddafi, both Muslim, sang along. Able God felt a sudden surge of emotion and struggled to keep himself from breaking down in tears. He did not succeed. The song tore at the pain in his heart like a fishing hook.

"Praise the Lord!" Patricia said, bringing the singing to an end amid a resounding chorus of hallelujahs.

"Our Father and Most High God," she proclaimed before launching into prayer. The boys closed their eyes and bowed their heads, some getting down on their knees. Able God found his attention drifting away from the prayer. With the back of his palm, he wiped the tears from the corners of his eyes. Even though he did not know the lost boy's name, he felt like he had lost a little brother. The boy must have been about the same age as Calistus when he'd dropped out of school. Able God wondered if the boy had also dropped out of school to embark on their treacherous journey. His attention drifted back to the prayer. He prayed for the boy to be protected from the heat and dust of the desert, from wild animals and poisonous snakes. Then he prayed for him to be found, not by bandits but by those who would help him, maybe take him back home. Now Able God felt feverish. His forehead burned, and his body ached. Moments later, the prayer ended, and Ben Ten took over.

"We thank the Almighty God for journey mercies," Ben Ten said after taking roll call. "As you can see, we are in Libya. This is Sabha, and we are not too far from Tripoli. I will ask our Tebu drivers to park the pickups when we reach the city, and we will go to our accommodations. Like Agadez, Sabha is not a place to roam about. Here, we need to be even more careful. There are thugs on the streets called

Asma Boys. Have you heard of Asma Boys?" He paused for an answer, but no one said anything. He plowed ahead.

"I know you all need food, water, and rest, but this information is
for your safety. The Asma Boys kidnap Blacks on the streets. Those
bastards will lock you up at gunpoint, torture you, and make you call
your families at home for ransom. They will tell them to send the
money through Western Union or a bank transfer. If your families
had money to give kidnappers, would you be out here hustling? Of
course not, but these boys don't want to know that. If they don't get
money from your families, they will waste you. May God continue
to protect all of us."

Half of the group responded with an amen before Ben Ten ordered them to get back in the trucks.

Before reaching the city, they passed through barricades cobbled
together with old fridges and burned-out cars. Ben Ten paid off the
armed men keeping guard at the barricade, and they were waved
through. They drove past rough walls peppered with gunshots, walls
where the plaster had fallen away in great chunks.

26

The streets of Sabha reeked of sweat, sand, and spices. The wide streets were paved with crumbling asphalt and lined with date palms, shops, boutiques, and passageways. Labyrinthine alleys wound past nondescript compounds and low-lying houses.

Ben Ten led them to a dirt-floored house with an open-air courtyard that was tucked into one of Sabha's back alleys. A herd of goats was rooting around the trash-strewn compound. In one corner of the courtyard, a crumbling concrete staircase led to a roof terrace.

Before they went in, Ben Ten tried to convince Patricia that she had to be separated from the group.

"Patricia, in Sabha they don't like it when men and women mix together," Ben Ten insisted. "This compound is divided into two. The women's section is on the other side."

Able God found the idea that there was a place where genders didn't mix very suspicious but also knew Ben Ten would always get what he wanted.

"What kind of nonsense is this? After what we have gone through together?" Patricia protested, her face a wall of defiance. "Why do you want to put me in the midst of strangers?"

"It's not like that, madam. They say, when you are in Rome, you behave like the Romans. This is what they want here, and we have to abide by their rules," Ben Ten replied. "Everybody here is a stranger to you anyway. Nobody here is a member of your family, are they?"

"So what? So what if they are not my family members?" Patricia asked, anger in her eyes.

Able God saw that another long fight was brewing, and the thought of it made him feel weak.

Ben Ten told her the women's quarters were less crowded and that they had bigger rooms and real beds. Surprisingly, she assented.

Inside the men's quarters, a single large room was crammed with bunk beds, its windows shrouded with musty checkered curtains. Mouse droppings littered the dirt floors. Able God felt weak again. He sneezed once, then twice, as he tried to commandeer a bunk bed. Pepe and another boy reached it before he did. He looked around for Morufu, who was also searching for an empty bunk. When Able God finally found one, he invited Morufu to take one of the beds.

A little later, Ben Ten came in with loaves of bread and tins of sardines. They all rushed to get the food and ate like ravenous beasts. Able God had no appetite, but he knew he needed energy. He gobbled up his food almost in one gulp, then clapped his hands over his mouth to prevent himself from retching. After the meal, he drifted off to sleep.

Able God woke up sweating. He sat up exhausted, his eyes searching the darkened room. Maybe it was the heat in the room. Maybe it was his feverishness. The room was almost empty, and the wooden bed frames no longer held any mattresses. There were no voices outside, only snores. He stumbled from his bed and walked toward the window. The ground undulated before his eyes. He gripped a bunk bed to steady himself and walked on, then parted the curtains and peered out. The travelers were asleep on mattresses spread on the ground, bodies piled on each other, limbs tangled. Ben Ten was nowhere to be found. Able God saw a perfect opportunity to make his getaway. He staggered back to his bed, taking deep breaths, his head swirling. He bundled his belongings, zipped his bag up, and slung it over his shoulder.

Able God glanced out the door before stepping into the cool night air. He shivered. The stars were out, and the air smelled fresh. He took off his shoes, hung them around his neck by their laces, and tiptoed to the long, dark passageway leading to the pedestrian gate. His legs wobbled, so he leaned against the mud walls for support as he quickened his steps. His head thumped and his eyes were dizzy, but he kept moving. The pedestrian gate was chained together and fastened with many locks. Did he think Ben Ten would just leave them behind without securing the place? What had he been thinking? His head weighed heavily on his neck. He glanced up as he considered trying to scale the gate. The gate, though not too tall, was topped with barbed wire. He dragged himself back to the quarters.

He tried to drink water from the tap in the compound but had difficulty swallowing. The boys stirred in their sleep. One of them woke up and went to piss beside the fence. Able God considered taking his mattress outside but decided it would make his fever worse, so he went back to the empty room and curled up on the bed, trembling. He clenched his jaw. Nothing to do but wait for dawn.

Hours later, he awoke from a dream in which he was back home playing chess with Morufu when the police barged in and grabbed him. They dragged him outside, as his parents looked on in distress. Mr. Hastrup stood beside them, his head cocked to one side, a satisfied grin on his lips. Able God wanted to stop and speak to his

parents. He wanted to tell them he was sorry for being a disappointment. He wanted to tell them he didn't mean to kill anyone. The police wouldn't let him. They dragged him into the back of the van as he
kicked and screamed. Before the van drove off, he heard his mother
screaming out his name.

In the van, Dr. Badero was sitting across from him, a piece of
glass lodged in his bleeding neck. He pounced on Able God, his eyes
popping out in anger. Able God put his thick hands on the neck of
Badero, who gasped for breath while blood spurted from his gashed
neck. Able God woke from the dream perspiring.

> ● ▲ >

"Is that Ben Ten?" Able God asked Morufu when Ben Ten walked
into the quarters the following morning.

"What?" Ghaddafi asked, turning to see. A confused look gripped
his face.

He had shaved off his beard and was wearing a clean T-shirt and a
fresh pair of jeans. It was obvious that most of the boys barely recognized him when he clapped his hands to bring silence to the room.
Usually they sealed their lips as soon as he appeared and waited for
his instruction like hungry dogs.

"Today is a good day!" he said, smiling. His face looked rested,
and it seemed a heavy burden had been lifted off his shoulders. Able
God wondered what his new appearance meant for all of them.

"We are close to the Promised Land. The rest of the journey will
now go on smoothly. I have arranged jobs for you here. I will be gone
for two weeks. I will travel to Tripoli to prepare the journey to Europe. Everything will go smoothly from now on, by the Grace of the
Almighty God," Ben Ten said, pointing a finger toward heaven.

Able God did not believe a word of what he said, but he also wasn't sure it mattered what he believed. Ben Ten took roll call, and the boys began to pack up their belongings.

Two pickups, a Datsun, and a large black 4x4 Jeep were waiting outside the gate. A man was standing in front of the truck. He was tall and light-skinned, with an angular jaw, an aquiline nose, and a pencil mustache. Beside him was a tall pregnant woman whose skin was marred by old smallpox scars. She wore four gold bangles on each wrist and rings on all her fingers. She had a face mask covering her mouth and nose like she didn't want to breathe the air around her.

"Let me introduce you to Mr. Serge. He is one of our consultants. He will take good care of you," Ben Ten said, pulling yet another smile from the day's seemingly endless supply. Serge said nothing to them. He simply nodded, a weak smile on his mustachioed lips.

Ben Ten gestured that it was time to leave, and they all headed to the vehicles. Able God clutched his bag, trotting behind Morufu to the back of the pickup. Ben Ten drove the Datsun. Serge and his woman got into the Jeep.

As the convoy moved through the city's zigzagging roads, Able God looked around. He stared at the crowded storefronts, the Italian colonial-era buildings, the graffitied houses with loose roofing sheets flapping in the breeze, the unplastered brick houses in half-open compounds, the walls covered with peeling posters, and the old billboards with pictures of Muammar Gaddafi in military uniform and dark glasses or campaign messages from his toppled regime. The noise made Able God dizzy. They drove past a public park where groups of old men played chess and checkers. That got his attention.

He noticed a group of people huddled under makeshift tents in a trash-strewn parking lot. Some lay on tattered pieces of cloth spread on the ground. They were tall, gaunt, dark-skinned men wearing worn-out clothes or rags, their hair matted and their flip-flops unmatched. There was no doubt in Able God's mind that they were migrants—possibly from Eritrea, South Sudan, or Somalia.

Able God took a closer look and realized that some of them were watching the convoy with morose eyes. He met one man's gaze and was persuaded that the fellow was looking directly at him. He focused on the fellow, cropping him out of the messy backdrop formed by the parking lot. For a moment, Able God caught the fellow grimacing as if he were swallowing poisonous phlegm. The fellow then shook his head slowly. Able God continued to look at him until the vehicle passed the parking lot. Minutes later, Ben Ten's car swerved onto the highway and sped off. The rest of the convoy turned up a dirt road. The gears crunched, and his vehicle bounced along the uneven dirt road, raising a cloud of red dust.

A thought kept echoing against the walls of Able God's mind, even though the idea seemed dangerous to him. He looked down at the road. The pickup was moving slowly enough for him to jump out without hurting himself too much, but he would be in the middle of nowhere. The convoy was going farther and farther away from the city. He thought about the quiet boy they had left behind in the Sahara and decided he would wait till they reached their destination before attempting an escape.

Soon, the cars growled up to the summit of a hill and stopped in front of a gate. It swung open, and Serge's car moved in, but the pickup vans did not follow. The gate opened again, and a truck drove out to meet them. Burly bearded guards with pistols, rifles, and dogs jumped down. They wore face masks and latex gloves. The guards shouted muffled commands in Arabic, gesturing for the boys to get down. The dogs barked and strained against their leashes. In no time, the group was assembled in front of the gate, huddled in a single mass, deep anxiety written on their faces.

Able God's heart was pounding, and he was covered in a cold sweat. He knew something was not right. Feeling the panic in the air, he edged closer to Morufu and elbowed him to get his attention. He wanted to tell him that his instincts had been right all along. Wanted to tell him it wasn't too late to find a way out. But before Morufu could turn to him, one of the boys bolted.

A guard took aim, and a terrible blast hit the air. Another followed. For some reason, the bullets missed the target, throwing up dirt on the road. Able God ducked, checked his body to see if he'd been hit by the ricochet. A third shot rang out, and the boy fell forward onto the ground, blood spurting from a gaping wound in his neck. He twitched and wailed until he became gape-mouthed and still. There were screams, sobs, and shouted prayers. Able God felt a stream of piss trickling down his thighs. His hands started trembling, the way they'd trembled after Dr. Badero died. The guard shoved his pistol back into its holster and bellowed some words in Arabic.

On the guards' orders, the boys lined up in three columns. One after another, the bearded guards frisked them while some of the boys choked back tears. The guards took everything they found, including phones and money. They ordered the boys to raise their hands and spread their legs wide. Ordered them to open their mouths. Searched the insides of their ears. Prodded every recess of their bodies. Able God was one of the last to be searched. A bearded guard with a Kalashnikov slung over one shoulder cocked his head and looked down at Able God's wet trousers. He chuckled. Able God was now beyond shame. He just wanted to live.

The guard's stare lingered for a while, then his forehead wrinkled in a rictus of disgust. He snatched the bag from Able God that contained the chess set, one of his last and most treasured possessions on earth, and waved him along. Able God could not do anything to protest. He wouldn't have dared try, even had he been in the frame of mind to do something.

Be calm and do whatever they ask, and everything will be fine.

When they had finished searching the group, the gate swung open again, and they let the boys in. They drove past a beautiful white house surrounded by flowers and trees. Serge's car was parked out front. They drove past dormitory blocks and continued to a fenced compound choked with tents. There they found more people like them.

27

Able God typically wolfed down his meals while standing because the guards gave them little time to eat. They emptied their bowels in the bushes beside the chain-link fence that surrounded the camp. At night, the camp never went completely quiet. Late night discordant coughing evolved into inmates clutching handkerchiefs spattered with blood-stained sputum in the morning, the result of their coughing fits. According to his daily mental account, it had been three weeks since the guards escorted them to the gated compound crowded with tents, yet it felt like an eternity. Able God wished time would pass quickly so that perhaps the end of their agony would be near, but time moved slowly still.

The fence was low enough for them to scale it if they wanted, but where would they go? How would they find their way to freedom through the desert? It was fear and not the wire fence that made them prisoners. Old inmates never missed an opportunity to pass down stories of what had happened to those who'd tried to escape.

The tents in the camp were made of sticks, rags, and old tarpaulins. They had no beds, so they slept on mats. The compound was filled with garbage, which provided a breeding ground for rodents. It was not uncommon to hear the squeaking of baby mice at night.

Able God once saw one of the inmates sweep their pale, squirming bodies out from underneath rotten wood. They also had to deal with bugs of all kinds: cockroaches, bedbugs, spiders, scorpions, and dragonflies. Occasionally, a serpent would slither into the camp and cause a commotion—not because the inmates feared the snake but because they wanted to eat it. They would scramble for sticks, stones, or whatever they could find and lunge after the creature. All they needed to make a fine snake-meat dish was a small fire and some salt, nothing more. Some inmates were known to consume the rodents as well.

They drank piss-colored water from a shallow well outside the compound. The guards rationed their food and made them stand in line for meals. The inmates shuffled in long queues, holding battered aluminum plates. Able God was hesitant to join the line when they first brought food; he was shocked and then insulted by the idea that he was queuing for food like a beggar. It took him less than five minutes to recover from his bruised ego before joining the group, but the line was so long that there was nothing left by the time it was his turn. Able God quickly learned that he could not avoid the daily indignity of fighting for food. The next day, he waited at the entrance of the camp, jostling for a spot at the front of the line, and subsequently got into a fight for his once-a-day ration.

For the most part, the guards took little notice of them. They addressed the inmates collectively through a megaphone. When they had to deal with inmates individually, the guards treated them like they were diseased. If the guards weren't wearing face masks, they would pull their shirts up to cover their noses when they had to talk to the inmates. They battered them with slaps. They beat them with sticks and sand-filled rubber pipes.

No one left the camp except on labor calls. A bearded guard

showed up in the mornings and evenings to take attendance. There were no visits, no unauthorized outings. In the mornings, a guard walked to a bell hanging by the gate, grabbed the rope, and pulled it, sending out the first call through the camp. There was usually a pause before the guard pulled it again—down and up, down and up. The bell's tolling became almost deafening.

Sometimes the noise was not enough to rouse everyone, so guards barged into the tents of those still sleeping, waking the inmates with canes. It became increasingly difficult for Able God to sleep at all, and when he did, one part of him was always awake, bracing for a blow or a whip. After waking them up, the guards would herd everyone into a single line and load them into paddy wagons driven by light-skinned men whose faces were covered with *tagelmusts*. The men hardly spoke to them, and sometimes Able God wondered if there was any shame or guilt beneath those masks. Perhaps the men saw them as mere chattel? The wagons carried the inmates to their work sites and brought them back late at night. Since there were no showers, the inmates usually slept without washing the filth and stinking sweat from their bodies.

Then the time came when a dusty water truck rolled up the hill. The truck growled and screeched, tossing sand up from its tires until it stopped. Within seconds, the guards showed up, and the truck driver pulled out a hose to serve a long line of filthy inmates. The light-skinned inmates were ordered to the front of the line while the rest followed. Able God watched as a guard instructed them to stretch their cupped palms under the hose. That was all they got. Some splashed water on their patched faces and necks before making way for the next in line. Others drank as much as they could in quick gulps. The guard was impatient and had a whip slung over his shoulder, so the line kept moving. Able God approached the tank, and when it was his turn to drink, he did not let go. He took quick gulps and positioned his head under the hose with his mouth open so the cold water could rush down his throat freely. The guard barked orders, but he didn't budge. He closed his eyes and took mouthfuls of refreshing water before swallowing. He allowed some to wash down his face and drip down through his filthy shirt. He was not going to let anyone deny him this moment of pleasure. The guard's whip cracked, and he felt a sharp pain tear through his back. One guard held him by the scruff of his neck, as another whip stroke landed on his back. He yielded but left pleased: he'd consumed water.

In the evening, Able God did not sleep in the tent; he spread his mat out in the open. He preferred to sleep outside, especially when the stars were bright and he could watch the constellations. He did not mind the mosquitoes that feasted on his blood or the flies that buzzed in his ears. The stars were not out tonight, but the lacerations on his back blazed every so often, and he thought exposing his back to the cool breeze would help. The stench of urine and insecticide hung in the air. A spectral cough floated in as if from a distance, and he saw someone doubled up by a violent coughing fit.

Able God tried to make his mind become an escape hatch. He had once seen a video of Magnus Carlsen playing ten games of chess simultaneously with his back turned to the boards. Carlsen never laid his eyes on any of the 320 chess pieces, yet he recalled where they were and which moves to make to defeat his opponents. He called out each move with precision until all his enemies had been vanquished.

Able God also tried to picture a board in his head: a board with black and white squares on vinyl, just like the one they had snatched from him, only bigger and brand new. He took stock of his pieces and the ones belonging to his imaginary opponents. He conjured up a strategy for his opponents, a famous move—Kasparian—and mapped out his own set of paths to attack, defend, and eventually win. Then he tried to conjure up new moves, but they got scrambled up in his head. Once that happened, the rest of the game fell apart. His chess pieces vanished one after the other, leaving behind an empty checkered board. Moments later, even the black and white squares disappeared. All that was left was a blank board. Then he felt his back burn with pain.

› ● ▲ ›

Able God looked forward to the moments they spent in the paddy wagon being ferried to and from the farm. The inmates were hardly ever allowed to speak casually during work, and they were too tired to do anything when they returned to camp. In the dark wagon, they sang together, shared horror stories, stories of beginnings, and stories about stories. They spoke of their families and loved ones.

There was Magodi, whose family had been butchered by al-Shabaab and who had had no choice but to run for his life. Tesfay had fled the oppressive dictatorship in Eritrea and vowed to go back to change his country after succeeding overseas. Desmond had left Ghana because Anslem, his brother, told him to come join him. Anslem had traveled the same treacherous path three years earlier, and he was now in Europe and doing well. Drought had driven Abshir from Somalia.

Billy was convinced he was born in a body with the wrong nationality—he was born Senegalese, but he had always known he was French. Confidence had seen a Facebook ad and decided to pursue it. Anas, a fisherman, thought crossing the sea would be easy. What he hadn't expected, though, were all the obstacles he'd face before reaching the sea. Haruna had languished in a detention camp in

Libya for over a year and had been sent back home to face his family empty-handed.

"When you fall off a horse, you have to get back in the saddle," he told his fellow inmates.

There was God Is Good, who'd been told by a prophet that his glory could only shine once he had ventured beyond the shores and that staying in his native country meant courting misfortune. There were, of course, the boys from the abandoned building with their hopes and their addictions. The time they spent sharing their stories and their grief brought them comfort. It gave them a sense that they were not alone.

Those cooped up with Morufu were often made to listen to football commentary from a Philips transistor radio. Able God was not always enthusiastic about riding in the wagon with Morufu, even though he did not fault him. His love for the game of football did not extend to fanaticism. In Able God's eyes, a football fanatic was an African who cheered for an English football club. Rooting for national teams and playing five-a-side football was enough for lovers of the game.

Morufu followed the Chelsea football club. He couldn't afford to buy the club's all-blue merchandise, but he made up for it by talking nonstop about which players had been bought and sold and for how much, tracking every game, every win, every loss, placing bets on his team, and getting into heated arguments and even scuffles with fans of Arsenal, Liverpool, or Manchester United. The one thing that struck Able God as truly strange was that Morufu never mentioned Chelsea when he talked about his aspiration to play for a club in Europe. In fact, he never mentioned any particular club.

"Which club will you play for when you get to Europe?" Able God asked Morufu as they journeyed in the paddy wagon that day.

"I don't know yet," he said, his transistor radio cradled close to his cheek. "When I get there, I will know. Maybe I will qualify for the feeder team first."

"What's a feeder team?" asked a Somali with a narrow head that tapered to a pointed chin.

Able God answered, "A feeder team is a club from the lower division. If you play well, they graduate you to the real team."

"Wait, you are talking about football, real football?" asked the Somali with a little grin in the corner of his mouth. The eyes of those in the wagon filled with surprise and laughter.

"What do you mean 'real football'? Is there fake football?" Able God said in defense of Morufu. He was feeling bad for starting the conversation in the first place. Fiddling with the knob of the transistor radio, Morufu seemed impervious to their mockery. He'd found the rickety, taped-together transistor radio in a heap of garbage near the camp. It was a noisy contraption, with static bursting forth and vanishing.

"Up blue!" one of them shouted.

With that they could no longer contain their amusement. Laughter echoed in the metal box. Able God had witnessed people mock Morufu many times, but this time was different. Usually, Morufu would smile while mockers goaded him with laughter, but he would also have a pained look on his face. This time his smile was unadulterated, like the smile of someone to whom nothing else mattered.

They slid from side to side as the road twisted, but Morufu kept the transistor radio balanced. The radio crackled to life and spewed forth the commentator's baritone voice. Morufu's face lit up.

A special BBC sports roundup featuring the very best football coverage from the English Premiership. I am Toby Burking, and as this exciting season gets underway, why not sit back, relax, and enjoy some great goals and some magic moments from the game between Chelsea and Liverpool?

Soon the focus shifted to the sound coming out of the broken radio—the rapid-fire talk, the feverish excitement, the screams and half screams. That Able God enjoyed—or at least he loved watching Morufu's reactions as he sat on the edge of his seat, his face tight with tension, his nose twitching. He would flinch and kick and tap the floor with his withered leg.

The words formed into images in Able God's head. He could picture the stadium, filled with spectators in colorful jerseys and costumes, blowing vuvuzelas. He could imagine the lush green pitch and the nicely kitted players sweating it out in the arena. He even imagined an attacker on the left running toward the goal. His pulse kicked up a notch.

"What a run! He passes to the first left winger and number 10. Is this a goal? Yes! It's a goaaaaaaaaaaaaaaal!"

Noise erupted in the wagon, as Morufu raised a clenched fist and sprang to his feet. He went around slapping and squeezing shoulders, his ruined teeth on display. When he came to Able God, he embraced his friend and shook him vigorously in unfettered excitement. Able God found himself making snickering sounds of pure joy.

28

Serge and his burly bearded guards came to the tent to lead them to the dormitory blocks. Able God, who had not fully healed from the beating of the previous week, didn't have to wonder for too long why they had been led there. The guards halted in front of a phone booth outside one of the blocks, and for a moment, Able God could not believe his eyes. Were the guards going to allow them to call their families? He had no desire to call anyone until he reached his destination, but still, he was surprised by the good gesture, or so he thought. A few moments passed, and they formed a straight line in front of the phone booth, the dark-skinned inmates before the light-skinned ones. Serge gave the signal, and one of the guards went to the booth.

The first inmate stepped forward and was addressed by the guard in Swahili. The inmate looked shaken. The guard picked up the receiver and dialed the numbers the inmate called out with a trembling voice. The guard let loose a stream of loud, threatening words into the receiver, and a wave of murmurs swept through the crowd. The guard handed the phone to the inmate, who broke down in tears as he spoke in Arabic with the person at the other end. Moments later, the guard signaled for the call to end, and the next inmate inched closer.

Serge brought out a pack of cigarettes and began to smoke. Able God looked at the inmate next to him, who had a gleam of amusement in his eyes and a hint of anxiety on his face. He didn't need to understand Arabic to know what was going on. He had once again made a fool of himself thinking, even if but for a moment, that anything remotely good was going to come from their little excursion to the phone booth. It was not enough that they were treated as property; now their captors wanted to extort money from their poor families. They were not only slaves but hostages as well.

Able God thought about the shame and sorrow his parents would suffer if they were contacted. Besides, they had no money, no property to call theirs, so Serge and his band of evil guards would not get anything from his parents. The question was, what would be the consequences of not paying the ransom? Death? More work? Maybe this was the end of the road for him. For Able God, the next several moments went by in a blur—lots of begging, crying, and screaming into the telephone. The guard addressed Able God in Arabic when it was his turn.

"English," Able God responded to the guard's words, after which the guard said, "Family, number."

Able God swallowed. "No family."

"What?"

"No number! No family!" he responded more sharply, courage in his voice. If he was going to die, he would die knowing his family had not learned of his condition. He was not a coward. He was not weak.

"You have no family? Are your parents dead?" Serge said after taking a drag from his cigarette, the light end brightening, and blowing the smoke out, never taking his eyes off Able God.

Able God wanted to insist that he had no family, but something nonsensical tumbled out of his lips as though there were hot coals in his mouth. Somehow, hearing Serge's voice made the sense of danger that had taken hold of his body assume a more fearsome quality. His heart fluttered—no, it wasn't a flutter; it was more like a thump. Serge approached with piercing eyes.

"I have no time to waste here, my friend. Give us the number of someone at home we can contact!"

Able God wanted to give in. He always complied without hesitation. That was how he had survived. He was, however, tired of surviving. Now he wanted to be free of this suffering or for the end to come.

"I have no family," he muttered.

Then a smile swept across Serge's lips as if he were in on some secret. Two guards stepped forward and grabbed Able God by both arms, hurling him to the ground and crushing his chest against the asphalt. They pushed his face, which he had tried to keep clear of the ground, against the surface of the verandah. He eventually stopped struggling. They dragged him to his feet, roughing him up all the way to the door of one of the dormitory blocks.

> ● ▲ >

The dormitory block, dark with dust and grime, was surrounded by a low fence. Vehicles and motorcycles lined the dirt yard within. Before Able God's hands were handcuffed in front of him, he opened his mouth to speak but thought better of it. He figured talking could make his situation worse, even though he wasn't sure what they were going to do to him. They moved into the dimly lit reception area, but they did not stop there. No one addressed him. The guards herded him on. They walked through a dark, gray-walled passage that led out to a concrete courtyard in the back of the building.

"Where are you taking me?" Able God said finally. No one responded.

"Tell me where you are taking me," he said, his voice arcing toward panic, his body trembling.

Instead of answering him, they stopped and proceeded to tie a piece of black cloth over his eyes. Before two guards dragged him inside, he struggled to break free, but the officers were strong. His anxiety shot up. From beneath the blindfold, some illumination seeped through, even though he couldn't see anything in front of him. He heard the jingling of keys.

He told himself to calm down. Struggling would only make things worse. Gripping his arms, the guard dragged him down what Able God could tell was another corridor. The little light soon disappeared, and he could feel darkness grow around him as they walked on. Finally, a heavy steel door opened, the reverberation making his head ache.

He staggered into a hot and airless room. He stiffened his nostrils against the wave of pungent smells that assailed him. Someone pushed him onto a metal chair, and the steel door slammed shut. Now he was sure he was the only one in the room. The stench was a bit more distinguishable now. Blood? Vomit? A new fear surged within him. The room was now quiet except for some little dripping sounds.

Drip, drip, drip . . .

He turned and twisted on the chair. He leaned on one shoulder to try not to put too much weight on the other.

Drip, drip, drip . . .

He stood up slowly and took careful steps, trying to feel his way around the cell to unearth anything to help him out of his dire situation. Sweat washed down his face. A few moments passed, and he heard heavy, quick footsteps coming toward the steel door. He scrambled back to the chair. The door opened.

Drip, drip, drip . . .

When they tore the blindfold from his eyes, it took him a few seconds to adjust to the semidarkness. Serge faced him, and a guard was standing behind him. The guard was gaunt and shorn-headed, his eyes noticeably sunken into their sockets. The room was without windows, as far as Able God could tell, and there were hooks attached to the concrete ceiling. A flashlight beam shined on him.

Drip, drip, drip . . .

Serge set down the flashlight, pointing the light at his face. He had a malicious glint in his eyes, and Able God suddenly felt a strong desire to poke them out.

"Do you know why you are here?"

Able God was confused by the question, even indignant. He would not dignify it with an answer.

"You cannot talk?"

He said nothing. A lopsided grin appeared on Serge's face. Serge leaned toward him as though to reveal a terrible secret.

"Okay, I will tell you why you are here. You are here because you have refused to contact your family, which was a big mistake because now we will do it the hard way. Not only are we going to make you give us their contact, but we are also going to record everything and send it to them."

Able God broke into peals of laughter. He was no longer in control of how he reacted to the situation. It was as though something had snapped within him. Fuck Serge! Fuck Ben Ten! Fuck Akudo! He stopped laughing abruptly and spat in the officer's face. Betraying no emotion this time, the officer wiped Able God's spittle away. He then gestured to the guard behind him.

Shorn Head interlaced his spindly fingers together and twisted them. They made a crackling noise. Able God burst into laughter again. Shorn Head rammed a clenched fist into the side of Able God's face, and pain surged through his head. He blacked out.

> ● ▲ >

When he came to, he found himself on a floor drenched in water with a metal pail beside him. They had dragged the table to the corner of the room. He felt tremendous pain in his head and jaw. Blood hissed in his ears and dripped into his mouth. He looked up to find Shorn Head peering down at him.

"Stand up, my friend!" Shorn Head commanded.

His voice echoed loudly in Able God's ears. Able God struggled to his knees and attempted to heave himself onto the chair. He knocked over the metal pail and the chair, tumbling on the ground again. Shorn Head picked the chair back up, then grabbed Able God by the collar, pulling him up. Able God noticed a cell phone held up by a tripod facing him. Serge spoke.

"Let me make it easy for you. We can make this quick if you just give us a number to call. Your parents? Your wife?"

Able God stared at him, smiling disdainfully. His mind was as muddled as a bowl of porridge. They grabbed him, then slapped a second set of handcuffs on him. They hauled him over to stand on the chair and attached the shackle to one of the iron hooks on the ceiling. Able God's arms pulled on the hook he was shackled to, his knees buckling under him.

Shorn Head kicked the chair out from under Able God's feet. His arms were drawn up, suspending him a few feet off the ground. His right shoulder made a popping sound, releasing pain so horrendous that a terrible scream came out of his throat, and he blacked out for a moment. When he came around, he was panting heavily. He was certain he was breathing in not air but hatred and pain. His fingers felt numb.

Shorn Head marched out and returned with a baton, a metal rod, and a flat iron bar. He arranged them carefully on the table. He picked up the baton and twirled it around.

"Are you ready to give us a number?" Serge asked again.

Able God spat a mouthful of blood-laced spittle at Shorn Head. He twitched his fingers for blood to flow again. He was not going to budge. Maybe if they put him to death, the suffering and humiliation would end. With the baton, Shorn Head hit his knees, the soles of his feet, his back, and his face. Able God swung back and forth from the hook as Shorn Head pummeled him. Able God swore at himself, then at Shorn Head, and in turn, Shorn Head tried to silence his screams by hitting him ever harder. But the time came when Able God could no longer scream. For a while, he thought he was going to die from the pummeling and the unbelievable current of agony burning through his veins. Blood pooled in his mouth. His eyes swelled shut. The waves of terrible pain racking his body had extracted all the energy from his voice and his being. Along with the saltiness of blood, fragments of teeth now filled his mouth. But he could not spit them out without considerable pain, so he allowed them to escape through the corner of his slightly open mouth. Slimy wetness slowly moved down his forehead, over his swollen cheeks, and dripped on the floor. He still felt excruciating pain in his dislocated shoulder. When Shorn Head struck him, he would catch his breath and wait for it to pass.

Shorn Head paused for a moment, walked to the table, and set down the now bloodstained baton. He picked up the metal rod and walked back to Able God. Minutes later, he switched to the flat iron bar. Able God now made little whimpering sounds, drifting in and out of consciousness.

"Are you ready to give us a number?" Serge barked.

Able God answered not a word. He would not give the bastards the pleasure of conquering him. He would rather die.

"We have a stubborn one here!" Shorn Head said, irritation in his eyes. He marched out of the chamber, then came back carrying a burning kerosene stove with his bare hands. He set it down below Able God. The officer spoke.

"We are going out for a smoke. No one will hear you from outside when you scream, so . . ."

The stove was already spreading warmth in the room. Able God knew it would not be long before the smell of his singed flesh filled the torture chamber. It dawned on him that his tormentors would not let him die. Able God decided he could no longer bear the suffering. He gazed in their direction with his good eye. A muffled sound from him and a vigorous nod of the head indicated his willingness to write down a contact. The men moved the stove away and slid the chair back into position. They let him down gently. He collapsed to the ground. He tried to get up but realized he could not move his right arm. He leaned on one shoulder to try to get up but fell back, pain cleaving into him. They helped him up, and with unstable hands, he wrote down his mother's number.

29

That same day, Ghaddafi helped pop Able God's dislocated shoulder back into the socket, something he had learned from his prison days. Still, Able God got constant headaches from his broken teeth and could barely eat anything without agony. His vision was blurred, and there was a taste of bile in his mouth. When he ate, vomit would rise up in his throat. Pain described every word that came out of his mouth. Not that there was much to say. The camp fell into a strange silence. The only sounds that came out of their mouths were the sounds of anguish as the inmates nursed their broken bodies. Hours after he came out of the torture chamber, Able God learned that even those who had complied with Serge were tortured, because their families had no money to give. Ghaddafi came out of the torture chamber with busted lips and black eyes. Morufu, who had bruises all over, kept complaining of discomfort inside his body.

Sometimes Able God wondered what his parents were going through and if their hearts would be able to bear the heap of trouble he'd left behind. He also knew there was no point in looking back. Able God knew how this would end. It was a matter of time before Serge started threatening to kill them, and he would likely carry out his threat.

The week came when they were assigned to work on a farm harvesting dates. They were driven over the mountains out into the desert, where they arrived at an oasis with spring-fed ponds and a grove of date palms. More guards awaited them there. The grove was enclosed with a barbed-wire fence and surrounded by watchtowers staffed by guards armed with machine guns. The date palms rose as high as ten meters above the ground and strained under the weight of the clusters of wrinkled ripe dates, each bunch covered with a mosquito net to protect it from birds and insects.

Three farmworkers demonstrated how the harvesting was done. A farmworker dressed in tattered jeans, a dirty plaid shirt, and a baseball hat climbed to the top of the palm with a sickle in his hand. A second man climbed halfway up while a third man waited on the ground. After removing the mosquito net, the first man cut a bunch of dates from the palm. He lowered the cascading bunch to the second farmworker, who lowered it to the man on the ground.

The farmworkers showed them how to tell ripe dates from unripe or rotten ones. They showed them how to hang the bunches over horizontal frames, sort the ripe dates into grades—first, second, or third—and box them for transportation. The foreman did not take questions or repeat the demonstration.

"Too easy, my friends! Too easy! Step one, pluck! Step two, drop! Steps three and four, you sort and stock!" the foreman said before he set them to work under the watchful eyes of the guards. The inmates were divided into groups, and some were handed sickles.

Harvesting at the grove was not as easy as the foreman said. Able God was assigned to drop bunches for the next three days. The clusters were heavy, and the foreman made them work so fast that Able God ended up sweaty and nauseated. His broken body made the task almost unbearable. He could not complete any task without great pain.

He was glad when a splinter from a prickly frond lodged itself deep into his palm, and they moved him to the sorting area. The foreman—who seemed to know just enough English to carry out his job—didn't want him "bleeding all over the dates."

Able God tore a strip of material from an abandoned mosquito net and wrapped it around the bleeding wound. He soon found out that picking and sorting the dates was not any easier. Again, the foreman didn't want him to bleed all over his dates, so he could only use his good hand to do the work. As if picking dates with two hands was not tedious enough.

"You too slow. Quick, quick!" The foreman leaned forward and shouted in his ear whenever he slowed down, his breath reeking of rum.

Morufu was assigned to transport the bunches from the palms to the sorting area, a task that wouldn't have been a problem if not for his disability. He hobbled along, pushing a wobbling wheelbarrow filled with piles of dates back and forth, groaning as he pushed his load. Sometimes he did not make any sound but winced in pain and sweated profusely, his feet covered with dust. He labored more and more slowly. Sometimes he halted to lean over in a furrow to collect himself. Many times Able God thought about lending Morufu a helping hand, but his body was hardly strong enough to complete his own task. He once tried to convince the foreman to assign Morufu to the sorting center, but his request was denied.

"I will push the wheelbarrow. I will do his job! He can do the picking. Pity his condition, sir. Please pity him!" Able God begged the foreman after the initial request. The foreman peered at him as suspiciously as an immigration officer might. He had just opened his mouth to say something when a call echoed from one of the palms about a hundred meters away. They needed his attention. The foreman gave Able God a last once-over and turned to go.

Later that day, Morufu staggered back once again, carefully balancing his pile of dates. He pushed the barrow forward a little, then lost his balance, his legs buckling under him and his eyes rolling back. The collapse was followed by a guttural sound from his throat. Able God rushed over to him.

◦ ● ▲ ◦

On the way back to the tent, the paddy wagon went on total radio silence. Although Able God and other boys had poured water on Morufu's face, talked to him, and lifted his head, he was unable to talk or move his body. They made him sit up and rest his back against the cold metal side of the wagon. Able God sat beside him and watched as a rope of saliva formed between his parched lips, stretching and shortening with his deep breaths. His bony chest rose and fell rapidly. For the first time since they'd left Nigeria, Able God noticed how emaciated Morufu had become. His eyes were hollow and his cheeks sunken. Morufu was mere bones covered with flesh. He had hardly any muscle left.

When they got to the camp, Able God helped haul Morufu out of the wagon. They dragged him through the piles of bedding, clothes, and trash and propped him up against an electric pole. Morufu began panting heavily, almost gasping—a sign Able God recognized as an immediate precursor of death. The guards either did not recognize the urgency of the situation or didn't care. Able God was seized by panic and walked angrily to a guard.

He grabbed the guard's shirt and shook him furiously while

screaming, "You have to take him to the hospital! Please do something! Please!"

The guard dealt him a quick slap across the face that sent him reeling. When Able God steadied himself, the guard began punching his face with clenched fists. Pain surged through his head, and his ears rang. After four strikes, Able God started parrying the blows with his arms, which seemed to anger the other guards, who now came rushing over. Their hands and sticks battered him until his knees gave way and he crashed to the ground. He tried to get back up, but blows rained down on him, causing him to dissolve into a pulpy mass of pain. He heard frantic footsteps. A round of bullets rang out, and for a moment he thought he had been shot.

When Able God was finally left alone, he was writhing on the ground and could barely see out of one eye. His mouth was a wound, his lips burned, and he could hardly move his jaw. He staggered to his feet and glanced at Morufu.

Morufu's head was now drooped on his chest, and his legs were flung wide apart. A guard walked over to Morufu, raised a stick, and prodded him in the chest. He flopped to the ground, his throat rattling before he went limp. Dead.

▸ ● ▲ ▸

The resounding clang of the bell woke Able God the following morning, but he could not move without considerable pain. He had fallen asleep where he'd been left the night before, face swollen and stained with blood. He had no clue as to how he'd gotten to his tent, but he did remember crying in anguish most of the night.

Now he heard the guards shouting as they hurried people along. A grave recollection flooded his clouded mind. The more he remembered, the more he rejected the idea that Morufu was dead. He could not be dead.

Head swimming, eyes dizzy, body racked with pain, Able God struggled to his feet, stumbled out of the tent, and made for the electric pole. He gritted his teeth. Morufu's body was still on the dusty ground, his eyes and mouth wide open like the corpse in the Sahara. *He could not be dead.* He wanted to stride on toward Morufu, but someone ordered him to halt. A hand grasped his shoulder. It was one of the guards firmly pushing him away from Morufu, forcing him to keep walking to the wagon instead. He did not resist.

The journey to the palm grove was quiet. Throughout the day, Able God hid his pain under a stiff grin and went about his duties in a perfunctory manner. The events of the day before had hollowed him out, and he was overcome by a profound sorrow. Worse, he was unwilling to come to terms with it. To come to terms with it was to again be reminded of his grim reality.

The return journey was even quieter. Able God scanned the sullen faces of the inmates in the wagon and sighed. His eyes fell on Morufu's transistor radio, which was still tucked in the corner under the metal bench opposite him. That radio had helped keep alive his dreams of playing football.

Able God averted his gaze, but he glanced back a few moments later, as though the radio were compelling him to look at it. Without thinking, he squatted gingerly and reached out for the radio. He flipped the switch on and fiddled with the knob. Static crackled out at each slight turn of the dial. A tear filmed and glistened at the corner of his good eye. It glinted, waiting to fall. The dial caught a signal as a voice crackled out.

This is the BBC Sportsworld, bringing live sports from around the world with news, interviews, and analysis . . .

The tears rolled down his cheeks now. He began to wail, but each sob sent a wave of pain through his body, so he gathered his strength and mourned his friend in silence for the rest of the journey. Morufu's corpse was still lying by the electric pole when they got to the camp. Able God wanted to go to the guards again and plead with them to find a way to contact the deceased man's family, to search his phone contacts or something. He would appeal to their humanity. Maybe they would send Morufu's body home to his family, and his corpse would not have to rot out in the open without honor in a strange land.

Able God mulled over the idea in his head for a while, then decided he was again being naive. Hadn't he tried to convince himself he would soon make enough money to cross the big sea into the Promised Land? Hadn't he told himself the bearded men would pay them since going home was not an option? Would the guards have treated him that way if they'd had any scrap of human kindness left in them?

Soon after they got to the camp, the guards came bearing shovels, led a group of boys to the edge of the fence, and ordered them to dig a grave. Able God watched them as they took turns with the shovel while the day darkened. The guard soon left, and Able God snatched a shovel from one of the boys. His hands trembled with grief as he scooped up the earth.

› ● ▲ ›

Able God sat in the shade of his tent, wrapped in an old blanket, and gazed into the distance. His tears had gone, but his eyes were red. The electricity had gone off, plunging the camp into darkness. Mosquitoes were buzzing and biting. Beyond the gates, off on the horizon, stood the darkened hills of Sabha. It was cold after the day's work, and trash was drifting in the breeze. He was wheezing just like Morufu had before he keeled over.

He stood up, stepped into his tent, and got out Morufu's transistor radio from beneath a pile of rags. He walked around the camp with his eyes searching the ground, then stopped to pick up a rusty six-inch nail. He made his way to Morufu's grave and sat down on a pile of sand beside it. He got to work, tears pooling behind his eyelids. The radio made a screeching sound as he slowly carved small letters into its plastic case. His hands shook. He paused to wipe the snot from his nose, then continued. When he had finished, he dusted off the radio to reveal the inscription etched across the surface.

MORUFU, THE GREATEST FOOTBALL
CHAMP OF OUR TIME. TUALE BABA!

"This is for you, my friend," he sniffed, then planted the radio on the heap of sand that covered Morufu's body. "This is for you."

30

Able God snapped to attention when Serge's black Jeep arrived at the camp in a cloud of dust, its headlights cutting into the night and illuminating the camp. Serge pulled up at the gate of the camp and stepped out with a smile, greeting his guards more enthusiastically than usual. He seemed drunk.

Serge ordered the guards to unload a bundle of firewood from the Jeep, then he got out some matches and built a fire. He gathered twigs and wisps of dry grass to feed the flames. Soon, he had a roaring fire, the wood snapping and crackling with every dancing flame, casting elongated shadows on the ground. Sparks flew from the firewood. Serge went to the driver's seat, and Ma'luf music boomed out from the car stereo. He swayed to the rhythm of the music, tapping his fingers while the guards looked on. Suddenly, a flash of remembrance lit up Serge's face, and he told his men something Able God couldn't quite make out. There was a burst of jubilation. He went back to his car and returned with three bottles for his men.

Serge raised a half-filled bottle up to his mustachioed lips and swung his head back, draining the contents. The liquid trailed down the sides of his jaw, sinking into his darkened collar. His men burst into laughter. Then they danced and went to the vehicle for more bottles. They chatted, sometimes in English and sometimes in broken Arabic. Able God felt bitterness well up inside him.

The spectacle was interrupted when Serge turned off the stereo, grabbed a megaphone, and ordered his men to unlock the gate. He lurched toward the bell and rang it once. He then spoke into the megaphone.

"My lovely girlfriend gave me a son today! She gave me a son!" he drawled, gesticulating wildly. His words hung in the air for a moment, and when the applause came, it was scattered. Most of the inmates feigned broad smiles—that was it. Serge shot a glance at the megaphone, frowning at it as though the machine hadn't managed to transmit his special message. He spoke into it again, repeating the same words. More people applauded the second time around. Even Able God felt compelled to join in. They wouldn't want to make the slave master angry, would they? Besides, Serge was the happiest Able God had seen him since they'd met. In fact, it was the first time he'd seen him say more than a couple of words.

"Thank you. Thank you very much. Tomorrow will be a day of celebration. You will celebrate with me," he said.

Able God did not know what Serge meant. Nor did he care. Serge went back to his truck and soon was gone.

⟩ ● ▲ ⟩

The ringing of the bell did not stir Able God awake, and not until a guard came to his tent did he stand up sluggishly and stare through reddened, sleep-deprived eyes at the man. Several minutes later, the wagon jerked to a sudden halt, and Able God looked out through the window slats. They had stopped in front of the hostel next to Serge's house.

Soon the lobby of the hostel was teeming with bodies. Able God, now inside the hostel, was still not sure what was going on. He cast a nervous glance at the sofas, the large TV, the long hallway next to the flight of stairs, and the clean white curtains. Was Serge moving them here? The guards led them upstairs to the common room, where stacks of towels were piled on a large table, a small bar of soap placed on each towel. There were laundry baskets filled with assorted clothes. Able God was mildly puzzled and a little suspicious.

"Take this, wash! Scrub!" one of the guards said, pointing first to the stack of towels and then to another hallway with doors on both sides. He spoke to them like he was telling a dog where to shit. They formed a line and proceeded into the rooms.

After about thirty minutes, Able God found an open spot. The shower was already warm by the time he slipped in behind the shower curtain. The grime of several weeks washed off him as the stream of water hit his body, sending discolored water into the shower drain and spreading a soothing warmth over his skin. He recalled Maracanã and the water tap in front of the beautiful house. Remembered how refreshing the water had felt after sweating out on the pitch. Able God was unable to look back on the past without experiencing inward anguish.

Maracanã was where his treacherous journey had started. Maracanã was where he'd met Morufu. Their brief friendship had largely benefited him, and although Morufu hadn't seemed to mind the unequal tally, it didn't make Able God feel any better about his death.

Had his life been screwed up long before his involvement in the murder? He was no longer sure that Akudo and Ben Ten were the problem. Perhaps his dire situation was not just the product of an unfortunate set of events. He quickly tried to tally every mistake he could remember throughout his whole life, every wrong turn he'd

taken that had led him to where he was. Then he realized he was embarking on a futile task and stopped.

Able God dried off and headed back to the common room, where
he was directed to the laundry basket to pick out a new shirt. He
dressed upstairs in one of the bed-lined rooms. The process was
rowdy: inmates struggled for spots in the shower and bumped into
each other, but the guards maintained the calm as much as they
could.

After cleaning up, they were herded to a dining hall on the first
floor, a spacious room lined with wooden benches and tables. A
sweet aroma filled the room, as the fumes of sizzling food wafted
from cooking pots. At the other end of the dining hall, five brown-
aproned women were spooning food onto plates. The inmates
walked awkwardly into the empty dining hall, looking around like
lost tourists. Able God was suspicious of the kindness.

The aproned women served them hot meals: rice with vegetables in a spicy sauce. The inmates hunched over their plates and ate
greedily. Able God sat with Ghaddafi and Pepe. He lifted the first
spoonful of rice and sauce to his lips, savored it, then eagerly gobbled
up his meal, his sense of wariness shoved to the back of his mind.

As the food turned to mash between his teeth, tears welled in
the corners of his eyes. He had been so hungry for so long that he'd
stopped taking pleasure in eating. For him, eating had been merely a
means of staying alive. Eating a delicious meal reminded him of how
deprived he'd been of life's simple pleasures.

◗ ● ▲ ◗

They drove to Serge's mansion. The stately home was appointed with
a grand piano, rugs with geometric patterns, leather sofas, polished
pine flooring, crystal chandeliers, cabinets filled with stemware, and

baseball paraphernalia. Serge gave the inmates a hasty tour—the living room, the swimming pool in the back. Nothing more. He was cheerfully courteous.

Outside the mansion, the bearded men were stacking bundles of cash on a large desk. The man behind the desk moistened the tip of his finger in a small bowl of water and began counting out stacks of notes.

"Single file," he barked.

The cashier gave the first inmate his stack without so much as a glance. The boy looked at the notes with surprise, then folded the wad in half and stuffed it into his pocket.

"Next!" shouted the cashier.

‣ ● ▲ ‣

"Today is not a day of work! It's a day of celebration!" Serge told them after the money had been distributed. "My men will take you downtown this evening and leave you to spend your money however you like. But you only have two hours. Just two hours, so decide what you are going to do before you get there. Please enjoy yourself. Drink, take a woman. Merry! You deserve it!"

There was a moment of silence that lingered. As the silence lingered, it seemed to take on meaning, and before long, the inmates were staring at each other in surprise. Able God was apprehensive. He still worried that his past could catch up with him. What if the Nigerian police had narrowed their leads to Sabha? What if they'd been in contact with the police in Sabha to arrange for his arrest? Then again, there was no functioning police force in Sabha.

31

The guards stopped at the rendezvous point, a yellow mosque with a green domed roof that was visible from all directions, and let the inmates loose on the gritty streets.

Two hours.

Able God walked with them down crooked streets lined with bullet-riddled walls, stalls and shops with ubiquitous blue doors, signs written in Arabic, streetwalkers flagging down vehicles, old men in filthy kaftans smoking pungent hashish in little courtyards, traders and angry passersby, the smell of cheap perfume, mint, and leather tanneries, wreckage and rubble and the dim red of broken streetlights—noisy streets crowded with vehicles and motorcycles.

Able God, Pepe, and Ghaddafi set off down the congested sidewalks until they reached a trashy mud-and-stone alley that curved into another street. Most of the streetlamps were broken, and a gloomy pall hung over the alleyway. The street was empty except for two black cats skulking about and a skeletal, limping dog that hobbled toward them. Trash, empty cartons, and broken furniture filled the alley.

Able God had convinced them to scour the streets for drugs—glue, tramadol hydrochloride, codeine cough syrup, Coca-Cola, and hashish—which they'd been surprised to find so cheaply. A trader who spoke good English even recommended a drug he called "jihad pills." The drug kept users awake for long periods of time, dulled pain, and created a sense of euphoria, according to the trader.

Able God told his friends that their gathering would be in Morufu's memory, but in reality, it was more about reliving the comfort of the abandoned building. It was about celebrating freedom, however momentary. It was about the calm and excitement his body craved. The boys did not seem to care one way or another.

Able God sat down to prepare his cocktail while his two companions huffed glue from a plastic bag. He upturned three little syrupy containers into a two-liter plastic bottle, slowly pouring in the viscous ruby-red fluid. He added some Coca-Cola, which frothed and foamed. Finally, he dropped a couple of crushed tramadol tablets into the mix, screwed on the cap, and shook the bottle vigorously. Ghaddafi rolled a blunt, took a long drag, and passed it around.

They drank and smoked while anxiously monitoring the adjoining street. The potholed street was bright and empty except for the cars that sped past every few minutes. Able God stared into the emptiness, sinking into himself. For the first time in a long time, he felt his chaotic world slow down. A cool, pleasant sensation seeped into his body. His ears, however, remained alert to the slightest noise. He scanned the alleyway regularly.

The night wore on, and although Able God did not know exactly how much time had passed, he sensed that it was time for them to start making their way back to the wagon. He was about to open his mouth and say something about how they needed to leave when they heard heels clattering on the asphalt, and a lady emerged from around the corner into the dim light of the streetlamps. The lady wore a tight red dress that snaked around her figure, constricting her thighs beneath the shiny fabric. A black bag swung at her side. Her hoop earrings glittered and bounced against her neck as she teetered on her heels. She seemed inebriated.

Able God followed her with his eyes. She stumbled into one of the potholes, her knees wobbling before she regained her balance. There was a perplexed look on her face as she came to a stop and glanced around. She soon continued walking. A vehicle approached and slowed down as though to pick her up, but then it sped past.

"I used to have a girl as beautiful as her," Pepe said, a tranquil, wry smile spreading across his face. Smoke curled out of his lips as he passed the blunt to Ghaddafi. "Back in Congo DRC. I met her when I was working in the mines. She came with a tray of bread on her head for the mine workers. She sold every loaf of bread that day because she was so beautiful. More beautiful than anyone I have ever seen."

Able God suddenly started to laugh and reached out a hand to rub Pepe's head. Ghaddafi laughed, too. Their laughter died out as they realized Pepe had not finished speaking.

"I wanted her to be my woman, but she went for that bastard Guy-Guy Nzali," Pepe said, his voice cracking. "She went for him because he had money. He did not really have money, but compared to a fucking pauper like me, he was rich."

Able God found the tirade almost comical. He took the blunt from Ghaddafi and gave it a long pull, the smoke rising thick in the air.

Pepe paused, drawing a breath. He wrinkled up his face and tightened his jaw, as if to suppress the anger rising inside him. The lady in the red dress tried in vain to wave down another vehicle.

"I am going to make it one day, friends! I am going to make it in

Europe, and when I am wealthy, I will have as many girls as I want," Pepe said in a tearful voice.

He stood and faced the wall, unzipping himself. He pissed steadily against the fence. When he was done, he sniffed back his tears.

"We will surely make it, my friend! We will make it!" Ghaddafi said before wrapping the glue bag around his nose again.

"Nonsense! We will not make it if we stay here! We are prisoners here! We will die if we stay here!" Pepe drawled, his heavy-lidded eyes half shut.

"Don't say that," Ghaddafi said.

"Don't tell me what to say!" he responded angrily, peeling away from the fence.

"Calm down, young man!" Able God said.

"I didn't come all the way from my country to be a prisoner here! No, I didn't. Today is the day of my freedom! Today is the day!" Pepe said, swaying like a drunk man. "You see, I am going to try my luck with that beautiful woman right there!" he added, pointing in her direction.

Ghaddafi patted him on the shoulder as though sanctioning his decision. Pepe put his palms to his mouth to form a trumpet and whistled loudly. The woman shot a look over her shoulder, clutched her bag to her side, and walked away. Pepe went after her, whistling and catcalling. Ghaddafi followed him. The three of them turned a corner and vanished.

Able God gathered himself together and ran down the sidewalk, searching everywhere, bumping into people, pushing them out of his way. He thought he spotted them up ahead but lost track of them again. Their two hours had run out. He had to find them, and they had to go back. Able God slackened his pace when the traffic on the sidewalk got thicker. After stopping to look around, he pressed on again, his heart racing. He didn't know what exactly was wrong, but he knew something had gone wrong. He turned down a narrow street with shops on both sides and emerged on another street.

Out of breath, he came to a standstill. He found himself in front of the glass door of a barbershop bright with fluorescent light. The barber was cutting a child's hair. Behind him hung a portrait of Muammar Gaddafi. The barber peered at Able God from the corner of his eye. After a few moments, the barber waved him off with his free hand. Able God got the message and walked away. That was when he came to his senses. Who did he think he was, always trying to save people from trouble?

He heard the crackle of the local mosque's loudspeaker, followed by the muezzin's call to prayer. He looked for the dome and changed course.

He quickly found his way to the rendezvous point. On the way, he experienced a brief vertiginous wobble, and he had to put a hand on the wall to find his bearings again.

There was no sign of Pepe or Ghaddafi. The guards did not take roll. They ordered the boys to get into the wagon and drove off. Able God did not know what to think, but he was glad he hadn't been left behind. Should he be glad? What if Pepe and Ghaddafi had found a way to be free? What if the Asma Boys caught them?

Able God looked out through the window slats and saw a shed filled with mats. There was an ablution area beside it, a row of benches and taps surrounded by men preparing themselves to pray. Soon, the wagon moved on, and Able God was puzzled to see the woman in the red dress standing on the sidewalk, chatting and laughing with a man.

▶ ● ▲ ▶

The following morning, the bell rang vigorously, and the guards screamed. Able God woke up in a haze of shock and fright from the sudden noise. When he stumbled outside, he saw the guards fanning out around the inmates and tossing people out of their tents. The bell kept ringing. Serge's Jeep was parked in front of the gate alongside the three wagons. There were more guards than usual and dogs, too. Able God saw a look of fear welling up in some of the boys' eyes and struggled to contain himself. Soon everybody was up against the wall getting frisked by the bearded guards.

When that was over, five guards opened the doors of one of the wagons and unloaded a handful of inmates. Their hands were tied behind their backs, and their bodies were streaked with dust. A few of them were barely conscious, so the guards had to drag them out, their knees buckling and their heads drooping. Pepe and Ghaddafi were among them.

Ghaddafi's knees dragged across the dirt as they carried him forward. He had sand in his hair and mouth, and his clothes were covered in dust. Pepe was able to walk upright, but his face was badly swollen, and he had a nasty gleam in his eye.

The guards lined them up in a single file in front of the gate and ordered them to stay still. Serge stepped out of his vehicle, and silence engulfed the place. Able God's lips trembled with anxiety. He hadn't expected things to come to this, even though he still had some residual doubt about Serge's show of kindness. It had been a trap after all, and they'd fallen for it.

Serge stood in front of the offenders and turned to look at them. The silence was so dense it was suffocating. Finally, he faced the camp and spoke.

"When you let a dog go free, the good ones find their way back home. They may come back smelling of shit and trash heaps, but they always come home. You know why? Because a good dog knows the way to the house of his master. A good dog always finds his way back to his master."

All the muscles in Able God's body tightened. Serge paused and walked to the other end of the row, his hands clasped behind his back. The silence was only broken by the crunching of his boots in the sand.

"But you see, the bad ones think they are smart," Serge continued. "They think because they have been granted a bit of freedom, they can do without their master. So they roam the streets with their tails wagging. They hump as many bitches as they like. They refuse to come home. The problem is the bad dogs always end up dead. The streets always end up killing them."

Pepe tried to free himself, a howl rising from his throat quieted by a guard's knuckles. Serge's lips stretched into a sly grin.

"We are going to teach these dogs a lesson. Let this be a warning to the rest of you dirty Africans. Don't take my kindness for granted. You will be free once you make me back the money I invested to get all of you here. Business is business."

He waved his finger in the air as he spoke, and when he had finished he brought out a cigarette from his pocket. Able God wondered what Serge was talking about since in the caravan they had been treated like livestock. How much money could Ben Ten have spent in total? Of course, that did not matter now.

Serge walked back to his car. Some of the guards began to leash the inmates to the bumpers of the paddy wagons. They kicked and fought and pleaded. Pepe's struggle to untie his hands was futile. Ghaddafi mumbled prayers in Arabic. Able God could no longer bear to watch. The drivers switched on the ignition and zoomed off. The inmates' shrieks were drowned out by the roaring of the engines. The guards fired shots into the air, and the inmates hit the ground. Able God lay on the ground with his cheek pressed against the coarse earth as he breathed in air that reeked of blood and burning rubber.

32

Able God mounted the second rung of the ladder, his head aching from wet paint fumes. He poured out some paint, coated his roller, and began applying the blue paint to the graffitied wall, spreading it, working his way from top to bottom. After a while, he swapped his roller for a paintbrush. He climbed down a rung, dipping the tip of the brush into the paint, touching up his handiwork here and there. It had been a week since they had tied his friends to paddy wagons, but it felt like it had happened hours ago, the pain searing and fresh.

Their task was to paint the city's walls and rehabilitate the many surfaces that still had slogans from the Arab Spring and the civil war scribbled all over them. He had seen signs that read "GO TO HELL" and "FREEDOM LIBYA." He had seen murals depicting Colonel Muammar Gaddafi being squeezed by a hand representing the revolution or thrown in the garbage of history, or as a chicken in flight.

The graffiti had remained on the walls for years until a nongovernmental organization decided to cover them over. Serge had won the bid. The technique was simple and required no artistry: scrape the walls, then apply coats of paint, the thickness or color of the coat determined by the degree of desecration.

The inmates mostly painted over colorful murals scrawled with messages that were undecipherable to many of them because they were written in Arabic. Only a few of the slogans were written in English. Sabha, one of the dictator's last strongholds during the revolution, bore a few antirevolutionary slogans. One read, "No Black Europe!"—a message referencing Colonel Gaddafi's famous request that the European Union pay Libya five billion euros per year to stop illegal African immigration and thereby avoid a "Black Europe." A pro-revolutionary message on the side of a building declared, "Gaddafi is a criminal!" Another read, "Gaddafi, go fuck your mom!" Yet another proclaimed, "God is great, greater even than the colonel!" There was even a giant caricature of Colonel Gaddafi as a rat.

Able God spent his days moving around the city, except once when a fight broke out between the Qadhadhfa and Awlad Suleiman tribes and Serge instructed them to stay at the camp. Their work took them from the impoverished Tuyuri neighborhood with its unplastered buildings to the better parts of the city, where people gathered in coffeehouses that smelled of incense and sweets to drink tea or coffee and take drags from hookahs.

Seeing the city allowed Able God to study the lay of the land. As he walked from building to building, a paint roller in one hand and a bucket of paint in the other, he observed his surroundings. He memorized the names of streets and committed landmarks to memory. He contemplated possible escape routes. He observed every back alley and shortcut and all the areas devastated by the war. He studied the neighborhoods demarcated by de facto borders and controlled by tribal commanders. He knew where black-market fuel was sold on street corners.

He observed the guards and their smoking habits, thought about places to hide without being caught. He found out about a roundabout in central Sabha where freewheeling migrants spent their days scratching their balls and waiting for odd jobs. Employers sometimes came for them from Tripoli. Able God had heard about detention camps in Sabha that were run by the European Union. What if he turned himself over to them? Serge could have men there. Besides, he would still not be free. He considered ways to make it to Tripoli. Tripoli would get him closer to the Promised Land.

Able God discovered that time did nothing to reduce his fear of death. Death was a ruthless angel. The day Pepe and Ghaddafi had been dragged down the dusty road of the villa, they hadn't died right away. The guards took away the bloodied men. Able God knew he would never see them again, even if they survived. There was no humane or quiet way of dying here. The suffering and death would not end no matter how many times Serge's girlfriend gave birth or how many visits they made to the hostel.

◗ ● ▲ ◗

Able God gently rolled down his faded, paint-stained jeans and peered at the guards from the corner of his eye. He took a deep breath while he waited for the guard on duty to turn his back and vanish around a corner to smoke. There were just a few minutes left before the day's work ended, and it was already growing dark. Nightfall would shield him. He understood how high the stakes were. He knew what would happen to him if he were caught. By the time they had finished with him, he would not be able to recognize his own features, assuming he survived their ruthlessness.

When his opportunity came, he wiped his clammy palms on his trousers and walked across the street. He made himself walk slowly, looking neither right nor left, whistling, striving to seem at once distracted and casual. He kept a steady pace, walking with long strides. He needed to get as far away as possible before the guard finished his cigarette, but running would reveal him. He quickened his pace once he was out of the guard's field of vision. His heart raced, and his breathing became more rapid as he walked. The air he breathed was stale. He walked past the municipal council building and made his way through the side streets, all the while looking over his shoulder. He heard footsteps and saw a blue-uniformed soldier approaching drunkenly. He waited, pretending to search his pockets for a cigarette, until the person passed. He released the air in his lungs and was finally able to breathe easy.

He made his way to the mud-and-stone alleyway, then rummaged through the dump in search of the biggest cardboard carton he could find. He flattened it and clasped it under his arm. He walked for half an hour until he found an abandoned railroad. On the other side of the tracks there was a crumbling building, a burned-out car, and a low fence. He waded through a tangle of grass, ferns, and wild sage as high as his waist to get to the car. Insects chirped. Grass sprouted into the car through its twisted and corroded metal. It was too dark to see clearly now. He wrenched the door open and slid in, spreading the flattened cardboard over the back seat and curling up like a cat. A deep slumber enfolded him within minutes.

He woke up shivering to a chirruping chorus of birds. All the bones in his body felt cold. Something crawled on him when he tried to stand up. He frantically brushed insects and dead leaves from his clothes while stretching his stiff back.

Able God looked outside at the tracks through the crumbling building. Serge would have sent his men to look for him by now. An abandoned railroad seemed like a place to hide. He knew he had to leave at once and try to hide in plain sight. But where? What if the locals informed the Asma Boys that they'd seen a migrant roaming about aimlessly? Being a migrant in Sabha meant being owned by someone. Serge probably had a deal with the Asma Boys, and they would return him to the camp in no time, shunting him from one nightmare to the next.

He dragged himself out of the car, walked over to the building, let his trousers slip to his knees, and squatted to shit. Flies droned around him, and he swatted them away as he contemplated his next move. When, after a few moments, he heard a sound, he quickly hitched up his trousers and hid behind the crumbling building's brick wall. Two stout men with rifles across their backs were plodding along the tracks. They chatted casually in Arabic as they peered around and approached the crumbling building. Suddenly, they stopped and made their way toward the building, guns drawn. A sudden fierce strength came to Able God's legs, and he shot off into the bush and scaled the fence.

◗ ● ▲ ◗

He only stopped running when he stumbled and fell. All the while, he heard men shouting, "*Waquf, waquf, waquf.*" It was only a matter of time before the big men ran out of breath and fired a shot, so when the shot rang out, he was sure he'd been hit. He hadn't been, but the loud crack gave him a jolt. He crawled through the grass, his body itching all over, his heart thundering in his chest. Being captured was not an option. A bullet in the back would be easy, he would bleed out within minutes. He hoisted himself up and darted forward. The men still gave chase, but he didn't hear another shot. He crossed the road and slipped through a maze of buildings painted pale yellow, looking over his shoulder to see if he was still being pursued, then stopped for a few seconds to catch his breath.

Eventually, he walked on. Almost immediately, he found himself on a palm-lined road. He could make out the Fort Elena Castle, built during the Italian colonial period. To his left, pencil-like minarets shot up above the clusters of low houses. He found a tap by a fuel station and drank from it. He was washing his face and hands when the attendant emerged from his shop to warn him off, stick in hand, face twisted with anger. He quickly took his leave.

Now that the sun was up, heat parched his throat. Fatigued and dizzy with hunger, he was not sure how he was going to eat. The locals didn't seem friendly, and stealing would only draw unnecessary attention. He roamed around hoping to find a fruit tree with any kind of edible fruit but found nothing. Exhausted, he stopped to rest beside a row of old fuel storage tanks before continuing past a cemetery and over to a string of stalls along a promenade. One of the stalls was full of watermelon arranged on a long table, cut in half and bagged in transparent plastic. Able God stood close to the stalls and peered at the watermelon, wondering what to do. His mouth watered as he imagined sinking his teeth into the succulent pink flesh, the sweet juice slaking his thirst before dribbling down his chin. A trader with a battered skullcap and soiled tunic waved him off.

He decided to find a place to hide before Serge got wind of his whereabouts—even if it meant going hungry. That meant avoiding the main roads and instead choosing back alleys and dirt roads. The farther he trekked, the weaker he became. To keep from lapsing into gloominess, he thought of home and his childhood. His birthday was in two weeks. His parents always called him on the morning of his birthday. His mother would call first, showering him with prayers and admonishing him to always lean on Jehovah's strength. Once she had promised to bake him a birthday cake in any shape he wanted, and he'd asked for a guitar-shaped cake, a request he later thought was ridiculous. But his sweet mother made it happen. She came home with a guitar-shaped baking pan for his tenth birthday. Calistus hadn't been happy about it and demanded his own special cake. The following year, his mother got a heart-shaped pan for Calistus.

Able God sat on the edge of a collapsed wall to rest his aching legs. He was despondent and racked with hunger and thirst. As a distant rumbling grew louder, he ducked behind the pile of rubble. A procession of tanks and trucks filled with men in military fatigues or djellabas passed along a nearby road, stirring up dust. They carried AK-47s and heavy machine guns with belts of bullets. There were armored cars with gunners in the turrets. Motorcyclists zoomed all over. They launched their front wheels off the ground; they lifted the back wheel and rode on the front wheel; they spun their wheels. The air was filled with dust, smoke, and the smell of burning rubber. He would have found the whole thing entertaining if it weren't so terrifying.

He held still, cupping a hand around his nose to keep from choking. Suddenly, something scurried beneath the rubble, making him want to spring up. But he didn't move.

For the next three days, he slept under culverts, covering himself with a prickly old blanket he'd found in the dusty back alley. The blanket smelled of old urine and made his body itch, but it protected him from cold nights and rat bites. He battled chills, fatigue, and headaches during the day and feverishness in the evenings. He could hardly lift his body. Hunger exacerbated his suffering—he had filled his empty belly with water from an irrigation canal and eaten a packet of soggy crackers he'd found in a garbage bin. His mother always told him food was the cure for sickness and that death was near if a man refused to eat. He dragged himself out of his hole and trudged ahead slowly, fighting for strength. He'd become less and less aware of his surroundings, and vigilance was no longer his priority. He staggered. He fell and got back to his feet. The world spun around him. He would keep begging for food. He decided he would steal if he had to.

He reached a part of the city crowded with people and vehicles. He looked around for food, shivering and cursing. The sight of two stray cows made him crave meat. A strange image flashed through his mind: a huge chopping block heaped with slabs of meat, covered in blood and entrails. The idea of eating raw flesh was not appealing, and he chalked up the image to an overactive imagination.

He felt weak and hollow, as if the slightest wind would blow him away. Soon his legs became too weak to carry him. The earth swayed, and everything blurred. He stood up but found himself right back on the ground, rising again, more slowly, this time holding on to an electric pole in a zombie-like shuffle. He found an alleyway and sat slumped against the wall. His eyes grew heavy, but he tried to keep them open. Maybe he should give in to sleep; maybe sleep would help him recover. Hadn't his mother always said that he should lean on Jehovah for strength? Now was the time to do just that. He would lean on Jehovah for strength. That night, the last thing he remembered hearing were footsteps and dogs barking.

"Are you okay?" A voice jolted him awake.

He scrambled to his feet, his legs barely holding him up. He reeled and fell over, gazing around wide-eyed.

33

A ble God became aware that he was in a tent that had been set up alongside the box truck. Then he realized that he lay on the gurney with an intravenous line taped on his arm and an empty fluid bag hanging on a rusty metal pole. For a few moments, he tried to orient himself, but his thoughts just kept jumbling up, memories muddling within memories, pushing out against the edges, fraying his nerves. He looked around and tried to get up, but brutal anguish racked the entirety of his body, so much so that he screamed. The doctor—a man with a pointed nose, gray hair, and tan skin—approached with a metal tray filled with implements and a replacement for the fluid bag.

"You are severely dehydrated," the doctor said. "You need to take in IV fluids and get a lot of rest."

"Where am I?" Able God asked, his throat terribly sore. He remembered holding on to the electric pole and falling.

"You are in a mobile run by Médecins Sans Frontières." The doctor started tending to his wounds using medical implements that had been arranged on a metal tray.

He looked around slowly. A generator rumbled loudly. *Médecins Sans Frontières* was inscribed on the box truck and on the safety vests of the mostly white workers. At the other side of the truck was a long, straggling line. The doctors saw patients one after the other, speaking to them via an interpreter who wore an oversize shirt and a beret. Most of the doctors pressed stethoscopes to their chests and wrapped blood-pressure cuffs around their arms before counting off pills from white plastic containers. One patient was taken into the truck to be treated privately. The place reeked of disinfectant.

"So where are you from? Do you have a family?" the doctor asked.

Able God watched as the doctor examined him, peering at the wounds on his arm and legs. The doctor gently cleaned and bandaged one wound, causing Able God to inhale sharply when the doctor's rough and calloused palm brushed his skin.

"Nigeria. I am from Nigeria. Can you give me a cell phone?"

"Yes, you will be able to contact home when you are better. Thank God they found you. Your wound is infected, so we will have to give you some antibiotics."

"Thank you, doctor . . ."

"Doctor Shaw, Greg Shaw."

"What happened to you?" Doctor Shaw asked.

Able God wanted to speak but hesitated. He felt his body grow tense. Was he out of Serge's reach?

The doctor smiled as he gathered his implements and set the tray aside. "That we are in a war-torn country doesn't mean we don't observe patient-doctor confidentiality," he said. "My job is not to make moral judgments. I am here for humanitarian work. But it's also okay if you don't want to talk about it."

There were a few moments of silence between them.

"Do you have a place to stay? If you don't, we have a shelter where we accommodate migrants. It's right next to our living quarters at the end of town. We can take you there, and you can leave anytime you want. We will make sure you are safe there."

"Thank you, doctor."

The doctor nodded and walked over to the truck. Able God became lightheaded, and his vision clouded. He rested his head back on the gurney and watched the fluid level in the saline bag dip as the contents flowed into his veins. Before he drifted off to sleep, his mind warned him not to trust anybody.

> ● ▲ >

Before Able God was transported to the warehouse, he sent a text to his mother. Doctor Shaw had given him a SIM card and a phone. The message was simple: MUMMY, THIS IS ABLE GOD. I AM WELL AND ALIVE AND NO LONGER IN DETENTION. DO NOT PAY ANYBODY MONEY. I WILL CALL YOU WHEN I CAN. With that, he removed the SIM card and handed the phone back.

Later that day, the MSF truck stopped at the monstrous outer gate of the shelter. The wall was easily eighteen feet high and viciously spiked. A gaggle of heavily armed guards in khaki pants and black T-shirts surrounded the gates. Some leaned against the wall, idly fingering their automatic rifles. Able God stiffened. The car seemed a few degrees hotter. On his way to the shelter, the thought of jumping out of the truck crossed his mind. He could pretend to have a full bladder to make the vehicle stop, then take off, but that would mean roaming the dry expanse of the town exposed to relentless danger. Better to stay where he might have a roof over his head and a hot meal. Besides, the chance that an international organization would be involved in anything nefarious was slim. *Exhale. Inhale. Exhale. Inhale.*

Before he stepped out of the driver's side of the truck, Dr. Shaw said, "The security is to keep our refugees safe, so nothing to be concerned about."

He shook hands with the guards and laughed with them. After a few moments of conversation, he walked back to the truck to get Able God.

"You will be safe here," the doctor said with a smile. Able God thanked him, then a guard led him in. He was no longer under the illusion that he would find safety anywhere in Libya. How much longer could he stay in the country before his luck ran out?

They walked past a reception area with peeling posters and stacks of wooden boxes and through an open space with bunk beds and mattresses on the floor. It was a little crowded, but it was better than any accommodation he had gotten since he left Nigeria.

"You will be sleeping here." The guard gestured toward a bunk bed beside a woman and her three children, then walked away, only to return seconds later with folded clothes. Able God sat on the edge of his bunk, scanning the warehouse. He let out a sigh of relief.

Moments later, one of the guards walked in, boots crunching, with a tray overflowing with mobile phones. The guard announced in English that the phones were for calling family. He walked around handing a phone to someone from each row before moving to the next. The mother got a flip phone, and her children, with flakes of white covering their shaved skulls and skins infested with eczema, huddled around her as she made a phone call. The children all spoke at once in a language he did not understand—possibly Swahili—to a person Able God assumed to be their father, but their mother swatted them away. She held the phone close to her ear, her voice high-pitched and frantic, her eyes teary. Able God felt tears sting his eyes.

Once they had finished, the mother handed the phone to him.

For a few moments, he only stared at it. By now, his family would have received the video of his torture, but he hoped the text message would prevent them from making any hasty decisions. What if it was not enough? What if Serge had told his parents that he would kill their son? Would they know Serge was bluffing? Able God quickly told himself to focus on what he could control here, now. He shifted his gaze to the mother and three children and gave the phone back to the mother.

"Thank you! No need," Able God said.

"You have no family?"

He hesitated and shook his head. "What are their names? Are these your children?"

"This is Abshir, his brother is Ciise, and the youngest one is Yasima," she said, pointing to them.

"My name is Able God."

"Good name. I am Hawra."

"How did you get here? Why did you leave your country?" he asked her.

"War. I no grow up knowing peace. I no want that for these children."

"What about your husband?"

"He is for Somalia. He was not allowed to leave."

Silence engulfed them.

"What about you? Why you leave your country?"

"Life is hard in Nigeria," he said, shifting his gaze to the door of the warehouse. A thought flitted through his mind and quickly took root.

Taking a deep breath, he sprang out of his bunk bed. He approached the guard and said, "Can I meet the person in charge here? I want to work. Give me anything I can do."

33

The manager, an *Arabo* named Abdulrazak, assigned Able God to work in the kitchen even though Able God was not authorized to meet him. His office was two miles from the warehouse. Not long after he got there, Able God discovered that conditions at the shelter weren't as rosy as he thought. Open pit latrines teemed with maggots, and the bathing area was flooded. The gutter, which led to a trash-blocked hole, floated with a greenish sludge and lumps of shit wrapped in nylons. The guards ordered the refugees to tidy up the warehouse when Dr. Shaw notified them that guests were coming. Otherwise, the place was left unkempt.

When Able God learned that the warehouse was a mere show center for EU diplomats, UNHCR staff, ambassadors, and donors, he was shocked by his own reaction. The more he knew, the more he wanted to know. He watched as heavily guarded envoys came to inspect the warehouse. They gave speeches before a barrage of microphones and mobile phones while cameras clicked away. During visits, the sick and wounded were locked in a secret cell in the back of the warehouse. When there were no visitors, they confiscated phones. Inmates were warned not to speak, and those who disobeyed were punished after the visitors left. Abdulrazak and Dr.

Shaw did the talking, and only Dr. Shaw showed up for meetings before their scheduled arrival. Abdulrazak insisted that everything was
in order except, of course, the three children with lice-infested heads
and their mother. He loved having them in the warehouse when the
dignitaries visited. Able God once overheard him say that the children made the warehouse look a little imperfect while preying on
their compassionate hearts to open their wallets. Able God reckoned
that by serving the center's interests, he would get special treatment
and live in better conditions. Maybe he could even ask for protection
from Serge.

Able God joined five others to wash the dented, soot-laden uten-
sils in the shelter's black-walled kitchen. He chipped off burnt food
from the base of a cooking pot with a crooked spoon or washed piles
of plates. Each day, he waited for the guards to whisk him away and
hand him over to Serge. He thought he could make friends with the
guards or find a way to make enough money to get to Tripoli. But he
was paid nothing for working in the kitchen except, of course, extra
rations from the cook. Three times a day, the refugees lined up at the
dining shed to receive food rations. A woman served the food from
a steaming pot, blowing her nose on her filthy apron every so often,
but people didn't mind.

Able God made some friends among the guards, if occasional casual conversations while smoking cigarettes meant making friends.
One of them even let him hold his Kalashnikov once and offered
a quick lesson on how it worked. Able God was spared when the
guards got angry or drunk and became mean or violent. It was soon
clear that he was no longer part of the migrants. Hawra eyed him
with a mixture of contempt and fear. She shielded her children from
him, but Able God did not allow this to affect him.

Two weeks after Able God got to the shelter, he heard motorcycles revving, followed by a barrage of gunshots in the molten air of the midday sun. Pandemonium unfolded. Screaming refugees darted in and out of the warehouse, while others dropped to the ground pretending to be dead. Able God felt no fear. Shock, maybe, but not fear. There was no time for fear. Able God crawled on all fours into a nearby gutter and slugged through filth in search of an escape. He peered over the concrete curb and saw a guard on the ground, staring with blank, upturned eyes. A thick line of blood flowed across the ground, gathering into a pool. The dying man's fingers twitched, his Kalashnikov close to his hand.

Without thinking, Able God sprang out of the gutter and grabbed the rifle. He ducked behind a pillar, turned his AK-47 in the direction of the gunfire, and pulled the trigger, firing several shots in the direction of the attackers. He again took cover and tried to think about his next move, his eyes raking the area. Men on motorcycles zoomed about, shooting indiscriminately. Multiple shots rang out as the attackers shot back at him. Able God closed his eyes and took a deep breath, waiting for them to exhaust their rounds. Then he reared up, aimed as straight as he could, and let loose a barrage of shots. A scream pierced the air. Able God felt something graze his left ear before he had a chance to react.

He took cover and was preparing to shoot again when he discovered he had run out of bullets. Blood now dripped down his shirt from his ear. Able God closed his eyes and waited for the shot that would kill him. He did not want to die this way, after surviving this long on this treacherous journey. Several moments passed, and the gunfire quieted down. There was a sound of motorcycles zooming off, then silence. Able God arose and looked around. Slippers, scarves, and shoes were scattered on the ground. Pools of blood sluiced on the concrete floor. People began crawling out from under covers, their clothes torn and shirts bloodied. They screamed, cursed, and clutched wounds from falls. Motorcycles lay sideways on the ground. An MSF van was riddled with bullets, waves of smoke rising from the chassis.

ꙮ ● ▲ ꙮ

Three days after the attack, Able God was transported to the office to meet Abdulrazak. The compound where his office was situated looked well tended, with manicured grass and neatly trimmed flowers. Inside, however, was a different story. Huge cobwebs hung low from the ceiling. There was dust everywhere: in the air, on the walls, covering the furniture, and lying thick on the floor. The windows were coated with filth, and blades of brown grass grew through cracks in the walls. Rodents and insects scurried from one place to another, leaving droppings everywhere. Thick drapes covered the windows, and the rooms were dark.

One part of the building was designed as an office, a spacious loft cleared of dust and filth and furnished with tables, chairs, and a sofa. The smell of rum, menthol cigarettes, and dust filled Able God's nostrils the moment he stepped inside. The room was almost dark. There was a small piece of frayed brown matting on the floor, some dusty picture frames on the walls, and a well-worn sofa facing the desk. The desk was large and free of clutter, except for an ashtray, a bottle of liquor, and a red candle, which provided the only illumination in the room and from which rose a thin plume of smoke.

As soon as he arrived, Abdulrazak motioned for him to sit on the sofa. A mustachioed fellow, he wore his hair in an afro, and his silk shirt was unbuttoned, displaying knotted chest hair. He had an unaccommodating expression on his dark, angular face.

"My guards told me what you did," Abdulrazak said, peering at him.

"I was just defending myself, sir," he said and sneezed. His bandaged ear surged with pain.

"Your gunfire scared them off. They were not expecting resistance. They planned a surprise attack, and it worked fifty percent. Three of my men are dead." He poured himself a drink.

"I am sorry, sir," Able God said, his mind returning to the image of the dead guard with vacant eyes.

"For months now, the Mehul gang has done everything to disrupt our operation."

"Why do they want to destroy a shelter?"

"Because we do other things."

"Other things?" Able God asked, and it immediately dawned on him what Abdulrazak meant. Everything made sense now. Abdulrazak was a smuggler. That was the only possible explanation for the attack.

"Does Dr. Shaw know what you do?" Able God already knew the answer.

A smile appeared on Abdulrazak's face. "You are a smart one!" He took a sip from his glass, stood up, and strode toward the dusty curtain. "We transport migrants to the boats in Tripoli. We move drugs around. We also do other things."

At first, Able God was taken aback by his audacity, but he reminded himself that he had been thrust into a world where morals meant nothing. Also, he now knew too much to back out, whatever that might mean.

"You will work for me from today," Abdulrazak said with a sense of finality.

Able God nodded earnestly and replied, "Yes, sir."

› ● ▲ ›

Able God leaned over the metal sink, cupping his hands under the tepid water issuing from a broken faucet and splashing it on his face. He looked closely at himself in a mirror for the first time in weeks. It was like looking at a stranger—a disheveled man with sunken eyes in a bony face, his skin ashy and scarred from the treacherous journey. There were scabs across his forehead and cheekbones from the torture. He kept his mouth shut so as not to reveal his ruined teeth. A few weeks ago, he would have been overwhelmed by a desire to cry. Instead, he buttoned up his khaki shirt, tucked it neatly into his trousers, and adjusted the holster that held his pistol, then took a deep breath and walked out into the night, where the commander and four guards waited with the Hilux pickup.

They drove ten kilometers out of the city before swerving off the main road into the bush, brushing past tall plants and swaths of dry elephant grass. They continued on through the bush to their destination, where the men unloaded tires and planks at the side of the road, concealing them with a heap of long-bladed leaves.

They sat on their haunches, sharing a joint and swatting away bugs, waiting a long time in the dark night. The only source of illumination was a flashlight they'd planted in the dry grass, its beam slanting up through the hazy air thick with ganja smoke, dust particles, and tiny flies. Able God wiped his sweaty forehead with the back of his hand and listened to the droning of insects, the scuttling of nocturnal rodents, and the faint sound of vehicles zooming past in the distance. All he needed to do was follow instructions, and everything would be okay. He would not have to hurt anyone. Able God sat down on the grass. There was a chill in the air. He took the joint from one of the guards and drew long puffs, trying to keep still and alert. They would leap into action when the time was right.

Glancing at his watch, the commander nodded to the men. It was time. They put on gloves and balaclavas. The commander slung a bag over his shoulders, and the others darted to the side of the road. The commander patrolled the area with his rifle while Able God and one of the guards built a roadblock, piling up tires across the road, then arranging the planks across the asphalt with nails pointing up. Able God's face was flushed and sweaty under his balaclava. Afterward, they went back to the bush and hid. They didn't have to wait long.

The roar of a cross-country bus grew louder before stopping with a pneumatic hiss. Its huge headlights illuminated the road. Able God whipped out his gun and cocked it while one of the guards sprang out of the bush shooting. Able God followed his lead, pumping bullets into the air. The bus driver came out and lay face down on the asphalt, as screams erupted from the bus. The commander barked at the driver, ordering him to his feet. The driver stood with his hands up. His trousers were soaked with piss. The commander shoved him toward the bus with the muzzle of his rifle. Able God followed close behind. The other four stood guard outside. The driver heaved the door open, and Able God stood at the entrance beside the driver as the commander went down the aisle, stepping over bodies prostrate on the floor of the bus and pointing his rifle at those still seated, telling them to lie face down on the floor. Screams filled the air, tears flowed, and supplications went up to God in many languages.

"Kneel down!" Able God commanded the driver, trying to sound stern. When the driver did not respond, he kicked the man in the back. The man dropped to his knees. The commander was still moving up and down the aisle, waving his gun and screaming threats. When he got to the first row, he stopped.

"Everybody out! Get out!"

Within seconds, the migrants were all out of the bus.

"Lie down! Lie down, or I will shoot you!" the commander yelled as he herded them to the middle of the road. One after another, the passengers lay flat on the ground. One migrant stood in defiance.

"You can't do this to us!" he said. "We are not animals—we are human beings! You can't take what we have left. We have come this far. You can't do this to us. We will have nothing if you take all we have!"

A guard charged him, ramming the butt of his rifle into his face. The man fell to the ground, clutching his face and screaming in pain as blood gushed from his mouth and nose. Able God's face itched. He rubbed it with the back of his wrist. They'd said he wouldn't have to hurt anyone.

"Everybody stand up!" the commander yelled, then unzipped his bag. Able God shot a disapproving glance at the commander but quickly repeated the instruction. The commander moved swiftly through the crowd, demanding cash and valuables. The migrants brought cash out of toothpaste tubes and from under their bras. They emptied their pockets into the bag. Women handed over their purses, men their wallets. The commander cleaned out every one of them. Then one of the guards had the driver open the luggage compartment and order the migrants to get out their suitcases. He opened bags and began tossing out personal belongings. Underwear and brightly col-ored blouses cascaded out of suitcases. Toiletry bags, shoes, medica-tion, towels, and various containers were strewn across the road. With the barrel of his rifle, the guard carefully lifted a pair of flimsy panties from a bag. He tossed the panties on the road and dangled a bra from the tip of his gun. Able God's nose itched; he looked around, wanting to be done.

In a matter of minutes, the commander had managed to fill his bag to the brim with cash and valuables. Able God saw a couple of vehicles halted some distance away. They turned sharply and reversed course. Moments later, they sped off in their Hilux. Able God removed his balaclava to take in the fresh air, but he was also glad to be done.

"We don't need their money," Abdulrazak had told him, and when he had asked why they stole from desperate migrants, he said it was to make them even more desperate. "Some of them will end up in the hands of Médecins Sans Frontières. They will bring them to the shelter. That's more money from the EU and UNHCR. We also have more people to send to Tripoli. Business moves. The chain must remain unbroken."

Able God found the logic of the operation impeccable but also evil.

> ● ▲ >

Able God received the keys to a Hilux truck the following day. Also, he moved to a new bedroom in what used to be a storeroom in the warehouse compound. The room was furnished with a queen bed, a small refrigerator, and an electric stove. He sat down on the bed to test its softness, then lay on his back, arms stretched out, eyes closed. This he missed, for he had not slept in a good bed in eight weeks. Somehow, the room reminded him of his small apartment back home. Able God felt a low and muffled resentment rising within him, climbing and spreading throughout his body. Distance had done nothing to assuage his pain. He reckoned that by now he had been relegated to cautionary tale status, a bogeyman for his cousins. He removed a SIM card wrapped in paper from his pocket and inserted it into a phone he had taken from one of the guards. The device spilled out blue light and was soon ready. After dialing his mother's number, he drew a deep breath. The phone rang for a moment, and there was a click.

"Hello?"

"Hello, Mummy?"

"Able God? Is that you?" his mother shouted from the other end.

He hesitated for a few seconds. "Yes, Mummy."

"Oh, my Jesus! Jesus, I thank you. My Lord, I thank you! They told us you were dead, but I told your father you are not. I had a dream, the devil is a liar," she screamed.

"I am not dead, Mummy."

Able God heard his father's voice in the background asking her what was happening. A few seconds later, his father demanded that she hand the phone over. He heard his father struggling with his mother for the phone and calling him a bastard. Able God hung up before his father got on the line. A heavy silence fell on his shoulders. He sat clutching the handset and blinking to stave off tears. *At least they knew he was alive. At least they knew.*

35

Two days later, Able God met Abdulrazak at a roadside hookah bar on the other end of town to celebrate his first successful operation. The bar's indoor area was full. Outside, there were trees and umbrellas with clusters of tables and bamboo chairs. Potbellied men in tunics and skullcaps and bald men in dress shirts sat smoking. There were men in casual clothes, too, who chatted while smoking ornate hookahs and sipping from cups of tea or sweating bottles of water. Food and desserts were also served. The air was dense with the aromatic smell of flavored tobacco and jasmine. Soft music poured from a small speaker inside the bar. Abdulrazak wore scuffed shoes and a starched brown khaki shirt with a green beret placed at a rakish angle.

Each guest had at least two phones, which they left on the edge of the table. Boys in black fezzes drifted back and forth as they attended to the guests. Cars pulled off the side of the road, and more guests filed into the bar as Abdulrazak and Able God claimed a table. At the center of the table sat an unused hookah with a glittering metal canister, a filter bowl, and two smoking hoses. No sooner had they taken their seats than a boy materialized and lit their tobacco. Abdulrazak puffed at the hookah right away, white smoke billowing from his mouth and nose. Able God looked around and spotted the VIP section of the bar through the open side door. The nook was cordoned off and only occupied by one couple, who sat side by side on a sofa, smoking and chatting.

Able God grabbed the other hose and took a drag. He choked on the aromatic smoke, whooped, then inhaled again.

"Congratulations, my friend!" Abdulrazak exclaimed, a fine sheen of perspiration beading his forehead.

"Thank you, sir," Able God replied, feigning a smile.

"I think you should stay here. I think we will do great things together!"

A Datsun pulled up alongside the bar, and a familiar figure stepped out with an unknown woman. Able God choked on the smoke again, this time out of shock. He coughed so hard he thought the pain would rip his ribs apart. Serge. There was no mistaking him.

"Easy, my friend, easy!" Abdulrazak said.

A torrent of questions surged through Able God's mind. He broke out in a cold sweat, his heart racing. Serge walked into the bar and began moving from one cluster of guests to another, laughing, shaking hands, and bumping fists. The woman smiled quietly at everyone and curtseyed. Serge seemed to be making his way to their table, which made Able God increasingly anxious, but he tried not to show it. But then Serge suddenly changed course and walked into the bar with his woman. For a moment, a combination of feelings roiled within Abel God, but it didn't take long for them to distill into a singular emotion—seething rage.

"You know him? You look like you see a ghost!" Abdulrazak asked.

"No," he responded, trying to keep cool. It suddenly occurred to him that his face might have given him away.

"His name is Serge. The mutherfucker runs a slave camp up north!" Abdulrazak explained.

Abdulrazak continued smoking, and Able God glanced back at the VIP section from the corner of his eye. Serge was talking to the couple. They gazed at him in rapt attention, their smiles painted on as though waiting for him to crack a joke so that they could all open their mouths and laugh. This pulled at Able God's nerves. The anger boiling inside frothed over, taking control of his body. Serge released a reverberating and repulsive laugh. Now Abdulrazak looked at Able God quizzically, his eyebrows hovering halfway up his forehead.

"Ah, you know him!"

Able God did not respond. Fear rose up in his throat. He shifted in his seat.

"Now it makes sense. You were there before MSF found you! You were an inmate!"

Abdulrazak adjusted his beret, leaned forward, and squeezed Able God's shoulders, speaking in hushed tones. "You know I could hand you over to him now for some money, but I won't do that. Because I like you."

"Thank you, sir."

"But you see, you have to make him pay for what he did to you."

"I don't understand."

"You are with me now. You can't be a coward!"

"I am not a coward!"

"Then eliminate him!"

"What?"

"Wait till he leaves, tail him, and shoot the fucker in the head."

Silence engulfed them. Then Able God excused himself and rushed into the bathroom. He breathed deeply and paced around. Abdulrazak sounded like he meant what he was saying. What if this was a test, and failure would make him end up in Serge's camp? What was in it for him?

He brought his pistol out of the holster and stared at it for a moment, then quickly reholstered it. Before returning to his table, he adjusted his shirt and tried to breathe slowly. Abdulrazak resumed talking to him, but Able God did not listen this time around. It was as if all sounds had been muted, and he was merely watching Abdulrazak's mouth flap open and shut.

After a while, people started leaving the bar and driving home. Abdulrazak was still talking and smoking. Serge was still talking and smoking, too. When Abdulrazak went to the bathroom, Able God looked around, trying to decide what to do.

Eventually, Serge, his woman, and the couple got up and waltzed out of the bar. Able God averted his gaze, waited for them to pass, then followed them to the street. Serge clasped his hands around the woman's waist as they crossed the nearly deserted street. The area echoed with their boisterous, flirtatious laughter. The couple seemed to have created an impenetrable protective bubble around him. The street had emptied out.

Abdulrazak returned from the bathroom and turned his gaze outside.

"Make sure you get a good shot," he said before leaving the bar. Seconds later, he drove off. Able God went to his car and sat behind the wheel watching them talk for another twenty minutes. He seethed with anger. The couple took their leave.

Before Serge walked toward the car, he pulled the woman to himself, and she ran her tongue over his lips. Seeing Serge kissing inflamed Able God with rage. For a moment, he tried to shake off the impulse, but the more he tried to resist, the stronger the urge grew. He told himself he was not a coward. Not anymore! Able God

THE ROAD TO THE SALT SEA   251

sprang out of his vehicle and ran toward them. They separated, and Able God aimed at him, pulling the trigger three times.

Serge did a little dance of death. The bullets were like punches pushing him farther and farther away till he fell to the dusty ground. The woman threw herself upon Serge's dead body, her cries loud and drawn out, like the howling of a dog. She had seen Able God's face. Able God pointed the gun at her and fired another shot, hitting her in the head. He dashed back to his vehicle and sped off.

Able God tried to empty his mind of thoughts as he drove home, but his hands couldn't stop shaking. After driving for ten minutes, he stopped the car and tossed the gun through the window like a contaminated object. The gravity of what he had done dawned on him, and for a few moments, he tried to convince himself that it hadn't really happened. Then he buried his face in his hands and poured out his grief.

36

Able God sat around burning pieces of furniture, smoking with the guards outside the warehouse and drinking gin from aluminum cups. He emptied his cup in one gulp. His head exploded with warmth. His eyes watered. He filled the cup again and gulped it down. A guard snatched the bottle away from him. Now he tasted nothing but felt a burning in his throat. The liquor was enough to warm his insides and take the cold away. He took a long drag on the joint. He closed his eyes and filled his lungs with smoke, allowing it to creep into his skull and finger its way across his brain. He jerked his head backward, lips curling. Smoke puffed out through his nostrils, vanishing into the dark night.

It had been two days since he went to the hookah bar, two days of living in denial. Abdulrazak had commended him for his courage and promised to protect him in case of any retaliation. He had assigned Able God to the group tasked with keeping the refugees in check and making the women conform to Islamic rules of dress. Able God had seen so many deaths in such a short period that he was beginning to think death was following him. Why, then, had death spared him? What was the purpose of his life?

The memory of Serge's face stayed with him just as he remembered the faces of others he had seen die. But this was different. Serge's death was by his hand. He saw Serge's face before he dealt the blow of death. He saw Serge's face as the holes opened in his body, a face filled with shock, a face that was unprepared for death. He could justify Badero by telling himself that he had to defend himself, and he could hold Akudo accountable. Without her, he wouldn't have been in a position where he would need to defend himself against Serge. There was no getting around the fact that this was no mistake. He had murdered two people in cold blood. Is this the person he had become, or was this who he had always been?

Hawra walked by, and one of the guards called out to her. He was short, muscular, scar-faced, with a small nose and fleshy lips. She came over to them.

"Where you going?" the guard asked her, slurring his words.

"I want to go pee," she said, looking surprised.

"You do not have to go all the way to the outhouse. You pee right there, in the gutter," he said, pointing to drainage a few feet away.

"Leave her alone!" Able God said.

"Hey, Mr. Nigeria, you can't tell me what to do! When did you come here to think you can tell me what to do?" the guard responded sharply. Able God decided he didn't want any trouble tonight. He blew a cloud of smoke into the air.

"Because I am a gentleman, I will escort you," the guard conceded.

For a few moments, Hawra looked at Able as though expecting him to do something. Before walking off with the guard, a look of disappointment came over her. Hawra walked slowly to the gutter, hiked her dress up, and crouched down. Able God turned away, but the guard kept looking at her. He just stood there, his head cocked drunkenly to the side, the crotch of his trousers bulging. When she was done, he pulled her to him. She screamed. He told her to shut up, but she persisted. He wrapped his arm around her neck and covered her mouth with his palm. She tried biting his hand, but he held her still, muffling her screams. All the guards sitting by the fire laughed except Able God, who was now irritated.

"Leave her alone! Stop!"

The short guard did not stop; instead, he pinned her to the ground. Able was overwhelmed by a desire to scream and lunge at him, but he did not yield to it. He walked away, made his way to his room, and began gathering his things into a backpack.

> ● ▲ ▸

He got to the bus station, where migrants sat in groups on the dusty ground, chatting or listening to transistor radios. Some crowded into the back of pickup trucks parked by the roadside, waiting for the drivers to arrive. Whenever a vehicle pulled over, about a dozen migrants rushed over to it screaming their heads off, each trying to get the occupants' attention. European Union–backed militias often raided the roundabout, spraying the air with gunshots and apprehending them, but when the situation cleared up, they would swarm back.

Able God halted when he caught sight of a group of men who were hunched over whispering by the roadside and looking in his direction. One of them broke from the group and lumbered over to him. He was wearing a T-shirt that was torn around the arm. On his dusty feet were flip-flops. Able God looked away as he considered breaking into a run. It was too late. The man blocked his way.

"*As-salaam aleikum,*" he greeted Able God, eyeing him.

"*Wa aleikum as-salaam,*" Able God responded, swallowing back spit. He glanced at him, hoping his face did not betray his feelings.

Able God hoped to God that the fellow was not one of the Asma Boys or someone loyal to Serge.

"Are you a member of our union?" he asked gruffly, giving him a quizzical look.

"No, but I am here to see Etim."

"Where are you from?"

"That man is my guest. Leave him alone!" a voice boomed from behind.

The speaker approached. He was a short, dark-skinned man with a gnarled scar on one cheek. It looked as though someone had carved it into his cheek with a fire-heated knife. Tobacco-blackened teeth protruded between his lips. He introduced himself as Etinamabasiyakka.

"Able God? You are Able God?" Etinamabasiyakka said. He grabbed Able God's hand and shook it vigorously. Able God nodded as he was led close to the buses.

Etinamabasiyakka and the driver argued heatedly in Arabic for several minutes, but the driver finally yielded and turned back to his business, his bald head sunk onto his shoulders. Etinamabasiyakka somehow had convinced the driver to put Able God on a vehicle going to Tripoli. Able God had gotten Etinamabasiyakka's contact when looking around for Nigerian smugglers living in Sabha. In Ibibio his name meant "When My Enemies Plan Against Me, God Never Allow."

"I have a friend, Kamil, who lives in the Souq al-Juma district," Etinamabasiyakka explained to him while they waited at the bus station. "You can work for him for a week. He will give you 250 dinars and accommodations. You will have to buy your own food."

He continued in a low voice, leaning forward, his tobacco breath in Able God's face and his gnarled scar straining. "If you beg him to let you work for one month, you can earn up to one thousand dinars. That will be enough for you to buy a spot in a rubber dinghy for the crossing, but it's very risky. I know you are targeting Italy. You don't have to tell me."

"Why haven't you crossed the sea?" Able God asked as he turned away slowly.

"My pastor doesn't want me to go yet. When I hear the voice of God, I will go! There is time for every fucking thing, my brother! May we not cross the sea when the Queen of the Coast wants her human sacrifice. Do you know the Queen of the Coast is the deity in charge of all the seas and oceans in the world?"

"Is there a church in Sabha?"

"No, my church is in Tripoli. I spend weekends there after the workweek. It is called the Sword of Deliverance Evangelical Ministries, and it is led by Reverend Chucks Adah. Don't worry, I will take you to church when I go."

Able God knew better than to trust a stranger with big promises, particularly an Arabic-speaking Nigerian with a long and complicated name, but he had to make a move before Sabha consumed him. He had a pistol in his backpack, wrapped in a piece of clothing. He would not take chances this time around.

Finally, Able God saw a pickup truck approach. Etinamabasiyakka jumped up and ran to the truck, pushing his way through the throng of migrants swarming around the vehicle, some already jumping in the back. There were some women with children among them, which only added to the turmoil. Plumes of dust rose in the air.

"Make una no rush this car! Na turn by turn! Na turn by turn!" Etinamabasiyakka barked after speaking to the driver. He pushed the migrants away from the car, then selected those he wanted to climb into the truck bed. He beckoned to Able God, who had been pushed to the edge of the small crowd. Able God squeezed through and clambered into the truck, crouching uncomfortably. He was next to a woman who wore a black niqab. Only her eyes and her gloved hands were exposed. Etinamabasiyakka pulled a yellow notepad and a pen from his pocket and scribbled something on the paper as the pickup van roared back to life.

"Here is Kamil's address in Souq al-Juma. He will be kind to you. Go in peace and may the Lord bless and keep you, my brother!" He raised his voice as he pressed the paper into Able God's palm.

"Thank you, sir! Thank you, sir!" Able God shouted.

"Don't mention, my brother. That's what brothers are for."

37

The drive to the coast at Gergarish was quiet. Able God shifted in his seat and peered out into the moonlit evening. His face was full of wary anxiety. For some reason, the stars were not out. It was very late, so there were few cars on the road, and the stalls were closing. Dealers were out on the streets in their tunics and skullcaps. There was a cluster of tents where people waited their turn to go to Gergarish to board the boats. Shifty-eyed migrants in careworn clothes and slippers lined up along the road under the glare of the lampposts. They were mostly sub-Saharans waiting to be hired for graveyard shifts. Able God had been told that sometimes the trucks that came for them carried them off to detention centers instead of construction sites. Able God imagined they also had dreams of crossing the great sea to Europe and needed money to pay the smugglers. It would be their turn one day, but tonight was his night. Once again, Able God allowed himself to hope. Time would pass, and some memories of the horrendous situation would become diluted in the routine of everyday life in Europe.

He had paid Kamil, Etinamabasiyakka's friend, almost all he had to get on the boat. The rest of the money he had wrapped up in a plastic bag, which he tied with a string around his waist, tucking it safely under his trousers. He had overheard the idea from a refugee in Tripoli as a good way to secure money at sea.

He had greeted the driver, whose face was covered, with a smile and a brisk handshake. No words were spoken. No words were needed. All he had to do was show the ticket he'd purchased. Guns were not allowed, so he gave up his weapon. Finally, he was hurtling toward a new life. This was the leg of the journey that mattered. If he had any hope, this was it. Although the sea was not yet visible, he knew it couldn't be far. The salty tang of sea air and the smell of rotting fish were stronger than ever.

Able God looked around, and his eyes fell on a woman close to the tent. His body tensed. Able God felt a stir of recognition, his heart pounding under his ribs. *It was her*. Akudo. Her face was gaunt, and she had bony collarbones that had sunk down into her chest, but it was her. Able God moved in closer for a better look. A young boy stood beside her, his hair shaved and eyes closed. He was dressed in an oversize T-shirt. No, not a boy, but her daughter dressed as one. He was certain it was her child. He felt a rush of overwhelming emotion after the initial shock had subsided. They were still alive. They had traveled here. How had they done it? How long had they been staying at the tent? In that moment, he realized that he didn't feel anger toward her, at least not anymore. He was simply relieved to see them. His first instinct was to rush up to them, embrace her and her daughter, inquire when they were taking the boat, and offer to assist if possible. But he restrained himself. He was nearing the end of his journey and was not going to let anything derail it. Furthermore, if they had arrived in Tripoli on their own and survived while others perished, they were capable of crossing the sea without his assistance. The driver called for the passengers to get on the bus, and Able God backed off, his eyes wet with a sheen of tears.

The bus moved into a convoy. Able God peered around as the buses took backroads and stopped after a while. Two men with covered faces and turbans were waiting for them. The migrants were ordered to get off and walk in single file. The men led the way. They passed under an arched walkway paved with white cobblestones, past single-story courtyards and windowless mud-brick buildings. They walked down crooked streets so narrow they could look into the homes on either side. Able God looked around uneasily, inspecting the buildings and peering through open windows. He was not sure what he was looking for, but the men he was following were smugglers, so he knew they were capable of anything. No matter how much hope he managed to summon, there was always a layer of hazy uncertainty that he had learned to accept.

They stopped at an old warehouse. The men handed them over to other turbaned men, who passed out small jerricans to use as flotation devices, if necessary. Then they were led down a sloping path to the rocky shoreline, and there it was. The sea shimmered before them in the moonlight.

The tide lapped gently at the ungainly boulders, leaving behind a strip of white foam along the waterline. Bobbing gently on the waves from pier-side moorings was a flotilla of old wooden and steel boats with chipped paint and rusted patches. The inflatable dinghies, which the men called Zodiacs—the name of the French company that made them—were farther out.

Able God sighed, inhaling the humid scent of the sea.

Close to the shore, away from the boats, there was a rowdy crowd of women, men, and children. They carried rucksacks on their backs or bundles of clothes and jerricans on their heads. Standing along the shore was a row of men who Able God guessed were Somali. Their faces were not covered.

The Somalis were wearing black combat trousers and torn T-shirts. One had a blade of grass between his teeth. Another, a dreadlocked man who appeared to be the leader, was sitting on a rock drinking from a bottle of water. They all had rifles slung over their shoulders. The driver shook hands with one of the smugglers, nodded, and left without saying goodbye. Moments later, the leader took another swig from his bottle, puffed out his cheeks, and spat a long, thin arc of water on the ground. He stood up and flung the bottle into the water with a flourish. Able God took a deep breath. One last leg of the journey and he would be free. Maybe he would learn how to put the past behind him. Maybe he would become a new person, with a new identity.

"Welcome! Welcome!" the man shouted, then signaled to the crowd to keep quiet. "We will start preparing for the journey in a moment. Please remember, when you leave this place, you are on your own. We are no longer responsible for your arrival in Italy. We can only pray that Jah grants you journey mercies."

Able God had been told that the rubber dinghies, which were only equipped with small motors, were not actually intended to go the full length of the journey. So sub-Saharan migrants were often sent out to sea in the hope that they would be rescued by the Italian Coast Guard and loaded onto larger ships that would take them to Italy. Able God was prepared for the journey. He had planned to gather provisions for the voyage—a sweater to protect him from the wind, some dates, biscuits, and oranges, a tin of menthol balm, a plastic bottle to piss into, and a fifty-liter jerrican to use as a floating device. If need be, he would swim for as long as his strength could carry him or cling to flotsam or his jerrican. He had thought about the different ways things could go wrong and what he would do. But then he found out he could only bring a single small jerrican because the smugglers wanted to pack as many people as possible on the boat. The limitations did not discourage him.

"The only advice I will give you is to pray that you reach your destination safely, and don't forget to be your brother's keeper," the leader said.

The crowd nodded in assent, but the words rang hollow in Able God's ears. He did not care about anything the man had to say; he just wanted to get going.

Moments later, the leader instructed his men to ready the boats for the journey. They fanned out among the crowd and began calling out the numbers of their groups. Able God kept his eyes trained on Akudo as she moved through the crowd, his chest suddenly heaving with anger. His mind whirled with questions. How did she find a smuggler? When did she leave? Who brought her to Tripoli? He half hoped they were assigned to the same boat so he could throw her overboard. They weren't. He decided he would find her if she made it across, even if it was the last thing he did.

He had no idea how much animosity he had for her until that moment. Without her, none of this would have occurred. He would have led a life of mediocrity working for the wealthy had he not met her. Without her, there was a chance that he might have gotten his big break, found a job, or made a connection to put himself in a better situation. He would never know, however, because of Akudo. But, once again, if this perilous adventure had taught him anything, it was what it showed him about himself. He was angry at her because of what meeting her had revealed about himself. Able God tempered his ill wishes. Her daughter, the poor girl, had been dragged into this mess, too. He could see Akudo was trying to save her. Would they survive the sea?

The smuggler in charge of Able God's boat asked for a volunteer to sit at the motor and steer the dinghy. Able God raised his hand, but a bearded man was chosen for the task. The smuggler gave him instructions about the motor.

"I will start the motor for you—you just have to drive it," the smuggler said. The bearded captain nodded slowly, evidently confused.

"Hold the tiller steady—steady, my man! Push here to go left and here to go right. Simple," added the smuggler as he demonstrated what that meant by moving his outstretched hand from side to side. The bearded captain seemed even more confused.

The smuggler noticed, so he added, "Worry not, my man! We will show you on the boat."

Able God wondered why he hadn't given the instructions on the boat in the first place, but he shrugged it off. The smuggler had not finished talking. This time he addressed the rest of the passengers. "Sit down straight. No move. Boat full, so if you move it will overbalance and throw all of you in the water," he said to them.

Able God wondered how they would avoid moving in the boat given how many people would be aboard. This ignited a new burst of nervousness. Moments later, they climbed into the boats.

The light-skinned migrants—mostly Moroccans and Syrians—who had paid more were loaded onto the wooden boats while the sub-Saharans were directed to the inflated rubber dinghies. They had no life jackets, only their jerricans.

Before Able God could react, the sub-Saharans showed their tickets and began wading through the waves. The water reached their waists by the time they neared the designated boats. A child whose father was carrying him on his shoulders broke into tears. What had begun as a murmur quickly grew into a barrage of shouts. Able God felt a lump rising in his throat as he hiked his trousers up to his knees, slung his bag high over his shoulder, and balanced his jerrican on his head. Taking one big breath, he waded into the sea. The water stung his skin with the cold, but he moved along. As Able God moved closer to the boat, he squeezed forward, water splashing everywhere. The smuggler was now beside the boat, directing them less by words than by gestures. Whenever he spoke, he shouted.

They were crammed into every corner of the boat with no room to stand up or lie down. After a lot of shoving and pushing and screaming, Able God commandeered a spot in the middle of the dinghy, pressed between a cluster of dirty bodies, and wrapped his hands around his jerrican. His eyes flickered anxiously.

Herding them all to the boats took a long time. Once completed, the smuggler pushed his way through tangled limbs to the motor in the back. He raised the anchor and cranked the recoil starter, and the motor spluttered to life. He choked the motor, set it to neutral, and explained to the captain how to handle the tiller. The roar of the motor drowned out his voice as he gesticulated. The boat lurched and reeled and moved forward, groaning under the weight of too much human cargo.

> ● ▲ ›

Able God gasped for breath. His back and legs and hips ached. He wrinkled his nose at the overwhelming odor of breath and armpits. He felt the heat from the boat's motor. The fear was palpable. The odor of piss filled the air.

When the boats first set out, he could make out the other passengers' faces. He saw hope hidden in their forlorn eyes and mouths. A mother cradled her infant in her arms while trying to pacify her toddler daughter. Families huddled together. There were boys and girls as young as five. He wondered when Akudo and her daughter would leave Tripoli and if they would make it. Perhaps he should not have abandoned them. How had he become so preoccupied with his own needs?

His own father never stopped touting his uprightness, and indeed, he was well respected for his strong opinions and uncompromising values. He always talked about how the "get-rich-quick syndrome" was destroying the country. However, when Calistus returned home with unexplained riches, he looked the other way.

"Don't be jealous of your brother. God will do your own for you!" his mother would repeat when he dared question the source of his brother's wealth.

When the matter eventually got to his father, he shrugged it off and sounded the same old tune: "When God blesses a man, things happen fast!"

Able God wondered what Calistus would think of him now—if he would be disappointed or just confused.

The sea grew louder, as waves heaved up and crashed against the speeding boat. The other boats were out of Able God's sight. The waves were not huge, but they were boisterous enough to cause a scare. There was a rising sense of panic, and to make matters worse, the captain could not see the waves in the dark, so it was difficult to hold a steady course.

"Easy! Easy!" Able God heard the bearded captain shout, as though speaking to a horse. Saltwater rose up and crashed over them, drawing gasps. When the captain saw that maneuvering the boat from side to side was not working, he revved the motor to propel the boat faster. The boat plowed through the water, spraying the passengers, but the turbulence eased after a while. There was a burst of applause for the captain.

A few moments passed, and it occurred to Able God—as though

the waves had jerked him back to his senses—that the captain did not have a compass or any kind of navigational device. But again, he reminded himself how the whole operation worked. The smugglers must have instructed the captain to just sail onward till they saw land or got intercepted by the coast guard. For a long time, he tried to stay still and keep his eyes closed. He kept telling himself that he was almost there.

38

The sea was cold and misty even though the sun had risen. Everyone was soaked and eager for the mist to burn off so the sun could dry their clothes. But the sea had not finished buffeting them. A sharp wind sang terrible, horrifying notes. The waves foamed white. The horizon narrowed and widened, dipped and rose. Two women huddled together, reciting the Quran. The captain gripped the tiller tightly, then pulled it toward him, which sent the boat into a curve. He pushed it back to turn in the other direction, and the boat lifted before dropping into a sickening fall. Able God felt dizzy, his stomach churning. He drew in several deep breaths as he tried to collect himself. Moments later, there was a retching sound from the other end of the boat. A child vomited, splattering those around him.

His clothes drenched and his body shivering, Able God clutched his jerrican. Water had been collecting in the boat, and now a puddle sloshed at his heels. His legs had grown so cramped and stiff from the cold that he could barely feel his feet. He rubbed his palms together to keep warm. Able God felt pressure in his bladder, but he held it in.

He thought he saw the fin of a patrolling shark in the distance and tried not to panic. Instead, he looked around to determine if anyone else had seen what he saw. It didn't seem like they had. Relief washed over him, but he felt a twinge of regret as his fantasy of swimming and clinging to the flotsam like a hero was shattered. He felt foolish to think that drowning would be the only danger if he were washed overboard by a wave.

The mist soon cleared, and the sun shone in its intensity. Their clothes dried, but the sun's heat did not abate. Able God unbuttoned his shirt and kicked the shoes off his feet, which had finally thawed out. He wiggled his toes and tried to give himself as much ease as the space allowed. He could see far across the water. No land was in sight. Seabirds glided through the sky. The Sahara and the sea were similar in many ways—they were places of vast loneliness. Both were relentless in bending everything in their grip to their will.

The sun lightened the mood and loosened tongues. Soon the boat buzzed with conversations in different languages. Someone was complaining about being cheated by the smugglers.

"Those bastards chowed my money. I pay five thousand. They give me rubber boat! They put those North Africans in wood boats with two thousand."

There were hums of surprise in the boat, and even Able God was shocked. Different voices erupted.

"Five thousand for a dinghy?"

"I paid two thousand!"

"I gave them three!"

"I paid one thousand five hundred. Monaco said it was not enough, so he took five hundred more."

"All that money and they pack us here like sardines!"

"Where did you get the five thousand to pay them?"

"We are sub-Saharans, my friend—that is how they treat sub-Saharans. Dark skin is a disease, a fucking disease!"

"North Africans are Africans, too!"

"They say we are the Africans. They think they are better than us."

"We are human beings, too. We should not be treated like animals."

"Fuck them. We will get to our destination, God willing!"

"Amen."

"We will make it!"

"Amen!"

Able God had known all along that sub-Saharans were treated with less respect than their light-skinned counterparts in North Africa. His harrowing experience in Libya had taught him that.

The passengers spoke about other things, mainly about places they had never been to—Italy, Greece, Europe, America. One of them said his ultimate goal was to reach America.

"My final destination is New York City. I will work in Italy for some years and move as soon as I make enough money. I will become an artist in New York City," he said.

"America is far away," someone countered. "You cannot reach there by boat."

"You can get anywhere by boat as long as the sea is kind to you! The sea will be kind to me when I want to go," he said.

Soon they had no more strength to speak. They nibbled on whatever food they had managed to stuff in their pockets and drank from their water bottles. Able God took just one cautious sip of water to wet his dry tongue and parched throat. He didn't know how much longer they were going to be on the boat, but he was determined to make it.

The afternoon wore on, and the sun slipped down behind a heavy mass of clouds on the horizon. Able God's eyes grew listless. Their bodies were too tightly packed in the boat for him to use his jerrican. The pressure in his bladder had worsened and the pain soon became unbearable. He had no choice but to allow the stream to flow. Warm piss trickled down his thighs, flushing his body with relief. Ashamed, he worried that the smell of his piss would fill the boat, even though his smell would have had to overwhelm the other odors to be noticed. He waited for someone to speak out or at least cast a disapproving glance. Nothing happened. Those closest to him covered their noses, nothing more.

The adults vomited, too. They also soiled themselves. The culprits neither gave a warning nor asked for permission. They did not speak, but their eyes were filled with shame. Some even covered their faces while they did their business. At first, the combined smells were unbearably nauseating and elicited more vomiting. But they soon got used to it, as the air became thick with foul smells.

39

A noxious odor began to issue from the engine, followed by a spurt of exhaust smoke. The engine sputtered and died, leaving the boat at the mercy of the waves. The captain pulled the motor's cord again and again to no avail. With no momentum of its own, the boat heaved in the choppy water. Panic took over the boat as people began choking on the fumes. The captain appealed to the passengers to stay calm. Able God also lent his voice, urging them not to move too much to avoid capsizing the boat.

The captain tried to pull the motor cord again, but the motor wouldn't budge. Murmurs turned into shouts. The boat yawed sharply to one side.

"Calm down! Please calm down! We will all die if you don't calm down," Able God shouted. He watched the captain poke and prod the motor, convinced the man didn't know what he was doing. Still, it was important to give the impression that the problem was being fixed. Able God announced he was going over to see if he could repair the motor, then he squeezed slowly through the crowd, stepping over tangled limbs and trampling on bodies. He checked the spark plugs and discovered they were blackened. After cleaning and dusting them, he rinsed them with some fuel from the motor, then slotted them back in, cranking the recoil starter again. No sign of life.

Perhaps he could take the motor apart? But with what tools? He asked around for a piece of metal with a sharp point, anything he could fashion into a tool, and managed to collect a couple of pens and some knives. With the knives he was able to remove some screws and strip some pieces from the motor, but he realized there was nothing he could do. Fixing the motor might not have been beyond his mechanical capabilities, but without tools, he would never know for sure.

Able God surveyed the crowd. His own fear was reflected in a host of exhausted faces. It was the fear that came from being confronted with death. The air was saturated with the smell of human waste, diesel fumes, and fish. As night fell, the passengers rested their heads on each other's shoulders and drifted off to sleep. The boat bobbed along in pitch darkness. Infants cooed.

The waves heaved up and down. Able God bit his lip hard to rid himself of fear. He wasn't sure which direction they were headed. What if they were lost? He couldn't be certain what time it was, but that didn't matter to him anymore. What mattered was to stay alive until the Italian Coast Guard showed up. On the boat, the sharp stench of piss mixed with a foul combination of seawater and shit. His shirt was caked with someone's vomit. No water was left in his bottle, and his tongue was swollen in his mouth. His thoughts turned to Akudo, and he wondered why she was the person he thought of at such a critical hour. Once more, fate had brought them together, but he had made the decision to resist it. Perhaps he shouldn't have left them at the tent in Tripoli. Perhaps he should at least have shown himself.

He drifted in and out of sleep. He counted to a hundred to stay

awake, the taste of blood on his tongue. His lip throbbed where he
had bitten it. He looked out at the horizon, expecting to see a ship
or land or something, but saw only the sea, a limitless pool of blue.
Long bouts of silence were punctuated by the cries of infants and
supplications to God.

⟩ ● ▲ ⟩

First, it was the distant growl of a ship's engine, then the blaring of a
horn, then a tiny dot on the horizon grew bigger and bigger until it
became like a mountain.

That took several minutes. Almost everyone on the boat shouted,
whistled, and waved as though the ship hadn't already spotted them.
Able God looked at the ship through tear-blurred eyes.

A new vision flashed by, and for the first time since he'd begun
the journey, the idea of reaching Europe felt real to him. He had no
doubts now. The possibility of a new life rolled around inside his
head and seemed solid.

He imagined kissing the land, grabbing fistfuls of soil and rubbing
them on his face. Yes, he would probably stay in a refugee camp for
some months, but he would eventually get back on his feet. He could
play chess in the city square. He'd get another degree or certificate if
he had to. He'd learn Italian. He would apply for jobs, any job at first,
then he would move on to corporate employment. His case would
not be an outlier. There were countless stories of young and talented
people who had failed at almost everything in Nigeria but went on
to prosper in Europe by doing the same things that hadn't worked
back home. It was as though a viable seed had been planted in the
wrong soil.

Able God choked with tears as the ship eased to a stop beside
the dinghy. Italian Coast Guard agents wearing gloves, face masks,

and red life jackets peered down from the railing of the ship as the migrants shouted with tears of joy. The uproar went into full gear when the crew flung down a ladder. They pushed and elbowed and screamed, every person for himself or herself. No working together. No solidarity. Only cries, screams, and swears. A crowd of people surged toward the prow of the boat, and the boat tilted, tossing half a dozen people into the salty water. Empty jerricans flew everywhere, as people grabbed on to whatever they could. Detritus floated about. The coast guard agents threw out life preservers.

Able God took small steps, clutching his jerrican as he pushed his way forward. He swayed and almost fell. He stood back up, sucking in air through his mouth. *"Easy, easy, you're almost there,"* he told himself. Soon, he found a way to grip the ladder and held on until they tugged him up. He clambered across the deck to the inspection area. He flopped on the ground, trembling as he looked down at those still on the dinghy.

"Don't move! Don't move! Keep calm. Don't worry. You are safe!" the coast guard agents shouted, but no one listened.

More people fell out of the boat, and some who couldn't get to a flotation device began to sink, gasping for air and flailing their arms. Three coast guard agents jumped into the water to rescue the drowning people. The coast guard agents pulled their gasping, choking bodies out of the water and back onto the dinghy, which was now half filled with water. One man had had his face submerged in the sea before he was rescued; another had to be resuscitated in the boat and spewed out foamy water from his mouth as he came to. There were not enough rescuers to save everyone, and soon passengers were surfacing face down, their bodies bobbing in the waves.

Able God shut his eyes and mourned quietly as the coast guard agents went into panic mode and the dying soaked the air with their screams. Tears misted his eyes, then quickly tumbled down his cheeks. Silent sorrow for the suffering he hoped to never experience again.

He stood up and sniffed back his tears. Surveying the horizon, he could see Italy from where he stood. It looked like a dot, but he knew it would become larger.

The coast guard put the dead in body bags and carried them on board. They treated the living like lepers. Officers wearing Red Cross vests searched them with masks and gloves. The officers blasted them with water from hoses while they were still in their clothes. They tossed towels and new clothes at the passengers as if fearing infection. Able God did not mind. Nothing was worse than the treatment he had already received. Now fate had brought him here—the same fate that made him cross paths with Akudo again. The anger he felt when he saw her in Libya had been washed away by the turmoil of the sea. The bitterness remained, but he rescinded his wish for her to perish at sea.

They were now within striking distance of Italy. He could see the Italian coastline from the deck—the granite headland, the lighthouse, the seaside mansions and cabins. The migrants crowded against the rail, craning their necks in the direction of land. When they had settled in, the ship changed course. He saw that the others looked as confused as he did, so he approached one of the coast guard agents, who turned his back to Able God. He walked up to a female agent.

"There will be an announcement soon," she said with a smile and walked away.

Two other coast guard agents called for silence.

"This ship is not going to Italy. It will take you to Malta," one man said, and the other man interpreted in Swahili for the refugees. "You will make your asylum claims in Malta, then we can take it up from there," he added.

There was scattered applause. Able God was shocked.

Malta. Why Malta? Why the sudden diversion? Did the Italian authorities not want them to dock in Italy? But then why would they send their coast guard agents to rescue them?

"More teams have gone out to rescue the others. We will not stop our rescue effort until we save as many lives as we can."

Able God got to his feet and shuffled along the deck. His head was flooded with a dreamy patchwork of flashes. Someone spoke to him, but he couldn't make out what he was saying. The words seemed like distant echoes. Able God struggled to combat his dizziness. He sank back onto the wooden floor of the deck. He tried to gather himself and to stay silent and still. He drew deep breaths until his panting slowed down. The ship chugged along.

"Malta!" he whispered hoarsely. "Malta!"

PURGATORY

40

There was a standoff at the military harbor in Valletta between the Italian Coast Guard agents and the Maltese authorities, and when the refugees finally were allowed to disembark, they were corralled into a detention center and processed by blue shirts. Later, Able God would marvel at the calmness of his response to life at the detention center in Malta. He should have felt panic and horror upon seeing the place, but so much water had passed under the bridge. He hadn't been able to take his mind off Akudo and her daughter since he arrived in Malta. When they leave, will their boat be diverted here or to Italy? He hoped they hadn't drowned at sea.

The center was a former airplane hangar surrounded by a perimeter fence topped with barbed wire. Heaps of garbage were everywhere, and parts of the center were flooded with sewage. The block houses were crammed with detainees, who slept in bunk beds. When Able God was shown to a bed in a cold corner, he found old dinner plates crawling with maggots on the floor beside his mattress. He later noticed that the detainees' bodies crawled with lice, scabies, and fleas.

Neither the cloying smell of the room nor the maggots moved him. His bunkmate, Maxime, would not stop talking and gave him an unsolicited crash course on how to survive in the detention center.

"This place is like purgatory," Maxime said. "No one wants to stay here. Everyone wants to go to Europe, but here you must behave yourself if you want to go to Europe, or you will be sent back."

Able God knew what purgatory was from having attended a Catholic primary school. Purgatory was a state of limbo; it was neither the world here nor the life beyond, neither heaven nor hell. At least purgatory was better than the hell he had lived through. Purgatory was also a place of atonement for sins. But Able God wasn't sure if he would ever finish atoning for the sins he had committed in Libya— and what did atonement mean in his situation, anyhow?

"If Bossman is happy with you, then you can be allowed to leave the center whenever you want. You can even invite guests with the right amount," Maxime said.

Able God immediately assumed Bossman was in charge.

"Bossman likes women, so if you are a woman, easy peasy," Maxime said. "As a man, you have to put money in his pocket. You pay the guards, and the guards give it to Bossman."

Able God smiled. The money he had strung around his waist would now be useful, but he must be judicious in spending it.

"Do you think they will bring more refugees here, more survivors?"

"I am not sure. If the coast guards haven't found them by now, they are probably dead."

Akudo and her daughter would not have boarded the boat after he left. Maybe they'd have to wait a few days before they were ready. Perhaps they didn't have enough money to get a ride and would have to wait several weeks. Able God decided to contact his parents.

"Is there any pay phone center here?"

Maxime nodded and said, "Tuesday mornings. Nine o'clock

sharp. That's the time for phone calls. There is a machine here in the yard. But you have to put your name down if you want to use it, and you only get two minutes to talk. The line is always long, and it's first come, first served."

Maxime later told a totally unrelated story about a sleepwalking migrant who moaned in his sleep. There was a soft ripple of laughter. The refugees had heard this story so many times that it no longer had the same effect on them. He told other stories and made wise-cracks. Able God soon realized that Maxime was the camp jester in addition to being talkative. Sometimes he spoke without worrying about whether the other person was paying attention. Other times people gathered to listen to him in the yard. He would crack jokes in a loud and jovial voice, his shoulders rising and falling in an uneven rhythm. His listeners would bellow with laughter or run to the other end of the yard in hysterics.

The atmosphere at the camp was strangely joyous. People strolled around in the yard, lifted weights, played card games, and listened to Maxime crack jokes. It was as though the whole camp had decided not to succumb to despair—or was happiness in purgatory a neces-sary distraction?

He did not sleep that night. Instead, he stared at the person snoring on the next bunk bed. He watched as the man drew in a noisy, hoarse breath. His face contorted as he exhaled in a whistle like the snort of a kettle. Able God counted how many times he snored. Perhaps Akudo and her daughter didn't make it after all. A little later, Able God closed his eyes and tried to empty his head of thoughts.

> ● ▲ >

The next day, after paying one of the guards some money, he was able to explore Valletta. He walked down one street, then another.

Outside the camp, behind the old city's gates, there were narrow cobblestone streets, steep lanes, and long stairways. There were ochre-colored stone walls, brick houses, and dense vertical buildings with wooden balconies painted red, blue, or green. Modern buildings stood side by side with ancient ruins. Canals crisscrossed the city, carrying ferries and boats on impossibly blue water. Tourists and backpackers swarmed all over the place. He resisted the urge to focus on anything.

He passed by clothing stores, outdoor restaurants, and cafés with their multicolored patio umbrellas, art galleries, and food trucks. He almost couldn't distinguish between tourists and locals because they all seemed to be dressed alike in their straw hats and shorts. He reckoned he could make a lot of money from the tourists—he just needed to find something they would pay for. The noon bells began to chime.

He found a square where men in their sixties in T-shirts and flower-print shorts relaxed on park benches. Pigeons flew and hopped about. A woman with a shock of white hair played the violin, the leather case of her instrument open for tips. He spotted a red telephone booth at an intersection near the square. It was dusty and probably didn't function anymore. Thoughts of Akudo popped into his mind unbidden, and each time, he resisted them.

His gaze fell on the middle of the square, where some men were playing blitz chess. Breath catching in his throat, he felt excitement flow through his veins as he hurried toward them, tripping over his own feet in his haste. He stopped to watch a game. The two men were playing furiously, as though in the final throes of the game. They tapped the clock every five seconds, their eyes fixed on the board. A small crowd had gathered and was watching intently.

Tap, move, tap, move.

Eventually, the bald middle-aged opponent slowed down. He finally reached out to the queen, picked it up deftly, and set it down on a white square.

The bald man's hand folded across his chest and a sly smile came over his face. The loser blew a deep sigh and held out his hand for a handshake in resignation. The group erupted into celebratory screams, fists in the air.

"Who wants to play? I have got all day!" the bald man said cheerfully, looking around. His words hung in the air for a moment.

"I will play," Able God said as he slipped into the seat. The man raised his eyebrows. He saw the look of surprise on the faces of the spectators. An idea struck him—or rather, he spoke almost reflexively.

"Twenty euros if I beat you," Able God said. They all roared with laughter. He laughed with them. The bald man coughed into his fist and cleared his throat.

"Okay, okay, I'll give you thirty euros if you win!" he said. The crowd cheered. Able God shifted in his seat.

It took Able God ten moves to trap the man's queen. As the game progressed, more people stopped to watch the spectacle. They whispered things into each other's ears as faces turned inquisitively back and forth. The bald man's grin drooped into a frown. With the flick of a finger, the king fell to its side, a sign of surrender. The man reached into his shirt pocket and handed Able God his winnings.

"*Grazzi!*" Able God said in the only Maltese he knew. The bald man asked to play a second game.

"Fifty euros if I lose!" he said. "But if I win, you'll give me fifty euros."

Able God took a deep breath, wiped his sweaty palms on his shirt, and shook on it.

He won.

Able God returned to the detention center with his winnings from the games, pleased with himself. He then left again to clear his mind. A cab took him around. They drove to the harbor with its craggy, honey-colored mountains dotted with dry grass and chalk-white stones. There, he lay on the rocks under the bright, cloudless sky. He let his mind relax, feeling the warmth of the sun on his face. He filled his nostrils with the salty Mediterranean air. He got to his feet and walked to the sea, touching the sand with his toes and feeling the water on his skin. The sea was choppy, just like it had been the night before he landed. He shook off the unpleasant memory of the crossing.

Before sunset, he discovered the shell of an abandoned migrant boat lying close to the boulders, rejected by the sea and washed ashore. He saw shoes and scraps of clothing and bottles.

"Save them please, Lord," he said, tears streaming down his cheeks.

> ● ▲ >

The following day, Able God approached a group of refugees chatting loudly and smoking outside the boundary fence. The air was thick with smoke. They cast dull glances at him without stopping what they were doing. He paused briefly, contemplating his next move. Maybe he would ask one of them for a cigarette. Before he could take any further steps, one of them beckoned to him. Short, muscular, scar-faced, with a small nose and fleshy lips, the refugee offered him a cigarette.

"New arrivals. Border patrol rescued new people from the sea," Scar Face said casually.

"What? When?" Able God perked up.

"They are being processed in the hangar. Why? Do you have family...?"

Able God hurried through the gates, eyes roving about. A long line stretched from the perimeter fence to the hangar. Men, women, and children huddled in emergency blankets. He slowed his stride, peering at each person along the line. As he walked closer to them, he kept telling himself he would turn back.

A guard planted himself in Able God's way and asked him to move along, which he did, but he had his eyes on the line. He sat on the bench, looking around for them as the line grew shorter. There was no sign of Akudo or her daughter. He buried his face in his palms. To calm himself, he told himself that they were either still in Tripoli due to a lack of funds or had made it to Italy instead. He gazed at the line again and saw that all refugees had been processed. He walked up to an aid worker who looked African to try his luck.

"Are more people still coming?" he asked.

"We don't know, but we will be ready for them if they do."

Silence.

"Do you have family on a boat?" inquired the aid worker.

He hesitated for a moment, then replied, "Yes."

"May God keep them safe."

"Amen, thank you," Able God said before turning to depart.

ACKNOWLEDGMENTS

My first debt is to God, the bestower of gifts, without whom I am nothing.

This book is the culmination of years of work, which included not just the labor required to produce the book but also all it took to become the writer that I am today. There is a Yoruba adage that says "eniyan l'aso mi. Bi mo ba boju weyin, ti mo r'eni mi, inu mi a dun, ara mia ya gaga," meaning "people are my covering, when I look back and see my people, I am happy, I am glad." The Yoruba concept of "eniyan l'aso mi" reflects a profound cultural belief in the significance of having trusted people for support when needed. My journey would not have been possible without the support of my family and literary community.

This novel began as a short story published by *AGNI* with the title *Sweet Sweet Strawberry Taste*. Many thanks to Sven Birkerts and Bill Pierce for giving it a home and the editorial support.

Boundless thanks to Julianna Baggott, who took me under her wing when she didn't have to and continues to lift me up to this day. Your faith has buoyed me through the years. This acknowledgement page won't be enough to tell you how much you mean to me.

To my mighty literary agent, Julie Stevenson at Massie & McQuilkin, whose steadfast support saw me through the years and who brilliantly steered me through the ups and downs. This novel is for you, and a thousand thanks would not be sufficient.

My gratitude goes to my early readers—Marie Silkberg, Cammie Finch, Hodna Nuernberg, and Leone Brander—who made this book a lot more readable than it otherwise might have been. And to Elissa Hutson and Jeffery Renard Allen, who were enormously helpful in tightening my manuscript during the throes of final drafting.

I give thanks to my publisher, Judith Curr. To my acquiring editor, Tracy Sherrod, for taking a chance on me and advocating for this novel. Although I regret that you were unable to see the project through, I doubt that this project would have been possible without you. To my editor, Rakesh Satyal, for stepping in, providing invaluable feedback for the crucial final draft, and shepherding the project to completion. Many thanks to the team at Amistad and HarperOne: Tara Parsons and Laura Gonzalez; to my publicity team, Ashley Yepsen and Ashley Candelario, and also to Amelia Possanza at Lavender Public Relations; to my production team, Amy Sather, Marta Durkin, and Elizabeth Berg; to my design team, Alicia Tatone and Stephen Brayda. Thank you for a job well done. I really appreciate you all for your support. Special thanks to Ryan Amato for the prompt replies and timely assistance.

Under Julianna Baggott's supervision, I wrote the first draft of *The Road to the Salt Sea* as my thesis while enrolled in Vermont College of Fine Arts's now-closed full-time MFA Writing and Publishing Program. VCFA changed my life, and I am grateful to this vibrant community of writers for the lifelong friendships I have made. Special thanks to my adopted family in Vermont: Dr. Jim and Doreen Hogle, and Paul and Michelle Acciavatti. I am grateful for Tavia Gilbert, Kerrin McCadden, Lenny Decerce, Lindsey Brownson, Lindsay Gacad, and Desmond Peeples.

Thank you to my former professors, some of whom have become friends and colleagues: Porochista Khakpour, Mary Ruefle, Janaka Stucky, James Scott, Trinie Dalton, Jessica Hendry Nelson, Miciah Bay Gault, Rita Banejee, Erin Stalcup, and Robin McArthur.

I was privileged to join the faculty of the VCFA low-residency MFA in Writing Program some years after I graduated from the full-time program. I am grateful for all my students and colleagues, especially the former chairs of the program, Connie May Fowler and Ellen Lesser.

I am grateful for my literary community in Georgia, where I got my PhD: Chika Unigwe, Karen Sims, Dylan and Danielle Fisher, Marisa Manuel, Jada Ford, Wanjiku Wa Ngugi, Deepa Varadarajan, Kate Easley, Dr. John Holman, Prof. Josh Russell, Dr. Sheri Joseph, and Dr. Randy Malamud.

Where would I be without the generosity of literary organizations that provided time, space, money, and community for me to write and share my work over the years? Thank you to the Word Diversity, the International Writing Program, the University of Iowa, the Island Institute, *Kweli Journal*, the Carson McCullers Center for Writers and Musicians, the Wellstone Center in the Redwoods, and the Norman Mailer Center.

My gratitude also goes to my colleagues and students at Penn State's Creative Writing Program.

Finally, my ever-loving thanks to my parents, Theophilus Ojo Kọ́láwọlé and Irene Omolara Kọ́láwọlé, as well as my eleven siblings, particularly my five brothers, Seun, Seyi, Dipo, Segun, and Leke.

ABOUT THE AUTHOR

Samuel Kọ́láwọlé was born and raised in Ibadan, Nigeria. His work has appeared in *AGNI, Georgia Review, Hopkins Review, Gulf Coast, Washington Square Review, Harvard Review, Image Journal, New England Review,* and other literary publications. He has received numerous residencies and fellowships, and has been a finalist for the Graywolf Press Africa Prize, shortlisted for the UK's First Novel Prize, and won an Editor-Writer Mentorship Program for Diverse Writers from The Word for Diversity. He studied at the University of Ibadan and holds a Master of Arts degree in Creative Writing with distinction from Rhodes University, South Africa; is a graduate of the MFA in Writing and Publishing at Vermont College of Fine Arts; and earned his PhD in English and Creative Writing from Georgia State University. He has taught creative writing in Africa, Sweden, and the United States, and currently teaches fiction writing as an assistant professor of English and African Studies at Pennsylvania State University.